PROS & CONS OF VENGEANCE

A.E. WASP

Kelpie  Press

To Zoe, for introducing me to Leverage and to my Dad for introducing me to heist movies.

The Masterminds

Charlie Bingham (45) - Deceased. Con artist, thief, blackmailer and probably a few more things.

Miranda Bosley (35) - Lawyer. Executor of Charlie's estate. Possibly Charlie's best friend.

Josie DuPont - (age unknown because she won't tell. Somewhere between 30-40 probably) Associate of Charlie's. International Woman of Mystery. Surrogate mother to the boys. Even Leo.

The Interested Party - a disembodied male voice . Seems to know everything that is going on. Speaks only to Leo and only over the phone. You can call him Al.

The Boys

Leo Shook (45) - FBI Special Agent. Currently on administrative leave for unspecified reasons. Bureau expert on Charlie Bingham. *Code name: Big Daddy, Silver Fox*

Castille (Steele) Alvarez (30) - Close protection specialist. Ex-Army Ranger. Former swamp rat from Georgia. *Code name: Rusty*

Carson Grieves - (age unknown) - Champion grifter and con artist. Date and place of birth unknown. *Known Aliases: Benjamin Waters, Peter Nobocook. Code name: Chaney*

Ridge Pfeiffer (21) - Thief. Not much of talker. Expert in old-fashioned safecracking, lock picking, and cat-burglaring. *Code names: Thing One, Spidey,*

Wesley Bond (27) - Hacker and social engineer. Social justice warrior. Literal red-headed stepchild. *Code Name: Neo*

The Poor Suckers Dragged Into This Mess

Breck Pfeiffer (21) - *Pros & Cons of Vengeance.* Ridge's twin brother and a victim of the bad guy Charlie had targeted. Ex-college student, ex-hooker. Steele's boyfriend. *Code names: Thing Two, Undercover Lover*

Danny Munroe (20) - *Pros & Cons of Deception.* First appearance *P&C of Vengeance.* Former competitive swimmer. Kicked out of his suburban Illinois home for being gay, Danny lived on the streets for a few years. His path crossed with Breck's in DC when they were both victims of the same man. Has Wesley wrapped around his fingers. *Code name: Arm Candy*

Davis Ethan (30) - *Pros & Cons of Desire.* Diplomatic Security Agent. First met the boys in *Pros & Cons of Deception* where he was undercover at the resort. Ridge stole his heart.

"ALL IN ALL, Charlie picked a decent place to die."

Palm trees swayed beneath a cloudless sky, and as I sucked in a salt-tinged breath of air, I felt the telltale tingle of an imminent sunburn on the few millimeters of my skin not covered by prosthetics, fake hair, or long polyester robes.

You had to love Florida. It was gorgeous when it wasn't trying to kill you. Even the rows of headstones in the cemetery seemed somehow cheery.

The woman beside me turned from her steady contemplation of the mourners ringing the newest gravesite and darted a quick look around, making sure no one had overheard.

Pfft. Like I would have let that happen.

"Keep your voice down, *Father*, before you blow your cover."

I stroked my long gray beard, partly to make sure it was still securely attached to my face, and forgave her for questioning me. It was the priestly thing to do, and I was all about method acting.

"I'm just *say-ing*," I sing-songed back. "Sun shining, birds singing a high, mournful song for that extra touch of drama. Florida has an A-plus funeral atmosphere. Ten out of ten. Charlie would have approved."

A man in the gathering narrowed his eyes at me suspiciously, and I returned his look with a benevolent smile, raising my hand in a blessing. The man promptly looked away.

"You are an *idiot*, and I swear to God if anyone recognizes you and pulls a gun, I am leaving you to fend for yourself. Understand?"

Ah, Miranda. She never tolerated my bullshit for long, which was one of the reasons I loved her. "Perfectly."

She nodded once, then resumed studying the black-clad men and women who stood chatting in small groups. "And it's hot as balls out here. Far from my idea of perfect."

"It's Sarasota in August, Ms. Bosley. *Hot as balls* is the only flavor weather comes in this time of year, unless you know someone who works miracles." I snorted. "Doubt they're big on miracles where poor Charlie ended up." I tilted my head down and widened my eyes meaningfully.

"I would appreciate your not implying Charlie may be roasting in some Old Testament version of hell. You might not care that Charlie is gone, but I'm... I am going miss him," she admitted. Her eyes looked suspiciously shiny.

I sighed, rocking slightly on the balls of my feet. "It's not that I won't *miss* him, Randa." I'd miss his gorgeous house with the enormous swimming pool that overlooked the beach, for one thing. Sunsets from that pool were *perfection*.

For another, Charlie was a world-renowned thief and information broker whose name was always spoken with respect. Without Charlie and his reputation opening doors for me, the world would be a much harsher place. But I wasn't exactly the sentimental type, and I doubted I'd spend a lot of time grieving. I'd see this one final job done for old time's sake, and then I'd ghost.

I figured Miranda wouldn't appreciate me mentioning any of that, though. Not while she was being all *melancholy*.

"It's just that... I think the best things about Charlie Bingham are things that will live on, you know?" I offered lamely.

She darted me a look, checking for sincerity, and I blinked guilelessly back at her. She sniffed.

"Also? It's worth noting that you're a giant, squishy marshmallow full of *feelings*."

She gasped. "Take that back!"

I folded my hands piously. "I'm pretty sure it's a sin to lie while impersonating a priest."

"You are insufferable," she said, shaking her head, but I talked over her.

"And the truth is, Miranda Bosley, beneath that sharky, lawyer-ish facade..."

"I think the word you're looking for is *professional*."

"You *care* about your clients."

"Charlie was an exception," Miranda said in a low voice. She narrowed her eyes at me. "The one and *only* exception."

"Oh, come on," I protested, nodding at a cute redhead who'd taken a seat in the third row back from Charlie's casket. I tried to give her the serious look of a man concerned with the state of her soul, but I'm not gonna lie, all I could see was her purse sitting unattended beneath her seat. It's like people *begged* to be robbed sometimes. "You were Charlie's attorney for, what? Ten years? You've known me for even longer. And you *love* me."

"So you say." She looked me up and down, taking in every detail of my outfit before exhaling a subtle huff of disgust. "But you insisted on proceeding with this ridiculous scheme..."

"Ridiculous?" I scoffed under my breath. "Listen, Randa, Charlie's time was up, and everyone knew it. Lots of people wanna get right with their conscience before they check out. Balance the scales. Right the wrong they've done in their lives. I don't think that's ridiculous, I think it's admirable! I'm glad to be a part of it." Laying it on a bit thick there, perhaps. I stroked my beard once more, briefly contemplating growing one for real. It was an oddly soothing gesture. "I can't help it if I'm enjoying myself along the way, babe. You know me."

"Yes, I know you, alright. And I knew Charlie." She turned toward me, putting her back to the crowd, and her hazel eyes drilled into mine. "Charlie should have faded into obscurity, unknown to the larger world, the way all the good thieves do. Instead, we're here having this *spectacle* of a funeral and blackmailing people into doing his work for him."

"Dude. Harsh," I chided. "Have some respect for the deceased."

"Not harsh, *accurate*," she corrected, spinning back around and blanking her face. "I can't believe either of us is involved in this. You do get that it's all insanely dangerous, right?"

"Miranda," I said in my most placating voice. "Honestly, it's gonna be fine..."

She poked me hard in the shoulder with one meticulously manicured finger. "Look at the men in this crowd, the men we practically forced to come here."

She nodded at a cherubic blond in the front row who sat with the preternatural stillness I'd only ever witnessed in psychopaths, assassins, and truly exceptional thieves. "That's Ridge Pfeiffer. He'd steal your soul and be two states away before you knew it was missing, friend. And then there are Castille Alvarez and Wesley Bond over there."

I followed her glance to a lone palm a few paces away from the main crowd, where a disgustingly handsome, black-haired, broad-shouldered, giant of a man stood protectively over a short, twitchy dude with dark red hair. I always thought Alvarez should have been a model, it would have been the perfect cover. Model slash assassin for hire. I guess there were worse faces to see with your last breath.

"You know Steele could kill you ten different ways before you could scream for help, and Bond could make a laser beam that would fry your corpse out of chewing gum and a magnifying glass."

I snorted.

"Do I even have to mention Special Agent Leo Shook?" she asked, raising one eyebrow pointedly.

"No, you do not."

"And don't forget Carson Grieves."

I frowned as I searched. "I don't see him." Come to think of it, I wasn't sure I knew exactly what Grieves looked like.

"Brown hair, brown suit, third row, pretending to salivate over the blonde in the low-cut blouse," Miranda said.

"Ohhh. Damn," I muttered, reluctantly impressed. "He's good."

"You sound surprised," she chided. "You shouldn't be. Carson could shoot you in broad daylight in front of twenty witness and no two would agree on what he looked like or if he'd even been there at all."

"Miranda, darling, why am I dying in each of these scenarios?"

"Because it's fucking dangerous," she hissed, even as she smiled and nodded at some signal from the funeral director on the other side of the gathering. "These men are not here to pay their respects to Charlie Bingham. They're not even here out of prurient curiosity. They're here because *Charlie* had dirt on them, because *you* invited them, and because *I* threatened to expose them if they didn't show up and play nice."

She turned to face me again. "And here *you* are, standing at Charlie's grave dressed up like... like...Rasputin-meets-Santa Claus." She touched her hand to the heavy silver cross that hung from my neck. "Sometimes I wonder if you're trying to get caught. To follow Charlie into that grave."

I blinked, stung. The woman was too fucking insightful, catching on to shit I'd barely ever acknowledged to myself. I grabbed her hand and held it lightly, a priest giving comfort to a grieving friend.

"First of all, I'm not getting caught," I told her absolutely. "That is not on the agenda, okay? I have never been caught, and I don't plan to start now. I'm a ghost, an afterthought. Charlie's invisible little elf. I'm not on anybody's radar."

I looked around at the men she'd mentioned, the men we'd invited here. They were men like me. Men like Charlie. Dangerous, but decent. Criminals, but ones who stuck firmly to their own moral codes. That's why Charlie had chosen them. "It's safer for everyone if they never find out who I am or how I'm connected to Charlie, and I won't jeopardize that. I'm not getting involved with Charlie's missions except from afar."

She looked at me for a long moment, then nodded.

"And second, I *may* be channeling Rasputin," I allowed, touching a finger to the hair above my temple. "But only in a Tyra Banks, *Rasputin-but-make-it-fashion* kind of way."

A helpless laugh escaped her, quickly turning to a sob. She rubbed her forehead. "Do you ever take anything seriously?" she demanded.

I sighed. "You know I do, Randa-Panda," I told her. "I take every part of this seriously. I took *Charlie* seriously. I take Alvarez, Pfeiffer, Grieves, Bond, and Agent Shook seriously. But I take the jobs they need to do, Charlie's unfinished business, even more seriously. And I'm thinking of this as Charlie's last hurrah, babe. One last con. We're gonna send him out in style. Yeah?"

She sucked in a deep breath and tugged at the hem of her black suit jacket like she was steadying herself.

"Once more," she said, without a trace of her earlier emotion. "Let me note that it's hot as balls out here."

I pressed my lips together to hide a smile as Miranda slipped back into lawyer mode. God, why was it that I always viewed serious, worrying, rule-following people as such a *challenge*?

"Quit your whining," I told her, stroking my beard again. "I'm sweating my ass off under this cassock."

"You could take it off. Even priests have to make accommodations for the heat."

"No can do," I said sorrowfully. "I've got nothing on underneath."

It took her a second, but when she finally processed my statement, her eyes widened and her jaw hung open for half a moment.

"You... you're not." She shook her head minutely. "You are *not* naked under that robe."

I wasn't, not entirely, but the look on her face made the lie worthwhile. "Wanna check?"

She looked so horrified, I nearly burst into laughter. Her eyes narrowed. "Your continued existence makes me question that whole *survival of the fittest* thing."

"Nine lives like a cat," I told her with a small smile.

"Only eight left if you manage to pull this off, *Father*."

The undertaker signaled again, gesturing me toward the unassuming podium set up at the front of the gathering. *Showtime.*

I turned to Miranda. "You do your part, and I'll do mine. For Charlie."

"For Charlie," she echoed, but as she turned to walk away, a man approached us.

Tall, with dark hair tinged silver at the temples, he had one of those lean, rugged, model-perfect faces where the jut of his jaw and cheekbones could cut diamonds. My heart recognized him first, pounding in my chest before my mind had fully identified him.

Special Agent Leonard Shook. The silver streaks in the hair at his temples made him look even more distinguished than he had previously, which was an impressive feat. Once the darling of the Agency, Shook was currently on a long, federally-mandated vacation.

Miranda's eyes widened at the same moment mine did, but likely for different reasons.

"Ms. Bosley," the man said politely. His eyes barely flicked to mine. "Father."

His voice was a deep, rumbling bass I'd heard in my dreams a million times. Though of course, the things he'd said when he invaded my sleep were far dirtier, and he'd sure as hell never called me Father... though I may have called *him* Daddy. Every morning after one of those dreams, when I woke up sweaty and aroused and alone, I'd tell myself that his voice couldn't possibly be as deep as I'd remembered, that my mind had been playing tricks on me.

But I'd been wrong. If anything, it was even more gravelly-sexy than I'd recalled.

"Father?" Miranda said sharply, widening her eyes.

Damn. While I'd been remembering my wet dreams, the man himself had been waiting for my reply.

"Pardon," I said, making my voice a little higher than it naturally was, and adding the slight Russian accent that was a perfect mimic of my grandmother's. "The heat. It... makes me light-headed."

Leo's brow furrowed, and he reached out one large hand to grasp my elbow, as though I might faint. "Are you alright? Would you like to take a seat?"

"No, no," I said, shaking my head, while the little demon in the back of my brain insisted, *Yes, please. Preferably on your lap.* "I'll be fine."

"Perhaps remove the robe?" Leo offered, and Miranda made a strangled noise.

"No, but thank you. It wouldn't be appropriate."

"Heat stroke trumps formality," Leo replied matter-of-factly. He reached for the hem of my cassock.

"No! No, my child," I backed up a pace. Did Russian Orthodox priests say *my child*? I couldn't recall. Suddenly I felt unprepared, caught out, exposed.

Maybe Miranda was right. Maybe I hadn't taken today seriously enough. I'd told myself it was important to come here, to see without being seen, so I could assess the situation and help Miranda behind the scenes later. I'd figured these robes would make me practically invisible—no one in this crowd of fences and crooks was likely to look too closely at a man of the cloth.

But then, I hadn't counted on Leo Shook. Jesus *fuck*. Why did this man get to me in a way no other person ever had?

I couldn't pinpoint exactly where or when my crush on Leo Shook had begun, but I knew it was before I'd ever seen him in person. The Javart to Charlie's Jean Valjean, their paths had crossed more than once and crossed once more closely than Agent Shook had known. He'd been Charlie's nemesis, always half a pace behind, and I swear, the cat-and-mouse antics were so amusing that even though I was nominally Team Charlie, I wasn't sure sometime if I was rooting harder for Charlie to escape or to get caught.

I took a deep breath. "There," I said in my high-pitched accent. "Much better."

"If you're sure," he said, unconvinced.

"Perhaps skip your remarks, Father," Miranda suggested. "I'm happy to say a few words about the departed on your behalf, and you can keep the funeral rites private?"

I nodded, taking the out she offered. "Perhaps, yes."

"I admit... I wasn't aware that Charles Bingham was a particularly religious man." Leo eyed Miranda skeptically.

Thank God he'd turned to *her* for answers. I wasn't sure I would have been able to stand up to that look. I'd crumble like a house of cards, give up the game before it had really started.

But Miranda, in her contrary way, absorbed his suspicion and used it to strengthen her backbone. "There were many things about my client that you didn't know, Agent Shook."

"Apparently. Didn't know Charlie was a blackmailer, for one thing."

"Blackmail is an ugly term," she said. "And an inaccurate one in this case. This is simply a business arrangement."

"Business arrangement," he repeated. "With whom? Charlie is dead. Dental records confirmed it."

And wasn't it curious how sad he sounded about that? We made a heck of a love triangle: me, Leo Shook, and Charlie Bingham.

"I have been authorized to negotiate the terms of the agreement on behalf of the Bingham estate, along with another interested party," Miranda said.

"An *interested party*," Leo snorted. "Christ. And who the hell might that be?" He tossed me an apologetic glance. "Pardon my language, Father."

That would be *me*, Mr. Interested Party himself, the man behind the curtain. The man who'd been left the task of redeeming Charlie Bingham and playing invisible puppet master to five very dangerous men.

I waved away Leo's apology and glanced down, focusing all my attention on the way the shiny black toe of my shoe peeped out from below my robe.

"Discretion is the most valuable service I provide my clients, Agent Shook," Miranda said.

"I don't give a good goddamn about your attorney-client privilege," Leo snapped. "I want to know how many people Charlie told what he knows about me. Or *thinks* he knows."

"Right this moment, only I know." Miranda studied her fingernails. "As I was saying, on behalf of the estate, I'm prepared to offer you and a select few others a job in exchange for certain... sensitive information you might find important."

Miranda shrugged lightly, as though she weren't coercing a federal agent in a cemetery in front of five dozen witnesses. The woman had more guts than anyone I knew; way more than Charlie had ever had; hell, more than the entire group of mourners put together. She also had a healthy respect for the law, which was why she was so damn careful about breaking it. "You have right of first refusal, and if you choose not to take it, then other individuals will be given the opportunity to bid for those goods."

"Those goods, meaning pictures of..."

Miranda cut him off with a sharp noise. "Not here, Agent Shook. We're having a select gathering back at the Bingham house after the service. You can ask your questions then."

"A select gathering."

Leo was like a parrot today—very unlike the calm, collected Agent Shook I'd come to know. I would have been more amused if my heart weren't still beating a mile a minute from the threat of being caught, and beads of sweat weren't literally rolling down my legs and puddling in my oh-so-proper shoes.

"*Very* select," she agreed. "You won't want to miss it. The house is up on Gulf Shore Road under the name of..."

"Bigolb-Autumn Enterprises. I know," he sighed.

He knew where Charlie had lived? He knew the stupid name of Charlie's shell corporation? *How?*

Miranda was startled and showed it. "How do you know?" she asked. "That information was extremely confidential."

"I've known for a long while," he said, sounding tired. He shook his head ruefully. "Only Charlie Bingham would create a corporation called *Big Old Bottom Enterprises* and think he could keep it a secret from everyone."

But it *had* been a secret. Not even the two or three people Charlie trusted with the truth had ever figured it out until he told them. Leo Shook was more perceptive than I'd given him credit for. And Charlie had been closer to getting caught than he'd ever dreamed.

Miranda and I exchanged glances. Mine said *holy shit*, and hers said *I told you this was dangerous, you idiot*.

This was worrisome. And yeah, fine, it was also a total fucking turn-on.

Leo ran a hand through his black hair. "I'll look forward to our discussion at the house, then," he said, in a tone that suggested it would not be a pleasant or peaceful discussion.

He turned to me. "Will you be at the house, Father?"

"Oh, me? No. No! Heavens, no," I tittered, painting an accent on every syllable. Even though I desperately wanted to be there, to see everyone's reactions in person, I knew it would be smarter for me to watch the proceedings from a distance. At least for now.

Leo nodded. "Well, then. Bless, Father?" he requested solemnly.

Jesus Christ. Of course the man was conversant in Russian Orthodox etiquette. *Of course he was.*

It was only thanks to the dozens and dozens of masses I'd attended with my Babushka Sonia that my mouth formed the words of the blessing, more muscle memory than conscious thought. I raised my hand, then offered it to him, as was customary, and he took it in both of his, lifting it to his lips for a kiss.

"Take care," Leo said, returning my hand to me. He nodded curtly at Miranda and turned away, taking a seat next to Ridge Pfeiffer.

I clenched my hand into a fist so tight I could feel the rapid beat of my pulse in each of my fingers. One simple touch, and he'd turned my stomach inside out.

Miranda was right; Charlie's last con was a dangerous game, dangerous for all of us. But it was too late to turn back now.

Thank Christ someone had been bright enough to leave the air conditioning on in Charlie's mansion. Dead men paid no electric bills, I guess. *Fucking Florida.* I'd been gone too long and had somehow forgotten how truly miserable the humidity could be. Sure, it could hit a hundred and fifteen outside of Baghdad, but it was dry heat.

I thought about taking off my suit, or at least my tie, but until I knew what the hell was going on here, I wasn't going to let my guard down.

Besides, I looked good in a suit.

"Nice house, huh?" Wesley said from behind me as I was busy assessing the layout of the house and cataloging any possible pinch points. Like I said, I didn't know what I was doing here, and I wasn't taking any chances.

"I've seen bigger." In my most recent incarnation, as close protection specialist and hired muscle to some very rich and very bad men, I'd been in mansions that made this place look like a pool house. Not that this place sucked. Not at all.

The cabin I'd grown up in could have fit in the foyer with room left over.

We followed Ms. Miranda Bosley, Charlie's attorney, single-file down the tiled hallway of the big house like a line of ducklings. Wesley was the only guy I knew and consequently the only one in the group I trusted enough to walk behind me. Even Ms. Bosley looked like she wouldn't hesitate to stab me in the kidney if she felt she needed to.

Seeing Wes at the funeral had been a surprise. A quick, stilted conversation had revealed that he was here for the same reason I was—we were both being blackmailed by Charlie.

I couldn't imagine what Charlie had on the kid. I'd only worked with Wes twice before, but he was more a gray hat than a black hat hacker; the kind of person who didn't mind doing the wrong things for the right reasons. A cross between MacGyver and Anonymous, the kid had probably been on a FBI watch list since he was twelve.

Wesley had triggered my protective instincts from our first meeting, but he'd never really needed much help beyond muscle. Sure, he could take care of himself with that jujitsu or whatever, but sometimes some people just needed their faces punched, and I was more than happy to do that for him. It was satisfying.

Now Angel-Face, as I'd taken to calling the gorgeous blond kid who'd been sitting a few rows ahead of me at the graveside ceremony, *he* triggered other instincts in me. Made me think things I probably shouldn't be thinking at a funeral. But then again, Angel-Face hadn't seemed exactly consumed with grief either. I hadn't been completely surprised to see him following Miranda after the funeral along with Wes and me. Very interesting. What had that choir boy done to be in such bad company at such a young age?

I fingered the challenge coin I always carried in my pocket as a reminder of all the things I'd survived and all the friends who hadn't. The familiar feel of the raised image soothed the niggling doubts in the back of my mind.

The fourth man in our little parade was the one who'd been sitting next to Angel-Face. I mentally dubbed him The Fed, because if he wasn't some kind of agent, I'd eat my hat. I figured the guy had to be pushing forty, or maybe he'd already humped his way over the other side.

If he'd been a simple cop pushing forty, he wouldn't be in such good shape. Guy looked like he could hold his own in a fight or a chase. Everything from his haircut to his body language, not to mention in the bulge of a shoulder holster under his jacket, screamed Fed. Of course, at Charlie Bingham's funeral, it was likely that more people were packing than not.

I couldn't get any read on the fifth man in the group, Mr. Anonymous. He was so amazingly average-looking, he was difficult to describe. He hadn't spoken once, so there was no accent or speech pattern to discern, and his generic dress pants and J.C. Penny shirt didn't give any clues to who or what he was. But I figured if he was part of our party, he wasn't your average, law-abiding citizen.

"Please sit, gentlemen," Miranda said, pointing at the collection of armchairs and sofas in the giant living room. Floor-to-ceiling windows provided us with a great view of the

Gulf. I walked to the windows, noting the drop to the beach and the stone staircase leading to the upper levels of the house.

"Please, Mr. Alvarez, if you don't mind." Miranda looked at me, and then looked pointedly at the other four men, who were already sitting.

Angel-Face had an entire loveseat to himself. What a waste. I headed his way, giving him smile Number Four, the one that said *I'm gorgeous, you're gorgeous, we both know it. What do you say we fuck soon?*

He looked at me with cold eyes and the thousand-yard stare I'd only seen on snipers and hockey goalies. It was like a bucket of cold water being tossed in my face.

Okay, then. I kept the smile on my face as I casually changed course. I took a seat next to Wesley, unbuttoning my jacket with one hand as I sat.

Wesley, the little shit, carved a plane crash and explosion out of the air with his hand, complete with almost silent sound effects.

"*Whatever.* Not my type," I said under my breath. It wasn't completely untrue. I liked my men a little more approachable, and, if I'm being completely honest, a little less together. I liked someone who needed me. Angel-Face didn't look like he'd ever needed anyone in his life.

Miranda crossed her legs at the knee, stilettoed foot tapping to some rhythm only she could sense. Somewhere on the far side of forty, Miranda was a handsome, slender woman with piercing hazel eyes that didn't miss a thing. She looked like she knew all our secrets. And judging by the letter that had dragged my sorry ass out of the swamp and down to the Suncoast, she did.

A middle-aged hispanic-looking woman in the kind of maid's uniform I'd thought only existed on television rolled in a fancy cart with a silver coffee service and a sweating pitcher of iced tea on it.

"Tea, gentlemen? Ms. Bosley?" she asked with the faintest hint of an accent. "Coffee? We have both."

Miranda closed her eyes and rubbed left right eyebrow. "Josie, what are you doing?"

The woman, Josie, straightened up and blinked. "It's hot, Miran... Ma'am. I thought you could use some refreshments after the burial."

Without opening her eyes, Miranda waved her hand, motioning for the woman to continue. The cart moved almost silently over the polished wooden floor.

"Ooh, aren't you *un niño bonito*," Josie said, handing Angel-Face his iced tea. I could swear she was a half a second away from pinching his cheek. Her accent was more south of the Mason-Dixon line than South of the Border. She probably spoke as much Spanish as I did: enough to order food, find the bathroom, and flirt.

Miranda sighed heavily as Josie rolled her tea trolley in my direction.

"Iced tea? You look a little warm." Josie poured me a glass before I could answer.

"Thank you, ma'am," I said, taking the blessedly cold glass from her. I sighed happily as I took a sip. The drink was one step up from tea-flavored sugar syrup, just like Mama used to make.

"Now you," Josie said, straightening up and looking directly at my face. "You look like trouble. Much too handsome. And you know it."

I grinned. I loved middle-aged women. You couldn't pull shit over on them. They could see right through you. Josie and my mama would get along just fine.

"Josie," Miranda snapped.

Josie's mouth tightened, and I swear to God she harrumphed. I had no idea what was going on between these two, but I liked this woman already. She served the rest of the group, then rolled her cart to a stop near Miranda's chair. She hesitated. "Do you need anything else? I could stay. Whip up some snacks?"

"No, thank you, Josie."

"You sure, ma'am?"

Truthfully, I could have gone for a couple of pizzas myself.

"I'm sure. And Josie?"

"Yes?"

"Put that ridiculous costume back from wherever you got it." Miranda tried to hide a smile behind her hand, but it showed in her eyes.

"You don't like it?" Josie pulled the white apron off. "I kinda like it. Makes me feel all *official*."

Miranda shook her head fondly. "Not necessary, Josie."

Josie handed her a black coffee in a delicate cup. "Whatever you say, Miranda."

"Thank you." Miranda took a sip and her shoulders relaxed a fraction. "I *will* call you after my meeting."

Josie nodded. She opened her mouth to say something, then walked away, shaking her head.

Well, wasn't that interesting? I'd been around a lot of wealthy people, including a few high-powered attorneys, and usually they barely acknowledged the help. The help certainly didn't speak to their bosses like that.

The late afternoon sun streamed through the tinted windows, glinting off the turquoise water and painting the room in a golden glow. Dust motes danced in the beams, and I noticed that dust covered the shelves and decorative accents in the well-decorated space. Charlie either hadn't used the room a lot, or he needed to hire actual maids.

"Let's get started, shall we?" Miranda said, reaching into her briefcase and pulling out a manila envelope. She placed it on her lap. "Before I get to the details of your assignment, I think introductions are in order."

"No, I think we should get to the point as quickly as possible," The Fed said. "I know three of these men, and I don't think we need to be *friends*."

Someone needed to punch that sneer off the guy's face. Too bad, because it was a very handsome one, if you were into that kind of thing. All rugged and Captain America-like, when he wasn't being holier-than-thou. Considering he was sitting in this room, though, and not out arresting bad guys, I guessed The Fed's halo was a little tarnished, so he could fuck right off with his bullshit attitude.

That was okay. There was more than one way to piss off a guy like him. There were a lot of things I hid about myself and my past, but being gay was not one of them. I hadn't survived being a scrawny gay kid just to crawl into a closet as a grown-ass man.

I leaned back in my chair, crossing my legs slowly, drawing his attention. As I shot my cuffs forward, and fixed the crease of my trousers, I eyed him up and down slowly, very obviously checking him out. Raising one eyebrow, I grinned.

"Oh, I don't know," I said, letting a little of the South Georgia swamp-rat seep into my voice. "I wouldn't mind showing you how *very* friendly I could be." I leaned forward. "If you got that stick out of your ass, Mr. Fed." Out of the corner of my eye, I could see Miranda sipping her coffee and watching us.

To my surprise, the guy raised his eyebrows and slowly checked me out from head to toe. It was hot, in a way, but I got the feeling the guy was observing every little thing about me and writing it down in some mental notebook. Like he could tell that my expensive suit had been a gift from a generous benefactor, and that I had stolen my Tommy John underwear from the dresser of one of my targets. Bad guys often had surprisingly good taste in clothes, and these had still had the tags on them.

The Fed shook his head. "Sorry, Alvarez, but I don't think it would work out. You're not my type. I like my men a little more respectable. And from what I've seen of the many slender young men you've had in your bed and other less comfortable places, I'm not your type either."

Wesley gave a long drawn out *oooh* and pointed his finger at me. "Need some cream for that burn?"

It took all my self-control to lean back slowly. How the fuck did this asshole know my name and who I slept with? I shot Miranda a look. She stared impassively at me. I kept forgetting she held all the cards. Now I had a choice to make. I could get all up in the Fed's face, or I could play nice. Considering how much I needed to get hands on whatever shit Charlie had on me, I'd try door number two.

I pasted a smile on my face. "Shot down twice in one night. Guess I've lost my touch."

Angel-Face burst out laughing, and even Mr. Anonymous was trying to hold back a smile.

"Aw, Angel-Face, not you, too?" I put my hand over my heart. "I'm crushed." I sucked down the last of my iced tea, wondering if Charlie had been kind enough to buy some whiskey before he died.

Fucking Charlie. This was all his fault. I'd had *one* run-in with the guy, done *one* job with him years ago. When I'd been ordered to shoot him by the woman we'd both assumed was on his side, I'd made the split-second decision to hesitate just long enough for him to get away. I didn't like double-crossers. And this was the thanks I got for doing the right thing.

I took a few deep breaths, trying to calm myself. Let's be real, I knew exactly what Charlie was blackmailing me with. If it got out, it would be bad not just for me and Uncle

Sam, but for the men I'd served with. I'd long ago come to terms with the things I had done, and Uncle Sam could fuck off for all I cared, but I'd die before I'd let my men pay for my crimes. No exaggeration. We'd put our lives on the line for each other more than once, and I would do it again in a heartbeat.

Miranda cleared her throat. "As I was saying, I think it's time for introductions."

"Why don't you let Mr. Fed do it?" I said. "Looks like he's got all the info anyway."

"It's Mr. *Special Agent*, to you, Alvarez. As in, Special Agent Leo Shook, FBI. Which means I could arrest you right here, right now."

Ha. I knew he was a Fed. Totally called it.

"Agent Shook," Miranda said. "As you are officially on administrative leave from the Bureau, I doubt that's true."

Now Wesley pointed at Special Agent Shook and laughed. "Oooh, burn *again*!"

Shook turned to him. "Who the fuck are you?" Shook said. "No, wait. I can figure this out. I can figure all of you out."

He pointed at me first. "Castille Alvarez. Also goes by *Steele*. Nice name, by the way. Very manly and original. Professional bodyguard and sometime hit man. Usually works for the bad guys, presumably because they have more money."

Hit man? Not fucking likely. I jumped up from my chair. "Twice," I said, holding out two fingers for emphasis. "I've killed two people in this job, and both times they were going to kill me first."

"On *this* job?" Mr. Anonymous said from his chair in the corner. He looked like the kind of guy who always found the dark shadowy corners to sit in, but his voice when he spoke was high-class and cultured, tinged with a la-di-dah British accent that made him sound like he had marbles in his mouth. "Have you killed in your previous positions? At least one of which was military, no?"

"Oh, he's got military written all over him," Angel-Face said.

"What is your name?" I blurted out. "I can't keep calling you Angel-Face in my head."

"Sure you can." He pushed his blond curls off his forehead and gave me a big smile. "You can call me whatever you want."

Great, now he was trying to flirt? I knew deflection when I saw it.

Special Agent Shook narrowed his eyes at the kid. "Angel-Face's name is Ridge Pfeiffer. He's a professional thief. Linked to a bunch of big jobs. He's flown under the radar for a while, but we've been starting to hear his name more and more."

He tilted his head at the man I'd dubbed Mr. Anonymous. "The guy in the corner trying to not be noticed is Carson Grieves, champion grifter and con artist. Implicated in a thousand and one crimes. Both of them are as slippery as the Teflon Don, so we can't make a bust stick."

He lifted his chin in Wesley's direction. "You're the only one I don't know," he said. "What's your role in this farce?"

"Farce?" I asked.

"Sham? Mockery?" Carson suggested. He had the same snooty accent all the bad guys in Dr. Who had, as if everything was vaguely amusing.

"Sounds better when he says it," Wesley said.

"Everything sounds better in a British accent," Ridge added. "It's a well-known fact. Just like a southern accent can lower your perceived I.Q. at least ten points."

"Bless your heart," I said as I gave him the finger. My mama raised me to be polite.

"I'm Don Juan Zero Juan Juan. People call me Zero," Wesley said. He grinned, making him look even more like a teenager who'd snuck into the grownups' meeting.

"No, you're not," Shook said, looking visibly, well, shook. His right hand reached for handcuffs that weren't there.

Wesley leaned back and stretched his arm across the back of couch. "Yeah, you're right. I'm just fucking with you."

Shook's body was still coiled as if he were going to leap up and tackle Wesley to the ground. I was starting to get the feeling I didn't know Wes's real story. I guess it had been kind of foolish of me to assume I did.

"Give me one reason why I shouldn't turn you in right now, Zero," Shook said.

"Nobody is turning anyone in," Miranda said sharply, cutting off Wesley's response. "Unless it's me. Remember that you're all here for roughly the same reason."

"I want to know who else is involved in this," Shook demanded. "Who are you working for, Ms. Bosley? Who's paying your bills? And how did Charlie Bingham die?"

Miranda smiled so evilly, a lesser man would have shit his pants. "The beauty of holding the cards, Special Agent Shook, is that I don't answer to you. Do the jobs Charlie has left for each of you, and you'll never have to see me, or each other, again."

"Works for me," I said. "Just tell me what I have to do, point me in the right direction, and I'll do it."

"I agree," Ridge said. "How fast can we get this shit done? I have things to do, places to be."

"Things to steal," Wesley said with a smile.

Miranda ignored the interruptions. "As you all know from the letters I sent you, Charlie's will left instructions concerning each of you gentlemen." She seemed to be choosing her words carefully, pausing between each sentence. "You've each had a connection with him in the past, and he is counting on your shared histories to...*encourage*...you to help him accomplish some tasks he was unable to get to before his unfortunate early demise."

"You mean he's blackmailing all of us from beyond the grave to do his dirty work," Wesley said, crossing his legs underneath him. "And if we do what he wants, you'll give us whatever dirt you have on us and we go on our merry way."

"Correct." She tapped her finger on the desktop, as though deciding how much to say. "Charlie was a master of information. He bought it, sold it, stole it, and leveraged it. He wasn't a model citizen from a law enforcement point of view." She gave The Fed an ironic glance. "But more often than not, he tried to be a decent person. Much of the sensitive information he collected, he never used. And some of the information, he tried to use for good. That made him some powerful enemies. If you want to know why Charlie's no longer with us, Agent Shook, that's your answer. Because he made enemies of the wrong people."

"Who?" Shook demanded. It sounded like he was ready to throw on some armor and ride out to avenge Charlie's death.

"That's not your concern," Miranda said softly. "At least not right now."

"But..."

"Charlie knew how many hit lists he'd landed himself on," she continued, ignoring Agent Shook. By the look on his face, the agent didn't like being ignored. "He didn't know exactly how the end would come, but he knew he wouldn't be able to avoid it. Not this time. So he decided to bequeath all of you, collectively, some of his most sensitive information. The tasks he left undone. The wrongs he wanted to right. And in exchange, you'll each get back the sensitive information he had on you."

She spread her hands flat on the desk. "These aren't jobs that any one person can do. They require a team of people with specialized skill sets, skills he felt the five of you possessed, as a whole. You will need to work and live together to complete them."

"Live together?" Shook looked like he'd bitten into a lemon. Probably thought he was too good for us. But he was here with us, and he wasn't storming out, which confirmed for me that there were some skeletons in his closet.

"Yes, Agent Shook. Charlie felt it would be the best way not only to ensure your compliance but to facilitate a level of bonding, if you will, between you gentlemen."

Angel-Face—*Ridge Pfeiffer*, I corrected myself. His name was *Ridge Pfeiffer*— snorted loudly. I agreed with him. The chances of this group getting together and braiding each other's hair were close to zero. I gave the whole experiment about three days if we all had to live in the same space.

Personally, I didn't mind living on the coast. It's not like I had a permanent place at the moment anyway, and this house was a lot nicer than most of the places I'd stayed. I could use a few more changes of clothes, though, and some other things I'd left behind on what I thought would be a quick overnight. Like my SUV. "What about our stuff?" I asked Miranda. "I've got some lucky underwear I left back in Georgia."

"We have people on standby waiting to transport your belongings here immediately, should you choose to stay."

"Not like we have much of a choice," Ridge said bitterly, speaking my thoughts. It seemed this whole thing was a done deal. Why were we acting like we could say no? We were trapped. I didn't think that was conducive to bonding either.

"There are always choices, Mr. Pfeiffer, as well as consequences for every choice." Miranda frowned slightly, her lips tightening.

Shook's scowl deepened.

"I think you will find that living here has many advantages," Miranda continued. "You have all of Charlie's resources at your disposal. This house, his cars, his private plane, all of his computer equipment. You'll have access to me, as well as a few other people Charlie trusted to assist you with these jobs. Whatever you don't have, you can acquire."

She reached into the large manila envelope she held on her lap, pulling out a stack of plastic cards. "Find the one with your name on it and pass them on," she ordered, passing out AmEx Black cards like they were Halloween candy.

I turned mine over in my hands. "Damn, never thought I'd see my name on something like this."

"No shit," Ridge agreed. "And for a good reason. Won't we be leaving a trail a blind man could follow if we use these? Shouldn't we be more, I don't know, circumspect?"

Wesley, Mr. Carson Anonymous, and The Fed all shook their heads.

"No point," Wesley said first. "Privacy is no more than an illusion now. I don't need credit cards to track you. I could trace you across the world even if you paid cash for everything and used a fake name, especially if you have a phone. I can use gravity, or LED lights in a store. I could even piggy back on the fucking Muzak playing over the speakers. If your phone's on and you're not on the Space Station, I can find you." He smirked at Agent Shook. "If I did that kind of thing, which, of course, I would never."

"Right," Shook said, voice flat.

"That's fucking terrifying," I said. And it also made it clear just how hard it was to physically steal shit in this day and age. Law enforcement could track a thief like Ridge just as easily as Wes could track a mark.

"Damn, Angel-Face," I told him. "If Agent Shook hasn't caught you, you must be really, really good."

He raised his eyebrows and tilted his head at me in answer, a silent *you think*?

"Old-school robbery," Wes said. "I dig it. Very retro." Then he stared at the ceiling, his lips moving silently and his eyebrows raising and lowering as if he were arguing with himself. "I'll need all my computer equipment, including the router and the servers. Even the cables, and the landline phones. I'll also need to check out Charlie's system."

Seemed like overkill to me. A computer was a computer. "Come on, Wes. There's gotta be a Best Buy near here. We have Black cards, we can get you all new stuff, the best money can—"

"Best Buy? Are you... are you *trying* to insult me? Would you tell Ridge to get his climbing rope from Walmart? Or tell Carson to get his fancy suits at Target? Do you have any idea how much my set up is worth, Steele? Tens of thousands of dollars. All of it custom-built, by me, to my own specifications, over a period of years, so that it can do exactly what I need it to, every single time!" Wes's eyes were wide, and he was practically panting. "I said I need my fucking stuff, and I need my fucking stuff."

"Down, killer," I said. "You want your stuff, we'll get your stuff."

"Everything you need will be provided, including any specialized equipment you have at your residences. If we could move this along, gentlemen," Miranda sighed. "I have several more appointments today."

"No rest for the wicked," I told her, wiggling my eyebrows.

She smirked. "As you're about to find out." To my surprise, the Dragon Lady grabbed an envelope from her briefcase and handed it to me. "You're running point on the first assignment."

I reached forward slowly, it as if might bite. I felt like the winner of a game show I hadn't wanted to play.

"Five assignments, five envelopes," Miranda announced. "And each of you will take the lead on one."

"Was that Charlie's instruction, too?" Agent Shook asked caustically.

"Nope. Mine." Miranda gave him a satisfied smile. "In my experience, criminals are like preschoolers, and the sooner you all learn to share the sandbox, the better for all of us."

"Should I open it?" I asked Miranda.

She inclined her head gracefully, but I hesitated. If the envelope contained copies of shit Charlie had on me, I sure as fuck was not opening it here and now. I didn't trust these guys as far as I could throw them. Not that I had anything to hide, but other people would get hurt if certain things were revealed. I flipped the coin along the back of my knuckles, over and under, while I weighed the possibilities.

The woman seemed to read my mind. "The information in the envelope is solely about the case we need you to take on," she assured me. "The rest of your information will remain private unless you choose to divulge it." She looked at the others. "And that goes for all of you."

Miranda stood up and fastened the clasps on her briefcase. "There are rooms on the second floor for each of you to choose from. If you have any logistical questions about the house or your belongings, Josie will be here. Otherwise, I expect you'll all know what to do." She gave each of us a last look. "Good luck, gentlemen. Charlie had faith in you, and for what it's worth, I do too."

I made the coin disappear into my palm, then slid it back into my pocket. Slitting open the manila envelope, I reached in and pulled out a stack of photos. Wesley leaned over to see and whistled in appreciation.

Holy fuck. Looked like three men getting it on. These were some hot pics, if you ignored the old guy in the middle, which was easy enough to do considering his face wasn't visible. But the two other guys? *Damn.* One had brown hair and killer abs, but the other had fair hair and the most incredible ass I'd ever seen. Lucky geezer. He had to be paying for it.

Wait a second. I held the pictures closer to my face and looked back and forth between the blond in the picture and Ridge. It was hard to be sure with all that distracting naked skin and those two bitable asses, but I thought I'd figured out what Charlie was blackmailing our thief with.

I slid the pictures back in the envelope and reached across the space to hand it to Ridge. "Hey Angel-Face, is there anything you want to share with the class? Perhaps some alternative revenue streams you've failed to divulge?"

Ridge took the envelope, looking at it as if it were filled with dog shit, and removed the pictures.

In his case, it might as well be dog shit.

"It's pics of a john with a couple of rent boys," I explained to Carson and the Fed, neither of whom had moved from their spots. "I have no idea who the client is, but there's a blond hooker with a truly *delectable* bubble-butt who's a dead-ringer for Angel-Face here."

Ridge shuffled through the photos once, twice, his expression set in stone. He pulled one out for closer inspection. A look of pain flashed across his gorgeous face, and I knew no matter what this case was about, I'd be helping him. I was a sucker for a gorgeous guy in distress.

"Well?" Wesley asked, unable to contain his curiosity.

Ridge handed the photos back, his jaw set hard. "That isn't me in those photos," he said. "It's my twin brother, Breck."

Britney Spear's *Work Bitch* blared from my cell phone, pulling out of a nightmare where I'd been drowning in freezing cold water, shivering so hard my teeth chattered.

I was simultaneously grateful for the save and pissed off at whoever was calling me at the ass crack of dawn. Okay, fine, technically it was the middle of the morning, but I'd always been more of a moonflower than a morning glory, so same difference.

Sadly, the freezing cold had followed me from dreamland and into the subarctic reality of my borrowed Dupont Circle apartment.

"What?" I barked into the phone as the dream receded and my heart rate slowed. I cracked open one eye. Harsh rays of sunlight peeked around the edges of my blackout curtains, searing my retina, and I closed my eyelid quickly.

"Have I got news for *you!*" said a man's voice. It dripping with the kind of glee that only came at other people's expense.

Shit. Emilio. Literally one of my least favorite people on the planet, and considering the people I'd been associating with recently, that said something.

My eyes popped open and I stared at the ceiling, cursing myself and my bad habit of answering the phone without checking to see who was calling. Now I would be stuck for ten minutes listening to Emilio's catty gossip as punishment.

Way to fail Phone Skills 101, dumbass.

Most people's internal voices probably sounded exactly like them, only bitchier. But, for better or for worse, mine sounded exactly like my twin brother. Ridge was identical to me in every way but one. He was a control freak with no filter who liked to call me *dumbass.* Still, I loved him more than anyone else on the planet. This made my internal voice comforting and annoying all at once, just like Ridge.

Christ, I missed him. Most of the time. But right now, I was glad Ridge had made himself scarce since I'd enrolled at George Washington University. He would kick my ass into the middle of next year if he knew what I'd gotten myself into and what I'd done with the tuition money he'd given me.

The kid who'd spent our entire childhood protecting me from bullies, the guy who'd taken the blame when we got caught lifting jars of peanut butter at King Soopers after our mom took off and left us without food *again*, and the man who'd forced me to take all the money he'd saved from his first big score and go to college since, '*One of us should make headlines for something besides stealing shit, Breck, and it ain't gonna be me,*' would sure as hell have something to say about the choices I'd made recently.

Prostitution hadn't exactly been on my five-year plan. Neither had been giving the money to our drug-addicted mother. But, as they say, plans change.

"Rocky, are you even listening to me?" Emilio demanded.

Rocky. Dumbest alias ever. Never ask a drunk, scared, homesick hooker from Colorado his name, okay? Because he might come up with one on the fly, thinking of the mountains back home, and get stuck hearing people yell, "Yo, Adrian!" for months.

"Not really. It's way too early to call if you expect me to listen," I yawned.

"It's nearly ten."

"And I didn't get to sleep till three," I snapped back without thinking.

"*Ohhh-ho-hohhhhh!*" Emilio managed to make the word teasing, admiring, and threatening all at once. "Does *Cisco* know you were partying last night?"

Damn it.

Cisco was our employer, our procurer, our... *okay, fine.* He was our pimp, and he would not take kindly to me partying off the books. Not that I had been. Unfortunately, Cisco also wouldn't take kindly to what I actually *had* been doing. He might have like the truth even less.

"A person can be up late without partying," I said. "I was home. Watching television."

"Hmm. So, if I asked around, or Cisco asked, nobody would have seen you at the clubs or hotels, right?"

Shit. Truthfully, I was on the security feed of a good half-dozen of the hotels Cisco's boys used regularly. But I hadn't been partying, I'd been trying to find Danny. No way was I sharing that information with Emilio, let alone Cisco, My only option was to double-down on the lie.

"Uh, *yeah.* I know it's a tricky concept, but that's what being at home means, honey," I drawled.

Emilio chuckled. "And where is *home?*"

That was a damn good question.

I rolled to my side in the big double bed and pulled the duvet up to my chin, luxuriating in the fake winter I'd created thanks to the window a/c and my complete lack of regard for the electric bill. Then again, it was easy to disregard the bill when I wouldn't be the one paying it.

I took a moment to wonder if Chad, the asshole from my *Modern Ethics and Culture* class who actually called this place home, was enjoying the Scandinavian backpacking trip he'd bragged about relentlessly all last semester. I'd certainly been enjoying squatting rent-free in his unoccupied apartment for the last few weeks. He probably would have birthed kittens from his asshole if he'd known I was living here, but I was watering his plants for him, so I figured it was an even trade.

"No one knows anything about you, Rock. When you gonna have us over for tea and cookies?" Emilio asked.

Never. Danny was the only friend I'd made in all these months, and even he didn't know my real name or where I crashed. "You know I like my privacy, Emilio. A girl's gotta have her secrets."

"Sure, Rock," Emilio said. "So, I suppose the reason you haven't been around the last couple weeks is a secret, too, right?"

The curiosity in Emilio's voice was a living thing, and for a brief moment I considered giving in and telling him the truth. But Cisco had warned me to keep my mouth shut about what had happened. Not there was much he could do to me. I was in this life voluntarily. I could always swallow my pride and ask Ridge for help. Danny was a street kid with nowhere to go, no one to turn to.

But Cisco was better than a teenaged girl at finding a person's weak spots and he promised Danny would pay the price for my loose lips.

If I spilled, Emilo would sell me out to Cisco faster than my dad had left town after seeing the plus side on my mom's pregnancy test.

So I'd say nothing to anyone until I could find Danny and get us both the fuck out of here. "Exactly," I said. "I'm taking some personal days."

"Uh huh. Well, it's time to get back in the game, sweetheart. Time to get dirty again. I have a job and I need you."

"Who's the client?" I asked, as if the thought of taking *any* john right now wasn't making me nauseous.

"Snow White."

Oh, *fuck*. No fucking way.

No one used real names in this business. Not the boys, not the johns. It was safer that way. In D.C., there was a real possibility that the Joe Smith you'd sucked off last night was gonna be on your TV the next day shouting about immigrants coming to take our guns or something, and if you so much as whispered his real name, you'd be slapped with a lawsuit and an eviction notice on the same day.

You learned early in this business: the most powerful guys were the kinkiest, and the deeper in the closet they were, the more vicious. And no one was more vicious than Snow White.

That psychopath was the reason I was holed up in his apartment. He was the reason Danny had disappeared, and the reason my plans had changed from *leave town as soon as I can pay Ridge back* to *leave town as soon as I find Danny*.

I didn't give a shit about college anymore, and I'd find a way to make the money up to my brother. Getting knocked unconscious while your friend was beaten to a pulp tended to make a man reassess his life.

"Yeah, I don't think I'm up for that," I told Emilio. "Thanks anyway."

"I say you are," Emilio insisted. "Or I'll have to tell Cisco you said no."

This was the price of his silence. Agree to do the job or have him start asking Cisco where I was last night. And if Cisco started checking things out, he'd realize I'd been looking for Danny, who hadn't been seen since the night Snow White beat us up. Cisco might use me to find Danny, and I was sure that if Danny was still alive, he didn't want to be found.

I pushed my head into the pillow case and slammed my free hand into the mattress over and over. Outside, I heard the rattle and squeal of a trash truck making its rounds. The deep notes of my upstairs neighbor's tuba fell through my ceiling. There were more than half a million people in this city, living half a million lives. I wasn't stupid enough to think all their lives were easy, okay? But I would have traded with any of them in that moment.

"Did you talk to Cisco about this?" I demanded. I couldn't imagine Cisco sending me to Snow White again. Not after the way the man had snapped two weeks ago, attacking both of us in a drug-fueled rage that had only ended when he passed out.

Then again, maybe that's exactly what Cisco would do. He wasn't the warm, fuzzy kind of pimp. If such a thing existed.

"Yeah. Cisco's the one who told me to call you," Emilio confirmed. "It's gonna be a big-ass party. Some kind of fundraiser he has every year. Like, old white folks in designer gowns drinking Dom and chatting about... horses? Stocks? Whatever shit rich folks talk about. But our john's a fucking perv, so you just *know* he's got this whole other party going on at the same damn time, right?" He chuckled admiringly. "Like, the wives think their husbands are all going off to the back room to talk business, but it's the kinda *business* that involves getting their dicks sucked or their brains fucked out. Last year was awesome. Tips were fucking incredible. Besides, you and I have fun together, right? We could put on a hell of a show."

Fun. Yeah. There was a time when Emilio would have been just my type. I'd fucking loved 'em dark-haired, dark-eyed, tanned, and fit. Sadly, I couldn't remember the last time I'd been honestly attracted to anyone. Sometime before I'd started seeing clients six months ago, though.

"Light and dark? Guys get off on that contrast," Emilio continued.

Guys got off on the fact that my blond curls and blue eyes made me look like some kind of cherub. Some of them wanted to defile me. Some of them wanted to worship me. All of them thought they were the best fuck ever, because they made it worth my while to let them think so.

Jaded? *Me?* Maybe a little.

"I don't know, boo," I hedged. "Let me think about it."

Emilio sighed. "Here's the thing, Rock. I'm trying to be nice, but there's really not a choice to be made here. Your buddy Danny ran off to who-the-fuck-knows-where," Emilio sniffed. "Called and told Cisco he's *out*. Like Danny can just *do* that, when you know he owes Cisco big time for the blow."

My stomach flipped. "Cisco heard from him?"

"Two nights ago," Emilio confirmed, and I closed my eyes in relief. Danny was alive, or at least he had been two days ago.

"Yeah, so when Snow White asked for him by name, Cisco sent his guys out to look for him. But he's a ghost," he added, confirming what I'd found after hours rambling around D.C. last night.

"So Cisco decided you're going Saturday. I'll text you the details. And if you don't show up, you better get lost for *good*, because Cisco's gonna take the bonus out on your ass."

"Fuck," I winced. I knew he meant that literally. But if Snow White was looking for Danny, I had way bigger problems than Cisco to consider. I was pretty sure Snow White wasn't interested in Danny for his dick-sucking skills, more likely he wanted to make sure Danny kept his mouth shut about that night. Permanently.

I threw the covers off and jumped out of the bed, pacing the small space between the bed and the window. Despite the a/c practically pumping out ice pellets, I was sweating. This was bad.

"You know, I don't get you, man. All this drama about doing your job," Emilio said, and I almost laughed. The guy had no clue what was really happening here. "You used to be one of the best boys in Cisco's stable. You were into it! You had *potential*."

He wasn't entirely wrong. My high school guidance coun-selor used to have an inspirational poster in his office – a picture of a rainbow-striped hot air balloon with the completely unrelated caption, "Whatever you are, be a good one!" I'm pretty sure Mr. Cheever didn't expect me to apply the motto to prostitution, but only because the educators of Alamosa, Colorado were singularly unimaginative fuckers.

I 'd never had any illusions about sex being some sacred, magical experience – it was fun as hell, end of story. So when I'd realized I was short about five zeros for my yearly tuition thanks to dear old Mom, and Cisco found me drowning my sorrows at a club one night and offered me a job, I didn't get all *Les Mis* about it. I said, *Why the hell not?* and decided to embrace it.

I mean, nobody ever dreams of being a rentboy, and there's zero career advancement, but I've never been the type to do something half-assed. And not to brag, but once I applied myself to practicing the oldest-profession, I was fucking spectacular at it. I was a professional, choreographing every encounter with detached precision. Men and women alike loved me. I was toned, I was groomed, and I'd perfected my skills.

The part about hooking that no one ever talked about was the weird kind of power there could be in hooking. At least, there was for me. Honest to God, the first time I knelt at a man's feet and heard him beg had been life-changing.

I couldn't tell you much about my first trick—not the fake name he used, not the bullshit background he gave me, not a single detail about his physical appearance. But I would never forget the Patek Philippe triple complication watch with a black alligator band and white gold face he wore. That fucking watch could have bought the trailer Ridge and I had grown up in. Hell, he could have bought the whole trailer *park* and a Bugatti.

But when I'd been down on my knees with his dick in my mouth, it hadn't fucking mattered that he could *literally* buy and sell me. It was me who'd had the power, and him begging me for release. As I kept him two seconds away from climax, I could have told him to do anything—bark like a dog, sign over his watch, tell me he loved me—and he would have done it, no hesitation.

I'd been in control. I'd felt strong. I'd felt *untouchable*.

Until I'd gotten incontrovertible proof that I really, really wasn't.

"Whatever your deal is, Rock, get over it," Emilio continued. "Remember Cisco decides when he's done with us." He paused. "And he's not done with you yet."

The phone beeped three times as he disconnected the call.

Awesome. Just fucking awesome.

I pulled on a pair of basketball shorts and a T-shirt and tried to steady myself by making a cup of the lemon tea that was literally the only thing in Chad's cabinet.

While it steeped, I called Danny again. And got his voice-mail. *Again.*

"Danny, for God's sake *call me*. Emilio said Cisco's looking for you and Snow White is looking for you, too. I won't make you do anything you don't wanna do, okay? I just need to know you're alright."

I threw the phone on the counter with a clatter and pushed the heels of my hands into my eyes. I needed a plan. A list. Step one was admitting I had a problem.

That's when you're dealing with addiction, dumbass.

The snarky words wrapped around me like a blanket, and for the first time, I considered calling Ridge. But last time we'd spoken, my brother was up to his neck in his own shit down in Florida.

And besides, I'd made a deal with myself when I let Ridge give me the tuition money. That it would be the last time I took his help. I'd be damned if I'd end up like our mother, using people until there was nothing left.

My MORNING BEACH run took me past mansion after mansion, each one bigger than the last, rising out of the purest white sand I'd ever laid eyes on. Must be nice to be rich. Technically, I was probably trespassing, but this early in the morning, I didn't think anyone would mind.

I nodded a hello at an old man fishing the surf from the shore. "Any luck?"

"Yeah. For the fish."

I laughed and kept going, my feet beating out a steady rhythm on the hard-packed sand below the high-water line. Sweat dripped down my face, stinging my eyes, but since every inch of my body was covered with sweat, there was nothing to do but endure it. Fucking southern humidity. Still, the slight breeze from the Gulf cooled me a little, and the gentle rolling of the waves was hypnotic.

I didn't listen to music when I ran; I liked the quiet. Running was my meditation, my time to get my thoughts in order as much as to stay physically healthy, and Lord knew I had plenty to consider after yesterday's cluster-fuck of a funeral and the aftermath. Cadences from my time in the service ran through my head, keeping time with my steady stride, and reminding me how much more fun it was to run without seventy-five pounds of gear strapped to me and with a view like this one to appreciate.

I'd been pleasantly surprised to find a fully-equipped gym in one of the outbuildings of Charlie's house, for those days when I just couldn't be bothered dragging myself the extra few feet to the water. This damn house had everything: sauna, hot tub, steam room, lap pool, wine cellar. Yeah, it really must be nice to be rich. I could definitely get used to the feeling.

For as long as I was here, anyway.

I slowed down when I saw the row of bushes separating Charlie's property from his neighbors, gradually reducing my speed until I walked the final few feet to the back of the house. As I passed the stone fire pit in the sand under one of the many balconies, Agent Shook stepped out from the gym.

Excuse me, *Special* Agent Shook. God forbid I forget that he was special. Though, seeing him like this, it wasn't hard to remember.

Shook's chest was soaked with sweat, he was breathing heavily. His body was hard with wiry muscles: the corded arms of a boxer and six-pack abs that were only possible through a combination of genetic lottery, exercise, and strict diet.

Yeah, I'd do him. I didn't have one particular type, and big guys like him were good for the kind of nice hard fuck I liked every now and then.

"Alvarez," he said as I came closer.

"Agent Shook." My eyebrows lifted as he handed me a towel.

"I saw you jogging up the beach, and you looked a little sweaty."

His gaze followed the towel as I wiped it across my chest and down my torso. He seemed to be enjoying the show, so I took my time, making sure to hit every spot. Since the only thing I had on were my tiny pair of running shorts, there were a lot of spots to cover.

"You must tan easily," he remarked.

"Nah." I hooked my thumb under the waistband of my shorts, inching them down on one side to show him the lack of a tan line. "Same color all over."

"Yes. Well." He crossed his arms over his chest. "You obviously take good care of yourself."

Was that almost a smile? "Occupational necessity, but thanks for noticing. And call me Steele, only my mama calls me Alvarez."

He frowned, the lines between his eyes deepening. I had a feeling they never went completely away. "She does?"

I smiled. "No. But if she *was* still talking to me, she'd call me Cassie."

"Cassie?" he smirked.

"She was the only one who got to call me that."

"Why isn't she talking to you?"

I heard the clink of plates and cutlery and what sounded like metal chairs being dragged across cement. A dog barked from somewhere nearby. "Let's just say she's not a big fan of my lifestyle choices."

His laughter caught me by surprise. "Which ones? I bet she's had a lot to choose from."

I shook my head and chuckled. "Pretty much all of them," I admitted. "Starting with my decision to enlist and ending with my announcement that I was never going to bring home a nice girl for her meet."

He rubbed his hand across his stubbled cheek. When he wasn't glaring at me like he wanted to arrest me, I could appreciate that Agent Shook was a fine-looking man. I appreciated a little stubble burn on my thighs after an encounter. He sighed. "Yeah, my parents weren't the biggest fans of those two choices either."

"You were in the service?"

Shading his eyes with his hands, he stared out at the water. "I'd kill for a cup of coffee."

That was a yes. But no way was I going to push the subject. A man was entitled to his secrets, and obviously each of us here had at least one. "I bet we can scrounge some up. Old Chuck probably had one of those fancy-ass cappuccino machines."

"He wasn't old," Shook said as we walked past the pool to the shaded patio outside the kitchen.

"Who?"

"Charlie. He was the same age as me. Still can't believe he's dead."

"Neither can I," Josie said as we got closer. "So sad." She'd forgone the maid's outfit today, opting for some lightweight capris and some kind of girly looking shirt. She looked younger in the casual clothes.

"Wow, Miss Josie, that looks amazing." I said as I caught a glimpse of her handiwork. She'd set up quite the breakfast spread on the big table on the shaded outdoor space. There were big bowls of cut fruit on the table and a full place setting at each chair. A toaster and a selection of bread and spreads sat on a long side table. Either she'd gotten here before the crack of dawn, or she slept here.

"You didn't have to go to all this trouble, Josie," Shook said even as he reached for a coffee mug and a metal carafe.

Josie spread her hands and shrugged. "What else am I going to do with my time, for goodness sake? Knit? Watch TV? I like to feed people."

I really wondered about the woman. What exactly was her job here, and who was paying her? Did she live on the property? Maybe in that small apartment over the pool house?

"Is anyone else awake?" Shook asked.

"Not that I saw, Agent Shook." She sat down in one of the chairs and poured herself a glass of orange juice from a glass pitcher that sat nestled in a bowl of ice cubes.

Shook poured a teaspoon of sugar and a healthy dose of heavy cream into his coffee and smiled. "Please, call me Leo." He lifted his cup to me. "Goes for you, too, Steele."

"I'm honored."

He quirked his lip and took a sip of the coffee, sighing in pleasure as the hot caffeine hit his system.

"I would have pegged you as a man who took his coffee black," I said, picking a slice of orange off the top of the fruit bowl.

"I put in my time with sludge. Still drink it at the office. I'm going to enjoy myself when I can."

"You're a wild man, Shook."

I went to take a seat at the table next to Josie when I realized how much I must smell. It wouldn't be fair to expose other people to that while they were trying to eat.

"Miss Josie, I'm gonna take a shower and then round up the troops and bring them down. Shouldn't take more than fifteen minutes. Is that okay, ma'am?"

"That's perfect, Steele, honey. And please call me Josie."

I shook my head sorrowfully. "I'm afraid I can't do that. My mama would fly down from Georgia and beat my low-class ass if I tried."

She laughed. "Fair enough."

"I'm going to hit the showers, as well," Leo said. "See you both back in a few minutes. I have a feeling we have a lot to talk about."

I agreed. I couldn't say I was totally looking forward to it, either.

I strolled in through the sliding door to Charlie's massive eat-in kitchen, which came with a corner breakfast nook large enough to seat at least eight people on the two couches. A fifteen-foot long island with a sink, oven, range and breakfast bar took up the middle of the room. Endless cabinets, and a sink large enough to bathe a Great Dane in, lined one wall. A wide doorway on the other side led to the living areas.

The large living room where we'd met with Miranda yesterday had a cathedral ceiling two stories high, and a two-hundred and seventy-degree view of the beach. Natural light flooded in through the floor-to-ceiling windows which opened onto the patio, just a few feet down from where Josie had laid out breakfast.

The second floor held six bedrooms – like anyone in their right mind would ever need that many – each with its own attached bath. When Miranda had told us we were all going to be staying at the house, which Wesley had immediately dubbed the Bat Cave, we'd each picked one of the rooms. We could have spread out amongst the buildings, but by unspoken understanding, we'd stuck together. Miranda might see this as a sign of our growing bond, but it was more like we didn't trust each other enough to let anyone out of our sight.

My first stop was Wesley's room. If I knew him, and I was realizing I really did *not*, he was still awake. The kid was mostly nocturnal.

Sure enough, he was awake and sitting at the broad desk that was the main reason he'd picked that room. For a guy who'd been bitching about being separated from his beloved tech, he'd sure managed to fill the desk with whatever he'd brought with him. He was wearing the geekiest headset I'd ever seen and snapping orders into the microphone that hovered near his mouth.

On the biggest laptop screen I'd ever seen, what looked like a hundred figures surrounded a giant snake-like monster, and it seemed like they were doing their best to kill it. I had no idea if they were succeeding.

"Shit, shit!" Wesley cursed. "Rad, get the fuck out of the AOE! Stay in range of the healer and everyone stack for buffs. Damn it!"

I waited until he threw his controller down in disgust.

"Bad game?"

"Bad group. Good game." He swiveled his chair to face me. "What's up?"

"Besides the sun?" I asked with a grin.

He swiveled back to the window where bright light seeped in around the edges of the curtain. "Huh. Look at that."

"Come downstairs, Josie made breakfast. I'm going to take a quick shower, and I'll meet you there."

"Sounds excellent. I could use some more coffee." He leaned back in the chair, yawned, and stretched his arms over his head.

"I doubt that."

Carson had chosen a medium-sized room that looked like it could've been in any mid-priced hotel in the country, which was probably why he had chosen it. I knocked on the door and got no answer, though I could hear voices inside. I waited a few seconds, then knocked again.

"Hold on." Carson sounded irritated. I heard him muttering as he unlocked the door and opened it a crack.

"Nice outfit," I said. Carson was half-dressed, and when I say half-dressed, I mean from the waist up, he was dressed as some kind of chef, his white jacket stitched with initials that weren't his. From the waist down, all he wore was a pair of boxer shorts with flamingos on them.

"Chef?" a voice called from the tinny speakers in the laptop perched on the dresser. "You there?"

I wasn't even going to ask.

"Be right back," Carson yelled over his shoulder in a distinctly non-British accent. He turned back to me. "What do you want? What time is it?"

"Breakfast time."

"I don't eat breakfast." His accent was back to that bored British one he'd used yesterday. He tried to shut the door on me, but I held it open with one hand.

"Miss Josie went to the trouble of making us a lovely meal, and we are all going to sit around the table and eat it. And then we can talk about the job." I was pretty sure the one bond that held us all together was the desire to get this over with. "The sooner we get this shit done, the sooner we're all free to get on with our lives. So finish FaceTiming your boyfriend or lawyer or whatever you're doing, and meet us out on the patio."

"Bloody hell." He sagged against the doorframe and started to run a hand through his hair before remembering he was trying to look respectable. "Is there coffee?"

"There is."

He rubbed his eyes and looked back at his laptop. "Time zones," he said in a vague explanation. "I'll be down soon as I can."

"I'll be waiting in breathless anticipation."

He snorted a laugh and shook his head. "Fifteen minutes."

He shut the door.

I took a shower before going to check on Ridge. We'd gotten off on the wrong foot yesterday, and it was probably my fault. Hard as it was to believe, not everyone responded positively to my charm. Ridge was prickly and defensive, and I knew there had to be a story there. Plus, I still wasn't one hundred percent convinced that this twin brother existed. I'd believe it when I saw them both in the same room.

Though if I ever did, I couldn't be blamed for my impure thoughts.

Knocking gently on Ridge's door got no response, so I knocked harder. Still nothing.

"Ridge?" Nothing.

"Angel-Face? You alive in there?" Still nothing.

It was early, maybe I should let him sleep? *No*. We needed to get started figuring out what Charlie wanted us to do, and how to do it.

Fucker could have given us directions or something like *your mission, should you choose to accept it...* But no, just some dirty pictures. If he weren't already dead, I'd strangle him. And I'd noticed how Miranda had snuck out before we opened the envelope, so we couldn't question her either. We'd have to work together.

Kumbaya.

I tried the handle, surprised to feel it turn under my hand. Huh. Guess Ridge wasn't too worried about anyone sneaking in.

The room was as cold as the inside of a refrigerator. In the dim light seeping through the heavily-curtained west-facing windows, I could make out the bed. I assumed the slight lump in the pile of blankets was Ridge's sleeping form.

"Ridge?" I called quietly from the doorway. I'd known too many people who came awake armed and looking for a fight for me to get too close to the bed. But nothing. He didn't even budge; his soft breaths the only sign he was actually alive.

"Ridge," I said a little louder. "Hey, Angel-Face. Wakey, wakey, eggs and bakey."

He mumbled into the pillow and flopped over, pulling the blanket completely over his head. It was unexpectedly adorable.

I really had to win him over. I loved a person who saw right through me and called me on my bullshit. That was the fastest way to win my heart. Well, to win my *friendship*, anyway. I liked my lovers a little more beguiled.

I had the horrible feeling that in order to change his mind about me, I was going to have to be real with him and tone down my flirtatious tom-fuckery. I walked up to the bed and squatted down before I shook his shoulder. No one liked some big guy hovering over them threateningly when they woke up. "Hey, Ridge, man." His skin felt soft. Nice.

"Go away, Alvarez," he mumbled without opening his eyes.

"Aw, is that any way to greet a friend?" At least he hadn't clocked me. I waited for a long second before realizing he'd fallen back to sleep. Damn, that was dedication. I tickled his ear gently with one finger. "Come on, Pfeiffer. We're burning daylight."

"Fuck off." He pulled the cover completely over his head, and I laughed.

"Come on, Grumpy Pants. Miss Josie made food special for us. She's dying to feed us. You don't want to disappoint her, do you?"

He sighed deeply as if disappointed in the entire population of people who woke up before noon. "Fine." He flopped the cover off his face with what I felt were unnecessary dramatics. "Is there coffee?"

"You know it. And bacon."

"Damn the woman. She knows my weaknesses." He blinked his blue eyes at me. "Give me five minutes, and I'll be down."

I stood up. "Great. And Ridge?"

"Hmm?"

"Miranda gave this one to me, but clearly it's going to involve you, too. We've really gotta talk about it."

He looked me in the eye and nodded. "Yeah. I know. After coffee. What time is it anyway?"

"'Bout seven-thirty."

"In the morning?" He sounded genuinely horrified. "Fuck my life," he said when I laughed.

"Five minutes, Pfeiffer. Wear something sexy." Okay, so the real me was kind of obnoxious, too.

"Go away. Pour me coffee." He sat up fully and stretched. I could tell he was completely nude.

"You know, what you're wearing now is fine. Just come like that. No one will mind."

I ducked the pillow he threw at me and left.

<hr/>

As promised, Carson had joined a freshly-showered Shook on the deck by the time I made it back down. He'd changed into white linen trousers with a sky-blue guayabera shirt. Like me, Shook had gone for the classic cargo shorts and T-shirt look.

"What do you wear under those?" I asked Carson. "Every time I try to wear linen, I end up showing off my underwear. Or if I go commando, you can see my package and even the fucking hairs on my ass."

"And no one wants to see that, Steele." Leo poured himself a fresh cup of coffee.

"Speak for yourself, plenty of people want to see this ass." I slapped it and sat down.

"Here you go," Josie said, setting what looked like an egg-white omelet with spinach and cheese in front of Leo.

"You don't have to do that, Josie. I can get my own food."

She waved Leo away and put the plate she held in her other hand in front of Carson. "Here you go, just like Mother used to make." The large plate was filled with a small buffet's worth of food, including eggs, weird bacon, baked beans, and something that looked like a cross between a hockey puck and a sausage.

"Thank you, Josie," Carson said, looking startled at his unexpected bounty. "It looks delicious."

"Yes," Leo said through a mouthful of food. "Thank you. Everything is delicious."

"I know," she said.

I leaned closer to Carson's plate, aiming my fork at a suspicious-looking red blob. "Is that a tomato?"

Carson slapped my fork away. "Eat your own food, Alvarez."

"I don't have any food," I pointed out.

Ridge came out through the door from the living room. He wore a polo shirt and slim-fit madras shorts with sandals. He looked like a model, like every white boy at every country club and golf course I'd ever seen.

"Have a seat, honey," Josie said, patting him on the shoulder. "I got some food special for you."

Wesley reached for the coffee carafe, but Josie yanked it out of his reach. "None for you, young man. I've got some chamomile tea with your name on it. Did you sleep at all last night?"

Wes opened and closed his mouth like a fish. "I'll sleep at some point, I promise," he wheedled.

"Mmm-hmm." She swept dramatically off the deck and back into the kitchen.

"Morning," Ridge said.

That seemed to be all there was to say. Leo and Carson ate. Wesley played with his phone, and Ridge and I poured ourselves some orange juice. I could hear Josie banging around in the kitchen, singing along to country music playing on the radio.

Take about three zeros off the price of the house, swap the Gulf for the Okefenokee Swamp, and I could be at home.

Josie came out with two more plates. Pancakes and bacon for Ridge, and a whole pile of food for Wesley.

"Josie, that's more food than I eat in a day." Wesley held up a piece of bacon and stared at it like he'd never seen one before.

"I know. I'm going to fatten you up if it's the last thing I do."

"What about me?" I asked. "Aren't you going to fatten me up?" I wasn't trying to be rude, but I was hungry. I had no problem going into the kitchen and making my own breakfast.

"I got something special for you." She went back into the kitchen came out with two bowls of egg and chili-soaked deliciousness.

"Chilaquiles! My favorite."

"I know," she said. "One for me, one for you." She pulled up a chair, squeezing herself between Wesley and Ridge. I got the feeling she'd picked that spot deliberately, to make sure they both ate every bite on their plates.

I dug through the bowl with my fingers, pulling out the crispiest piece of tortilla I could find. Making sure the chip was fully loaded with eggs, cheese, and salsa, I popped it in my mouth. I groaned happily. "Delicious."

She laughed. "Just like your mama used to make?"

"No. My mama left home when she was sixteen and left her family and her heritage behind. By blood, I'm Cuban. By raisin,' I'm as Southern as biscuits and gravy. I can barely speak Spanish."

She shook her head. "That's a damn shame."

The silence stretched awkwardly. The scrape of a fork against the plate and the caw of seabirds were the loudest sounds. The breeze from the water blew a napkin onto the floor.

"I'll get it," Josie said. After chasing the napkin across the deck, she went into the kitchen. When she came back, she was carrying two cold bottles of champagne. They hit the tiled table top with a clink.

"Give me your cups, glasses, whatever," she said to everyone.

Carson, Wesley, and I dutifully handed over our small juice glasses.

"None for me, thank you." Leo said.

Josie glared at him, eyes like steel. "We have shit to do, and I'm not going to sit here and watch you guys not talking to each other all day. So we're going to have some nice mimosas to break the ice, and then I'll leave you guys to talk about what you do. Remember the faster you do these things, the faster you can leave and never speak to each other." She paused meaningfully. "If that's what you want."

Leo handed her his glass.

"Who *are* you?" Wesley asked her, sounding impressed.

"I work—worked— for Charlie, the same way you all do. At least, I did when he was alive. And now I'm here to take care of you."

"Was he blackmailing you, too?" Ridge asked.

"Actually... yes. At first." Josie smiled, like the memory was a fond one. "I was running a con at a hotel in Chicago. Unfortunately for me, I picked Charlie as my mark." She rolled her eyes. "Turned out Charlie was running a longer con. He let me get away with my game for a while, but when he need some help with his, he told me he was onto me, and if I didn't help him out, he'd report me."

She took a long swig of mimosa. "So, I helped him. He asked me to stay. I stayed. The end. Now your turns. Geek boy, you first."

Wesley leaned back in his chair, sipping the champagne. His eyes were halfway closed, and I knew he wouldn't be able to stay awake long. "Me?" he demanded, straightening.

"Yeah, you."

"Um." His eyes slid to Leo. "You can't arrest me, right?"

"Not right now, I can't." Leo stared deadpan at him over the rim of his glass.

"Later?"

Leo shrugged.

"Boys," Josie said. "Play nice. Nothing said here actually happened. It's just a big game of what if." She emptied her glass, then reached for the bottle.

Leo stared at her, then grudgingly nodded.

"I blacked out most of the Eastern seaboard last year."

My jaw dropped.

"That was you?" Ridge asked, equally stunned. "Holy fuck! I owe you one, then. I was in the middle of a job, nabbing a painting that had gotten held up in a divorce dispute."

There were nods and groans of commiseration up and down the table, and it occurred to me how much of our collective business had to do with people's petty feuds.

"I was green as grass, and Murphy's Law was in full effect. In the week since I'd cased the place, the owner had redone his security system *and* redecorated his entire fucking house, so all my exit routes were blocked. I thought I was dead for sure. Then all the lights went out, the security system, *everything*. Bam. Pitch black. That was the only thing that let me get away. I thought it was my guardian angel." Ridge shook his head. "But I guess it was you."

Wes snickered.

"So where does Charlie come in?" Carson wanted to know.

Wesley looked uncomfortable. He drained his mimosa, then twirled the glass between his palms. "I guess Charlie was impressed. He found me."

"Of course he did," Leo muttered. "Fucking found Zero." He held out his cup for Josie to refill.

"And what did you do for him?" Ridge asked.

Wes raised one eyebrow. "*Stuff*. What about you?"

Ridge shrugged. "I'm a thief. Art mostly, jewels. Small, easy-to-steal stuff. Charlie tracked me down through this Albanian guy I've used as a fence. Needed me for a job. I needed money, he paid good. Pretty simple."

Leo snorted.

"What about you, Agent Shook? How did you get invited to this party?"

Leo's lips tightened into a hard line. "I'm not part of this. I've been tracking Charlie's ass for years." He shook his head. "Cat and mouse. Hopping all over the country. Every time I got close—and I got really close—he'd get away."

I didn't think I was imagining the faint hint of admiration in his voice.

"So what does Charlie have on you?" Ridge said. Asking the question I was dying to know the answer to.

"Nothing." Leo reached for a pastry.

"Bullshit," Wesley said. "You wouldn't be here if he didn't."

Leo tore small pieces off the flaky treat and tossed them to the small birds hopping around the deck, apparently not scared of us at all.

"Okay," I said when it became clear he wasn't going to answer. "It doesn't matter. What matters is, are you going to help us?"

"Help do *what*?" Leo practically yelled with frustration. He lobbed the remains of the Danish at the poor birds, who took off in a quiet flap of wings. "None of this makes any sense. Why give Steele pictures of Pfeiffer having sex? What the hell are we supposed to take care of?"

"It's *not me*," Ridge said through clenched teeth. "It's my twin brother, asshole. Breck Pfeiffer."

"Sure it is," Wesley said. "The mysterious *identical twin*."

Ridge scowled. I was pretty sure only Josie's presence between them kept him from hitting Wesley.

"Eat more," Josie said, nudging his plate toward him. She turned to Wes. "You, too. More eating, less fighting."

Wes obediently shoveled more food into his mouth. Then he grabbed his phone and started typing.

"Do you have the pictures with you?" Leo asked me.

"Yeah. I figured we'd need them." I picked the envelope up off the ground where I'd set it and pulled the pictures out. I looked through them, passing each one around the table as I finished. There were twenty-six full-color pictures in all. There were no clear pictures of the old man's face. "These look like surveillance photos, taken from a distance with a long lens. From the grain, I'd go out on a limb and say they were from a film camera. What do you guys think?"

Leo and Wesley flipped through the pictures. "It could be," Leo said.

"I can almost guarantee it." Wesley held the photos up to the sun, tilted it back and forth. "They look chemically developed, not done on a printer." He rubbed a finger across the face. "Yes. These are film."

"Okay. So, what?" I asked. "What are we supposed to do? Why are we supposed to care who is screwing who?"

"Because it's my brother, jackass!" Ridge said hotly. "He's in college, for fuck's sake. George Washington, up in D.C. He's supposed to be doing some kind of fucking internship this summer, not.... not... whatever the fuck that is." He waved a hand at the pictures in disgust.

"You wanna get on your brother's case, that's your business. I'm still not seeing how that's a problem for *us*, man."

"Can't you just call him and ask what the pictures are about?" Wesley said, not looking up from his phone. Whoever he was texting, they were exchanging messages fast and furiously. His fingers flew over the surface.

"You think I didn't try that?" Ridge retorted. "I've texted him a thousand times, no reply. My calls are going right to voicemail, and his mailbox is full. That's why I'm going to Washington and find out what the fuck is going on. Make him stop doing ... *that*."

"Having a threesome with an ugly old guy?" I asked. "I mean, it's a questionable life choice for sure, though the other kid is cute enough. But maybe the guy's got bucks. Or he's dynamite in the sack. Maybe your brother wanted a little strange. Maybe he was drunk." I snapped my fingers excitedly. "Maybe he's a professor and your brother's blowing him for money!"

Leo balled up a napkin and threw it at my head.

"What?" I demanded. "I saw it in a porn once. Or..." I coughed. "Maybe more than once."

Carson groaned.

"My point is, who gives a shit who he sleeps with? If he's doing it for fun, that's his concern. If he had too much to drink and made some bad choices, he'll learn from them. If he's doing it for money, more power to him." I shrugged. "I don't get my panties in a wad about where a man chooses to stick his dick." I looked at the pictures again. "Or, uh... chooses to have someone else's dick stuck."

"No," Ridge said, shaking his head resolutely. "No way is Breck doing that voluntarily. Someone is making him."

"I think Steele has a point. Maybe he's doing it for the money," Leo said. "Wouldn't be the first good-looking kid to do that. And nothing about these pictures speaks to things being involuntary. Even this one, where it looks like your brother's passed out and the old guy is slapping the other kid..." Leo hesitated. "If I'm honest, it looks like a slapping kink. And your brother looks like maybe he had too much to drink."

"No offense, Ridge, but if that really is your identical twin brother, he could be making bank. Especially if he's doing it in pairs. Bloody gorgeous, the both of you. People would pay a lot for that," Carson added.

"No," Ridge insisted. "He doesn't need the money. I made sure of it. His whole job is to graduate. I take care of the money."

"Well, actually," Wesley said slowly. "From what I'm looking at right now, maybe he does need the money."

"What?" Ridge said.

"I just ran a profile on him. Your brother is broke, Ridge. And he's taken a leave of absence from school for next semester. Great grades though, before. Three point eight GPA."

Ridge's jaw dropped, then he shut it so hard I was afraid he was going to break a tooth. The anger in his eyes promised a less than friendly family reunion was in the cards.

"I thought your equipment was still in Chicago?" I asked. "How'd you find that so fast?"

He held up his phone and shook it. "Turbo charged phone loaded with my own custom decryption software. Don't leave home without it."

"I know Charlie," Leo said. "Probably better than anyone here, except maybe Josie. He wouldn't be sending us to D.C. just to stop some guy from selling his ass. No offense. There has to be more than this. If it was just about your brother, why give the assignment to Steele? There's something more going on here."

"I agree," Carson said. "That is much too straightforward for Charlie. He wasn't blackmailing the guy, I assume." His accent came and went. I could hear bits of Josie's drawl and Wesley's broad vowels sneaking into his pronunciation.

We all looked at Josie. She shrugged. "Don't look at me. No one knew all the pies Charlie had his fingers in."

"Great," Ridge said. "Just fucking great."

Josie sat up straight. "I'm sure he had a good reason for this. Charlie was a good man."

We all snorted at that.

"He was," she insisted.

"He was a criminal," Leo said. "Like everyone at this table. And I am including you," he said to Josie.

She grinned. "I didn't say he was an honest, law-abiding man. I said he was a *good* man. You can be both."

Leo's eyes narrowed, and I could see him fighting to keep the words in. Not in Leo's world, you couldn't.

"Josie, is there any more information? Does Miranda know anything?"

"No. That's it. Pretty sure there are limits to what she can know without being disbarred." Josie smiled to herself. "Though I'm pretty sure if he was still around, Miranda might kill Charlie herself."

"Charlie has that effect on people," Leo said. He blinked. "Had. *Had* that effect."

"We're all spinning our wheels here. I need to get my brother," Ridge stood up. "I have ways of tracking him, and I'll go alone if I have to. Miranda said we could use Charlie's plane."

"Josie, fuel the jet!" I waved my hand imperiously. "I've always wanted to say that. But seriously, we have nothing else to go on. Looks like we're going to get Ridge two-point-oh."

Leo pushed his chair back and stood up. "I'll run these photos through some facial recognition, see if we can't find out who the brown-haired guy is."

"You think the other kid could be Charlie's target?" I handed over the photos I still held. "Not the old guy?"

"Could be both of them," Leo said. "You know how it is. No one is too young to go bad."

Yeah. I knew. "Come on, Angel-Face, you and I can clean up and come up with some sort of plan. Josie, can you make arrangements for us to fly into D.C. under the radar as soon as possible?"

She nodded.

"One thing," I said to Ridge as we started loading up the dirty dishes. "I'm a man of limited but very specialized skills. There's only one reason civilians hire me, and unlike your brother, it's not for my looks. Either Charlie thinks you, or Breck, or possibly both of you, need protection, or someone needs to be roughed up." Or worse. I really hoped it wasn't worse. I'd die happy if I never had to take another life. I used deadly force only as an ultimate, last resort, and everyone who hired me knew it.

"But who?" Ridge asked. "Who is Charlie looking to take down?"

Leo and I shared a look. Neither of us wanted to say it, but old men in bed with young boys brought up too many bad memories. Including some I worked very, very hard to keep down.

"Let's go get your brother," Leo said, "and find out."

I FINISHED MAKING the cup of lemon tea in Chad's otherwise barren kitchen and immediately regretted it. My stomach was too knotted up to handle even that. Chad's apartment no longer felt safe. I imagined Cisco's eyes tracking my every movement as I gathered my clothes and put them in a bag.

Danny had once mentioned that he liked to walk at Rock Creek Park, and since I'd exhausted all the likely places to find him, it was time to start searching the unlikely ones.

I grabbed my tea off the counter and headed to the living room to dump the cooled mixture on Chad's ficus.

The knock on the door startled me so badly, I spilled teawater all over the floor.

"Maintenance, Mr. McMickles!"

Poor Chad. If I'd grown up with a name like McMickles, I'd probably be an asshole, too.

"Uh. Busy now! Come back later," I called. Much later, like after I'd gone.

"Emergency," the maintenance man insisted.

Damn it. *"No hablo ingles!"*

"Abre la puerta, Señor...McMickles?"

Shit. Figured they spoke rudimentary Spanish.

I crept through the kitchen toward the door and peeked through the peephole, but all I could see was the base of the man's throat and a vee of smooth tan skin peaking out from the open collar of the blue button-up shirt all maintenance guys wore.

How fucking tall was this guy? I took a step back.

"I'm having sex!" I cried. *"Oh, God! Oh, fuck. I'm sooooo clooooose!"* My fake pleasure-moans were on point, if I did say so myself.

There was a momentary pause. "Sir, water is pouring into the apartment downstairs, and we think it's coming from your air conditioner."

Fuck. That could be true. That thing had to be gushing out water, cold as it was in here. Okay, looking at it objectively, it would have been nearly impossible for Cisco to have traced my phone here that quickly. And no one else knew I was here.

When in doubt, do the thing least likely to arouse suspicion. I slid back the deadbolt and opened the door. W*hoa.*

Like, *whoa,* this guy was tall. As in Jason-Momoa-tall. And the peephole had not done justice to the breadth of his chest, which almost filled the fucking doorframe. Apparently they built the maintenance guys like Aquaman around here.

Then *whoa* again, because when I finally forced my gaze off his chest I saw him grinning at me like I was the best thing he'd ever seen, teeth bright white against his tan skin. While I was used to men finding me sexy—that was *literally* my job—the looks they gave me were possessive and covetous and *hard,* nothing like this warm amusement that suggested Aquaman and I were in on a shared joke.

And then *whoa* one more time, because the dude licked his lips and said, "*So... was it good?*" in this deep, raspy voice that reminded me of the radio announcer on the easy listening station back in Alamosa. Damn if I hadn't lain in bed at night back in high school, listening to fucking clarinet solos and power ballads, just so I could jerk off to David Tremaine telling me tomorrow's weather forecast between songs. This man was a walking orgasm, and I felt a stab in my gut I barely recognized as lust since it had been so long since I'd felt it.

"W-what?" I stuttered.

"The sex," he said, leaning against the doorframe and leering at me like no maintenance man outside porn ever would. "Was it good?" How did he manage to make a good ole boy accent sexy?

Somewhere beneath the lust-filled part of my brain, distant alarm bells began to ring.

"Get out of the way, Alvarez," a distinctly familiar, distinctly *un-sexy* voice carped, before another body pushed forward, elbowing Aquaman in the gut. "And for God's sake, turn the pheromones off. Some of us are trying to breathe."

It was like looking at my own damning gaze in the mirror as Ridge shook his head at me. "What the fuck have you done, little brother?"

I stepped back, stunned. "How did you find me?"

He rolled his eyes and strode past me into the apartment. "Psychic twin powers."

"Bullshit."

"Better question, dumbass," he said, hands on his hips, "is why are you hiding?"

I snapped my mouth shut and ran both hands through my hair, leaning back against the kitchen counter. I closed my eyes.

The tuba player upstairs was still practicing, and if there was a god, when I opened my eyes, I would have somehow been transported upstairs to join the band. I cautiously lifted my lids and found Alvarez leaning back against the door with his arms crossed and his eyes still warm on mine.

He winked.

"Imagine my surprise," my brother continued, "when I got to that apartment in Georgetown I paid for, only to find that you hadn't been living there since *January*." He was angry. I'd known he would be. But he was disappointed too, and I hated that.

I bit my lip. "I needed a change of scenery. I've been subletting." More like crashing in random cars and benches around campus, grabbing hotel rooms when it was really cold.

"Yeah? A change of scenery? That why the school says you've taken a leave of absence for next semester?"

"You went to the school?" My eyes widened, and I took a threatening step toward him. "You had no right to pry into my life, Ridge."

"My paying your tuition says I do." He closed the distance between us like he was ready to throw down right there, right then. He'd do it, too. Neither one of us was the type to back down from a fight.

Aquaman put a hand on Ridge's shoulder, and *oh my god* the glare he got in return. Ridge was not a fan.

"Much as I would be totally into you and Angel-Face going at it on the kitchen floor right now," the giant said to me, "it wasn't his fault."

"Pardon?"

"It wasn't Ridge who did the prying, it was my friend Wes. Computer whiz." He mimed someone typing on a keyboard.

I frowned, completely lost, and looked to Ridge for an explanation, but he wasn't looking at me. "What?"

"*Wes* looked you up," Alvarez said patiently, like *I* was the idiot here. "To be honest, when Ridge said he had a brother, none of us believed him." He shrugged again, sheepish this time. "Especially when he told us your name was Breck. Breck-and-Ridge? And you're from Colorado? Who does that to a kid?"

Our mother, that was who.

But apparently his question was rhetorical, because he continued. "I mean in that situation, I woulda invented an 'identical twin,' too." He made air quotes with his fingers, then tilted his head to the side thoughtfully. "Or maybe not." He grinned. "Maybe I would've owned it, especially if I had an ass like yours."

"What the fuck are you talking about?" I demanded, but my blood ran cold and I was pretty sure I knew, especially when Ridge glared at Alvarez and yelled, "Jesus Christ. That's my little brother you're perving over, asshole."

"Yeah, I know." He leered. "Imagine how happy I was to find out there were two of you."

"I'm younger than you by thirteen minutes, jerk face." I walked forward and grabbed his face, forcing him to meet my eyes. "What the fuck are you doing here? What's going on?"

Ridge's eyes met mine for half a second before his gaze skittered away. He shook his head. "For fuck's sake, Brekkie, If you needed money, you could have come to me." His voice was low and dripping with pain. "You *should* have come to me. Dropping out of school, losing all that money. Doing... the shit you've done. It's like I don't even know you."

I dropped my hands and took a step back, then another.

He knew. *Fuck.* While I'd never intended for him to find out, I hadn't really known how badly I *needed* him to never find out until I saw his face just then.

I took a deep breath and stood as tall as I could, arms crossed over my chest. "I don't need your help," I said with what though was admirable calmness. "I'm handling it."

"By *whoring*?"

"Wow," I whispered. I was all about owning slurs and taking the power out of them. I'd heard them all over the years, and especially in the last six months. But I hadn't been prepared to hear *that* one. Not from my brother.

"Tell me I'm wrong," Ridge challenged.

I couldn't. But I shouldn't have had to.

"Pfeiffer," Alvarez said, glaring at Ridge. "Step back. Be chill."

"Chill? I'll chill when he tells me what he did with the money I gave him. Over *fifty thousand dollars*. And now that account is empty."

"You've been checking my bank account, too?" It shouldn't have been a surprise. It shouldn't have hurt as much as it did.

Alvarez grimaced, lifting one enormous hand to scratch his beard. "It wasn't personal," he said. "It's SOP when running a profile on someone."

I lifted my chin and blinked, first at him and then back at my brother who still wouldn't look at me. "Standard operating procedure when you run a profile on *someone*? There are only two kinds of *someones* who get profiles run on them without their consent: suspects and marks. Which one am I, Ridge?"

Ridge stiffened. "This isn't about me, Breck. Don't try to turn this around."

"It is one hundred percent about you," I told him. "You being a control freak, as usual. I took that money because you begged me to. But that doesn't mean you get to control my life. My choices are mine. *Mine.*"

"They're shitty choices! What did you do with it, huh? Snort it? Gamble it away?" Ridge looked at me finally, and I almost wished he hadn't, because his eyes were bleak and devastated. He shook his head. "Mom would be so proud, Brekkie."

The words hit me like a blow, knocking the air out of my lungs. "I...I can't believe you'd say that to me."

He swallowed. "So give me something else, then. Tell me you donated it to charity or something."

At that moment my brother, the man who wore my face, was a stranger to me. I knew the shit he was involved in and the people he associated with had made him hard over the years, but he'd never been that way with me. He'd always been on my side. *Always.* And I hadn't realized how much I'd relied on that until it was gone.

I shook my head. "I have nothing to say to you right now."

"Oh, you'll talk to me alright. You'll explain what the fuck these are about." He grabbed his phone and unlocked it, then thrust it into my hand.

Pictures. Dozens of them. Of me laying on Snow White's bed with my hands on his chest, while Danny sucked him off. Of me on my back with Danny on top, kissing while Snow White looked on avidly. Of me, laying on the floor in what looked like a drugged-out stupor while Snow White smacked Danny's face.

I clapped a hand over my mouth as the disgusting lemon tea threatened to make a reappearance and tossed the phone as far from me as I could. "Where did you get these?"

"I got them," Alvarez said. He walked forward and stuck out his hand. "We haven't been formally introduced. I'm Steele Alvarez."

He gave me a flirtatious smile that succeeded in distracting me for half a minute.

"Steele?" I raised one eyebrow. "Is that... one of those things where you try to pick your own nickname and hope it sticks? Like, when your name is Percy, and you tell people to call you *Punisher* or *Predator*?"

Ridge snorted and twisted away, running a hand over his face.

Steele's lips twitched, and he pressed them together. "No, it's one of those things where your mom names you Castille because of some story she read while she was pregnant and then nicknames you Steele because the only alternative is Cassie." He paused. "And she said I didn't look like a Cassie."

Well, that was the damn truth, anyway.

"I got those pictures as part of a... let's call it an *assignment*," Steele said, exchanging an eye roll with Ridge. "Or maybe more like a crusade that I was voluntold to join. The only instructions are to *set things right*. And I guess we'll know the job is done when we get... uh. Paid."

"This picture is your crusade?" I clarified.

"Yeah." He paused and laid a tentative hand on my shoulder. "We can get you out of here, you know. If money is the issue, you don't have to do that work anymore. You have people who care about you." He gave Ridge a hard look, daring him to contradict. "And we have access to resources. *Financial* resources."

I snickered.

They both looked at me like I'd lost my mind, and despite the seriousness of the situation, despite the gaping maw of shiteousness my life had somehow become, I couldn't help but laugh until I was doubled over and tears ran from my eyes.

"Let me understand," I gasped once I'd finally caught my breath. "You white knights took a look at this picture and automatically decided that the worst thing that could possibly be happening here is me having sex for money?" I looked at Ridge and snorted. "Because I should be saving my virginity for marriage?" I looked at Steele. "Because you've never had sex except with people you *love*?"

Ridge shuffled his feet but said nothing. Stubborn fucking control freak.

I sighed. "Step into the living room, dumbass. I'll clue you in."

GRACIOUSLY, I refrained from saying *I told you so* to Ridge as we followed the kid into the McMickle living room. Eyeing his cute little butt helped. But really, I'd told him ten times that I doubted Charlie would go to all this trouble just to keep his brother from hustling. People did it all the time. I'd seen kids way younger than them selling it in truck stops up and down I-95.

I figured the kid did it for some extra spending money, for the thrill, for no-strings sex, whatever. I gotta admit, part of me was wondering how much he charged.

Let me tell you, if those two decided to sell themselves as a twin-act, they would be two of the most exclusive escorts in the country in a matter of weeks. Hell, give me a camera and some massage oil, and I could have sheiks tapping their oil wells for a couple of hours with the twins by the end of the day.

I spent a few seconds imagining the photos while scoping out the apartment. It was a spanking new condo that screamed *daddy's paying the rent*. Whether it was daddy or *a* daddy was an open question. But there was no way Chad McMickles, twenty-year-old international relations student, was paying his own rent on this. I'd almost shit when I saw the rents in D.C. Holy hell.

Tension radiated from Ridge's back. He was trying to hold on to his anger, I could tell. But I also knew he was worried about the kid. He'd been pissed when he saw the photos, but he hadn't lost his mind until Wes had let him know the money was gone from the bank account.

"Hey, Sweetcheeks." I pinched the kid's ass. *Firm.* I caught his hand as he whirled around, fire in his eyes. Unfortunately, I didn't catch the foot Ridge slammed into the back of my knees. Damn, I hadn't expected that. I staggered, and it was all they needed. The two of them had me down on the ground before I could say sorry.

Breck ended up kneeling on my chest. I laughed, my hands going to his hips of their own will. Smart hands. "Damn, Colorado. I was right. I could get big bucks for the two of you together. The biggest."

"Yeah?" Breck asked. He didn't seem in too much of a hurry to get up. I rubbed my thumbs against his hip bones.

"Fuck you, Alvarez. And don't touch my brother." Ridge yanked Breck off me. I liked to think Breck was as unhappy about that as I was.

I stayed lying on the expensive hardwood floors. "Sweetcheeks, if you move just a tiny bit to the right, I'll have a much better view." The leg openings of those shorts were nice and wide.

"You're disgusting." Ridge tugged Breck away from me.

"I know." I pushed myself up to my elbows. "What I was asking, before I was so rudely interrupted, is what happened to the fifty K?"

Breck dropped into a stylish but uncomfortable looking chair with a sigh. He swung his legs over the arm. "Look. I did pay my tuition, I swear. You must have seen that."

"We did," Ridge admitted, sitting down on the surface of a glass coffee table directly in front of Breck. "But there were thousands—thousands—of dollars of cash withdrawals! There's only one thing you could need that much cash for." Ridge jumped up, pacing in the tight space between the chair and the table. "God damn it, Breck. We promised! We said we wouldn't touch any of that shit!"

Breck watched his brother, his eyes tracking him as he paced. "Wow. That's some first class detective work right there. Are you done?" he asked when Ridge paused for breath. "Did you actually want to hear what I have to say or just stand there and glare at me?"

Leaning against the stainless steel mantel over the free-standing gas fireplace, Ridge waved at him to go on.

"Thank you, that's so kind of you." Breck put his legs down and leaned forward. "And fuck you for going right to the worst possible assumption about why I'd need money. *Christ.* And you wonder why I didn't come to you for help?"

Ridge opened his mouth to argue again.

As much as it turned me on to hear the sass rolling off Breck Pfeiffer's tongue, I was in no mood to play family therapist. If I wanted to get out from Charlie's hold, I needed to find out what the hell I was supposed to *set right*. Since Breck obviously didn't need rescuing from hooking, our mission had to do with whoever that old guy in the photos was, I was sure of it.

"Enough!" I used my in-the-field voice, the one that made battle-hardened men jump-to. "Breck, what the hell did you do with the money?"

Breck turned and looked at me. He sighed. "I gave it to Mom." He flinched preemptively from Ridge's yell.

And yell he did. "Mom? Goddamn it, Breck! What the fuck were you thinking?"

Aw man, the kid looked guilty. Like a dog that knew he'd done something wrong and wouldn't look his owner in the face.

"I was thinking she was our mother and she needed it." His cheeks were red, and I wondered if he was telling the whole story.

"Brekkie..." Ridge looked like he'd been punched in the gut. "Come on. You know better. I *know* you know better. How many times over the years did she tell us she needed money to get clean or pay rent or get a new apartment, and every time she scraped anything together, she drank it or smoked it or shot it in her arm?"

"Yeah, well," Breck said, looking defiant and maybe a little embarrassed. "Clearly I'm an idiot, okay? Drop it, Ridge. The money's gone. Everything you gave me and more besides. Move on."

Aw, fuck. Talk about a tale as old as time. (Yeah, I like Disney films, don't judge.) Goddammit. I wanted to hate the woman, and I did hate what she'd done to these kids. But addiction, man. There but for the grace of God, and a very scary mother, went I.

I levered myself up from the floor to the sofa and reached for Breck, wrapping him in my arms.

"Aw, Sweetcheeks, you're not an idiot. But you do know better. It's never different with addicts."

He stiffened in surprise, but I didn't let go. This kid needed a hug bad. Wes's research had painted a picture of a man all alone in the world. He had no family outside of Ridge and no real friends. We'd only found him because Ridge had put a tracking chip in his brother's cell phone months ago as an emergency precaution, and Wes activated it as soon as we figured out Breck was no longer living in Georgetown.

Breck relaxed in my arms, even going so far as to rest his cheek against my chest. I barely resisted the urge to kiss the top of his head. I'd bet his blond curls were soft.

It was hard to remember that this was a *job*, but for everyone's sake, I had to.

"Breck. What was your grand plan, here? Were you ever going to go back to school? How were you going to pay for it?" Ridge eyebrows drew together, and he frowned. "*Hooking?*"

I could've told the guy that speaking the word like it was a disease wasn't going to help him get any information out of his brother, and predictably, Breck stiffened.

"Maybe. You can make insane money doing it." Breck paused. He raised his chin stubbornly. "But anyway, I wasn't gonna go back. Maybe it's time for me to start over somewhere new. Say goodbye to Breck Pfeiffer for good."

"And were you planning to tell me?" Ridge demanded, pain in his voice.

Breck looked momentarily guilty, but he recovered. "Right. 'Cause you make it so easy to tell you things, Ridge," he fired back.

God, these boys really were alone, weren't they? I'd gotten the feeling things were worse than Ridge wanted to admit to himself.

Ridge looked like he was going to argue, but I held up a hand to cut him off. With a final hug, I let Breck go. "First things first. I think we need to talk about these photos."

I could see Ridge wanted to bitch me out. I could see *who do you think you are?* and *you're not my dad!* hovering in his expression.

Breck's phone rang, belting out Britney Spears. He jumped and ran to the kitchen to grab it off the counter. "It's Danny!"

I followed him to the kitchen and snagged the phone from his hand. "Tell Danny you'll call him back after we chat."

His blue eyes nearly incinerated me. "Uh, how about *fuck you?*"

I held the phone up out of his reach, but he leaped up and grabbed onto it, dragging my arm down with his weight. Fucker was strong. More muscular than his brother, and mad enough that his knee was aiming at my balls.

"Breck, this is important. We need to know..."

"No, *this* is important," Breck gritted out. "Danny's my friend and the other guy in the pictures." He glared at Ridge. "The other *whore*."

I let Breck yank the phone from me. He answered it and I stood close enough to hear both sides of the conversation.

"Danny?"

"Rocky! Are you okay?"

"Me? Jesus Christ, dude. I thought you were dead!"

"Dead?" I demanded. I shot Ridge a glance and found him frowning at Breck like he was trying to see inside his brother's mind. "What the fuck?"

Breck waved a hand, trying to shush me, but his friend had heard me.

"Rocky?" he whined. "Are you alone?"

I'm no expert, but the kid sounded younger than the twins and terrified. Considering Breck had been seriously concerned the kid was dead, I was afraid he was going to bolt. "Talk to him. Tell him everything's okay."

"That's what I was trying to do, asshole," he whispered furiously.

Okay, he had a point. He glared at me and turned his attention back to the phone.

"Danny. Where are you? Are you safe?"

"For now. I guess. Who are those people with you? Did Snow White find you? Did he... hurt you?"

Snow White? What the hell had these kids gotten involved in? I remembered the picture of the old guy slapping that one kid in the face while Breck lay on the floor. Ridge had assumed his brother had been passed out from drugs. We all had.

I was beginning to think we had been very, very wrong.

"Nobody found me, except my brother. Well, Emilio called me, too. Fucker."

"Why did you answer the phone?" Danny's voice was panicked.

"Habit! He woke me up. Look, don't give me shit, Danny. Just...come here. I'm at—"

"No!" I snapped, putting my hand on his wrist. "Don't say where you are. Someone could be following him."

"Shit," Breck said, rubbing a hand over his forehead. "You're right. I know better than that."

Oh great. If one of the Pfeiffer brothers was agreeing with me, the situation must be dire. I'd only known Ridge for a couple of days and Breck for a couple of hours, but I could tell they didn't do anything they didn't want to.

"Danny, my brother and his, uh..." He trailed off with a look at me.

"Business associate," I supplied. "Temporarily." *Fellow victim of a dead man's blackmail* seemed a little bit TMI.

Breck rolled his eyes. "My brother and his *friend*—"

Ridge snorted. "Hell no," he muttered.

I clapped a hand over my heart and shook my head sadly. "And here I was picking out matching BFF tattoos."

Breck slapped me in the stomach.

"They're insane, but I think they can help us." Breck looked at Ridge. Ridge nodded, sure and confident. Breck's shoulders sagged. "I'll come to you instead."

"I don't know. Snow White's got guys looking for me." Danny's voice was barely a breath of sound, but he was petrified.

I started to grab the phone again, and Breck turned away, shielding the phone with his body. "Cut it the fuck out," he hissed. To Danny, he said, "What happened, Dan? I was unconscious for most of it, but I remember you were hurt pretty bad."

I took a deep breath. "Bre...Rocky," I amended at his quick head shake. *See? I pay attention.* "Please, may I talk to your friend? I don't know exactly what's going on, but I'm getting a general idea."

"And it's not good," Ridge added unnecessarily.

I glanced over at him and nodded before turning back to Breck. "Yeah, not good. And the kind of shit that you shouldn't be talking about on the phone, okay? We need to get you both to a safe location, and then we can get into the details of what the hell you've gotten involved with... and how we can unfuck it." *And how I can get my freedom back,* I thought but didn't say.

"Danny, did you hear that? We'll come and get you, okay?"

"N-no, man. I gotta go. It's dangerous, and..."

Breck gripped the phone with both hands. "One second. Please. For me, Danny. Please."

There was a long pause. "Do you trust these guys? Really?"

"It's my brother," Breck said as if that were explanation enough.

Danny snorted. "So? Family doesn't mean anything."

This time Ridge yanked the phone out of Breck's hand before I could and put it on speaker. "Danny? I'm... uh... *Rocky's* brother. And that means something to me. So when I say I swear we'll help you, you can believe it. Now just tell me where to meet you, and we'll come and get you."

"A crowded public place with a lot of security cameras," I said.

"Fine," Danny agreed. "Not like I have a lot of options. Tell Rocky I'll be at the place where we trailed that guy we thought was Adam Rippon."

Breck smiled at that. "Okay." He raised his voice so Danny could hear him. "We'll be there in about twenty minutes or so, depending on traffic. We'll text you when we're somewhere close, somewhere away from the cameras. Okay?"

He hesitated. "Rocky, you gotta be careful, man. If they're after me, they're probably after you. You shouldn't show your face."

"Is that so?" Ridge asked Breck. He shook his head in a way that suggested Breck had a lot of explaining to do.

Breck ignored his brother. "My brother's friend will come get you. He'll give you a code word..." He paused for a second. "I know! The name of your pet turtle!"

"Okay," he whispered. "Be careful."

"You be careful, too." Ridge hung up and handed his brother the phone.

"Come on," Breck said. "Let's go."

"Not so fast. We need a couple of answers first," I told him, laying my hand flat on his chest and pushing slightly.

Breck collapsed onto the leather couch with a sigh. He ran both hands through his curls, the same way I'd seen Ridge do when he was thinking. "Thank God. I thought he was dead. Jesus." He slumped forward, dropping his head into his hands. When his shoulders started shaking, Ridge sat down next to him.

He put an arm around his brother, pulling him into a hug, and Breck went easily. Proof that no matter how pissed off they still were at one another, they were a unit. I hadn't known Ridge was capable of that kind of loyalty, and my opinion of the guy shot up considerably.

"Brekkie, who's the old guy in the photos?" he asked.

Breck inhaled. "I'm not a hundred percent sure. Cisco, he arranged all the...all the dates. We didn't use real names. We called the guy Snow White. Stupid name, right? But he liked me and Danny. We'd been with him a couple of times. He was... fine. I mean, kinky as fuck, but then lots of guys are. He'd never been into the really rough shit."

He wouldn't look either of us in the eye, but I could see the red creeping up to his ears and down his chest. I swore one day I would see that flush from passion, not from embarrassment.

I also swore one day, I would kill this Snow White. Or at least break his dick.

"So you don't know his name? Would you recognize him?"

Breck nodded quickly. "Anywhere. In the dark."

Snow White had better hope he didn't meet Breck in the dark. The kid had murder in his voice.

"That night." He pointed at the pictures that had brought us to D.C., and his mouth trembled. "That night, we were at his house. For the first time ever. And he—something was different. He wasn't really hiding who he was? Like, not really. And I mean, he even said it was his house. Like I can't use the internet? Anyway. He was different that night. Meaner, saying really nasty things, calling us whores and sluts. He has this assistant... bodyguard... whatever, who'd usually wait out in the hall, and even that guy looked surprised at the way Snow White was acting when he let us into the bedroom."

"Fucker," Ridge growled.

I was going to cut off Snow White's dick *slowly*. With a dull knife. Everything about Breck made me want to protect him. To take care of him and keep him safe. To make him mine. It was a feeling that had gotten me in trouble many times before. Guys didn't always appreciate the caveman thing.

"Let me finish," Breck begged. "Or I won't get it out."

"Did he hurt you?" It was time to cut to the fuckin' chase. "Did he hurt Danny?"

"Yeah. I thought he was going to kill us," Breck said, voice flat. "He was on something. Had to be." He smiled without humor. "If there's one thing I learned from Mom, it's how to spot when someone's fucked up. His eyes were like little pinpricks. And he tried to get me to do lines, but I... I said no. Screamed it, actually. Which is when he backhanded me onto the floor." He swallowed. "I was mostly in and out of consciousness after that. But I know he whaled on Danny. Left him bloody. I tried to get up and help him, but I was useless. I, uh... woke up on a bench outside Union Station. And I had no idea what happened to Danny."

"Fucking bastard! I'll kill him," Ridge said through clenched teeth.

"You can't!" Breck grabbed Ridge's arm as if his brother was going to leap off the couch and run out the door. "I think he's a senator!"

Jesus fuck. Of course, he was.

"What makes you say that?" I demanded.

"It's not exactly uncommon around here, you know? Cisco's guys are the best in town, which means his clientele is connected." He shrugged. "But I overheard his bodyguard dude. He came in at one point when Snow White was passed out on the bed. He tried to wake him up, and I'd swear he called him *Senator.*" He shook his head. "As much as I could swear to anything from that night."

"Which senator?" Ridge asked as I pulled up a list of senators on my phone. One hundred senators. I eliminated twenty-three women and two black guys. Given how much skin I saw, I was fairly confident we were looking for an old white guy.

Breck studied the picture, enlarging it with his fingers. "That one," he said, shuddering as he pointed. "With the white hair. That's part of how he got his nickname. Well, that and the blow."

Ridge grabbed the phone and studied the caption. "Senator Harlan," he spat, jaw set. "Fucker."

Of course it was. John Harlan was the most vocal anti-LGBT voice in Congress, and that was saying something. A former pastor, he'd been 'happily' married to his wife for forty-five years. They had two perfect children, and he had a vocal support group that was more than happy to condemn millions of people to hell simply because of who they were.

Of course, he was fucking boys on the side.

"I'm going to kill him." I could easily make it look like an accident. I dusted my hands together, and I could practically feel the man's neck between my fingers. "No charge. I'll enjoy it."

"You can't just kill him," Breck said.

"Why not?" Ridge asked, looking at me as if to confirm that I could do what I said.

"Are you kidding?" Breck looked at me, and I shrugged. I'd beaten people up for way less. And while I'd always drawn a line between *personal security* and *assassin for hire*, I was pretty damn fine popping my cherry for this guy.

Plus, honest to God, this kid had riled every protective instinct I had. There was something about him that drew me in, something beyond the curls and the big eyes, beyond the bubble butt and the sass. Ridge was just as pretty, and he'd never affected me the way Breck did.

Breck needed me, whether he knew it or not. And… I kinda dug it.

"Okay, first of all, did you get the part where I said he was a senator?" Breck demanded, folding his arms and glaring at me. "There are only a hundred of them, you know? So folks tend to notice when they go missing." He rolled his eyes.

All I could think was that he was perfect for me. The idea of me killing the senator in cold blood didn't faze him at all. He was more concerned that we might get caught.

I opened my mouth to argue, to tell him that I knew a hundred ways to immobilize a guy without arousing suspicion, but he kept talking.

"Besides, that would be letting him off too easy." Breck looked at Ridge. "Those pictures on your phone. You saw what he did. He knocked me unconscious. He beat Danny to a pulp. I want him to suffer." He looked at me, and his eyes were burning with an emotion I knew intimately. "I want to take everything from him, and I want him to know who did it."

Yeah. I understood that. Breck needed vengeance. And I wanted to get it for him. "Damn right," I said loudly. "That's what we're going to do."

"How?" Ridge asked.

"I don't know," I said. I gave him a wry look. "But we know people who do."

It all became clear to me at that moment what Charlie's ultimate motivation had been. These weren't personal vendettas or petty crimes he wanted to be solved. He wanted justice, the kind he couldn't get from inside the system.

FOR THE LAST year my life had been more like a series of slow blinks and jump cuts than a coherent story. Sometimes it felt like I'd closed my eyes in one reality and opened them in another one entirely.

Ever since we'd learned there were forty-nine other states and six separate continents outside of our own, Ridge and I had talked about putting as much distance between us and Alamosa as possible someday. But in the meantime, we never left Colorado.

Then Ridge had gotten a huge score on some paintings—big enough to bring him some heat—and he'd come home yelling, "Breck! We're leaving. *Now*." So we'd left town in the dead of night like we were fleeing the zombie apocalypse.

Two days later, I'd found myself strolling a cold, empty beach in North Carolina, more than a little dazed, thinking, "Okay. So... this is my new life, I guess."

Same thing last fall, when my mom had come calling. The pitiful whines of "I need money, Brekkie," hadn't worked on me, no matter what I told Ridge, but the vindictive threats that followed had been pretty damn effective. She'd threatened to ruin everything Ridge had worked for. So I'd paid up... and then I'd taken the only kind of job I could find that had any hope of making that money back before Ridge found out and literally killed our mother once and for all. And as I was doing the walk of shame out of the Capitol Inn after servicing my first john, I'd had another of those weird moments of vertigo. "Wow. Okay. So this is what I'm doing now."

You might have thought I'd learn to roll with it, to accept my status as fate's fucktoy, but I hadn't. So when I found myself laying on the shaded area of a pool deck overlooking the Gulf of Mexico, twenty-six hours after Ridge had barged back into my life, I was not admiring the incredible view of the water, or the majesty of the huge-ass mansion we were staying in, or the way the sun glinted off the infinity pool overlooking the beach. And I was definitely *not* thinking, "Oh, well! I'll just make the best of it!"

I was fucking *pissed*.

I slammed my palms on the arms of my chair. "How much longer are they going to keep us here?" I demanded.

Danny, who was floating on an enormous pink raft in the center of the pool, lowered his sunglasses and squinted at me like I was insane. He was naked except for the tiniest pair of red Speedos, and practically glowing from whatever oily shit he'd basted himself with before coming out to soak up rays. "Um... Honey? I think the question is *how much longer will they let us stay?*"

I shook my head, fuming silently.

I didn't expect Danny to get why I was upset, not really. I mean, when we'd met up with him at Union Station yesterday morning, he'd looked *bad*. Gaunt and twitchy. Not like he'd been using, but like he'd spent way too many nights looking over his shoulder, without a hot meal or a safe place to sleep.

And unlike Ridge and me, Danny wasn't used to that kind of life. He hadn't grown up making do with scraps of food or stealing shit to keep himself fed. He'd been a soft, suburban twink before his uber-religious parents had kicked him out. Hooking was the closest he'd come to a life of crime. He'd taken one look at Steele, ten feet tall and bulletproof as he was, and had practically fallen to his knees in gratitude at being rescued. Now he was Team Steele all the way.

Not that I could totally blame Danny for that, if I were being honest. When Steele had taken the seat next to me on the little leather loveseat in the private plane that had collected us from Dulles, thrown his arm around my shoulder, and hauled me up against his side for the entire ninety-minute flight, I hadn't exactly protested. Or moved, except to rest my head against his shoulder. Or tried to hide my smile at the way Ridge glared at Steele from across the cabin the whole time, like he was daring him to make a move on me. Steele's attention had been more comforting than sexual and damn if I didn't like it.

There weren't a lot of guys who could stand up to that look from my brother, but Steele was either oblivious or he cared more about sitting next to me and offering me support than he did about my brother being pissed.

That idea made my stomach flip in a way that anyone who knew me as Rocky would find comical. I was the exact opposite of a shrinking virgin, but there I was, sinking under the weight of my crush on Castille Alvarez.

Josie, the housekeeper Steele had introduced us to, wheeled out a little metal cart with drinks. "Strawberry daiquiris, boys?"

Danny's eyes lit up. "God, yeah. Totally!" He paddled his raft closer to the edge of the pool, and Josie smiled fondly as she handed him the hurricane glass. It was impossible not to be protective of Danny.

But when she turned to me, I shook my head stubbornly. Sure, the drink looked delicious, and I was already sweating even though it was barely ten in the morning. But I wasn't here on vacation. I was here under protest.

She sighed and thrust the drink in my direction. "You're not hurting anyone but yourself, honey."

She was right. I knew it. My problems with Ridge and his high-handedness wouldn't be solved by refusing her.

I rolled my eyes and took the drink. "Thanks."

"It's not so bad around here," she said. "You'll get used to it."

"They took my *phone*," I said. And I'd understood it, mostly. They wanted to make sure we were untraceable. But it was another sign that I was a prisoner, not a guest. "Not sure I'll get used to life without the internet."

"I may have a solution," she said, narrowing her eyes thoughtfully. "Talk to me this afternoon."

"Yeah?"

She nodded. "Drink up. Leo's back, and they're getting the media room ready. Steele asked where you were, so I'm guessing it's only a matter of time before he comes looking for you."

I frowned but nodded. I had no clue who Leo was, or what the fuck we were going to do in the media room—watching *Weekend at Bernie's* seemed unlikely—but if Ridge or Steele wanted me around, it was a sure bet they were going to pump me for more information on Snow White.

I took a deep sip of my drink, ignoring the threat of brain freeze.

Danny heaved himself off the float, landing in the shallow water with a splash. Holding his drink above his head, he made his way to the steps and threw himself into the lounge chair beside mine.

"Hey, watch it!" I said as he rubbed his fingers through his long-ish brown hair, spraying water droplets all over the khaki shorts and polo I'd stolen from Ridge.

Danny looked at me, then deliberately repeated the move.

I reached over and shoved his head until he sank onto his own chair. I put my drink on the glass side table next to my chair and stood, huffing.

"Lighten up, Rock," Danny said, relaxing back into the seat and taking a long sip of his drink. "We're in *paradise*. Cisco has no idea where we are. Snow White can't find us. There are fucking *walls* around three sides of this place, man. Cameras on every door. There are worse things than being safe, you know?"

I frowned, looking down at him.

Like me and Ridge, Danny had one of those innocent baby faces that would keep him looking sixteen even when he hit thirty. But unlike Ridge's, or even mine, Danny's face was expressive and open. He couldn't lie for shit. The little line of tension around his mouth, despite his relaxed pose, and the way his gaze shifted quickly away from mine to stare at the horizon, said that something had happened that night at the senator's house, while I was in and out of consciousness. Something besides the beating and the trauma it had caused.

Even now, sitting in the warm sun behind those security walls, Danny was still scared.

A long, low whistle made me turn my head.

"Hell of a view out here," Steele said, striding towards us.

He could have been talking about the turquoise Gulf water, or the white sandy beach. Hell, he could even have been talking about Danny. But his eyes didn't move a millimeter from mine as he stalked closer.

The sun was suddenly a hundred degrees hotter. I grabbed for my drink and sucked it down. His dark eyes crinkled at the corners with his grin.

He was wearing low-slung cargo shorts and an insanely tight heather-gray T-shirt that clung to his broad chest like cling film and said, *Surely Not Everybody Was Kung Fu Fighting.*

Gah.

Hot Latino men big enough to break me in half had always been my weakness. But a guy like that, who also looked at me like I was more than just a collection of holes he could sink his dick in *and* wore ridiculous T-shirts? With that sweet-as-syrup Southern accent that peeked out every now and then? He was my kryptonite.

Eyes locked on mine, he took the pink drink from my hand without asking, wrapped his lips around the straw, and sucked slowly, cheeks hollowing with each long pull. When the glass was empty, he licked his lips, like he was chasing every single drop.

I nearly whimpered, and my dick perked up. I wondered if he noticed.

His gaze dropped to my crotch, and he smiled. Yeah, he'd noticed.

I cleared my throat. "Josie said you were looking for me. Come to escort me to the ball?" I asked, crossing my arms over my chest. I needed just a tiny bit of distance before I fucking *evaporated* from the heat in his eyes.

And damn if his smile didn't widen like he knew exactly what I was trying to do.

I couldn't help but return his smile. I was pretty sure I was grinning like a fucking fool, and I didn't care.

"That Miss Josie. So *helpful*." He grinned. "I was looking for you," he agreed. He turned to look at Danny for the first time and gave him a wink. "Both of y'all. You can come, too, if you want to, Danny. Wes—the redhead you met last night —has a preliminary report on the Senator. Thought you might be interested in hearing what he has to say."

I nodded. I definitely was.

Danny swallowed and shook his head, grimacing as he laid a hand on his stomach. "No. Uh. No, thanks. You two go ahead. I think... I feel like maybe I have a headache? Maybe too much... sun?"

Steele gave me a look that asked, *Is he for real?* And I replied with a shrug that said, *I know, he can't lie for shit.*

Steele nodded once, then smiled at Danny. "Sure. You feel better, okay?"

Danny nodded as if he had no choice but to obey Steele.

I snorted.

"I'll ask Miss Josie to bring you some water, too," Steele said, frowning at the drink in Danny's hand. "And maybe something to eat."

"Th-thanks," Danny breathed gratefully like Steele had offered him a new car instead of a bottle of water.

"No problem." Steele wrapped his arm around my waist.

He led me toward the three-story wall of windows that formed the rear of the main entrance hall, with its white stone floors, enormous oak front door, and the sweeping stone staircase that led to the second floor. From the stilted, two-second tour Ridge had given us yesterday, I understood that the bottom floor was mostly entertaining areas - a huge living room, library, dining room, and kitchen, plus an echo-chamber of a room with a piano and a bunch of plants. The second floor had six fairly small bedrooms - three in the front, and three in the back - each with an attached bath. And the top floor housed the media room, along with the master bedroom, which apparently no one ever went into, for reasons that hadn't been explained.

"Keep feeding him, and Danny's gonna propose to you," I teased.

Steele grunted. "He's going to be disappointed, then." He looked at me seriously. "I'm not the marrying type."

I nodded. I got that. Hell, neither was I. Romance was bull-shit, and forever was a pipe dream. All I wanted was respect.

"Besides," Steele continued, typing a message on his phone one-handed as we crossed the hallway and climbed the stairs, "Miss Josie lives for this shit. Stand still too long, and you'll become her new project."

"How'd you guys meet her?"

"She came with the house." He shrugged, his hand still firm around my waist. "How much has Ridge told you about the situation here?"

"Hmmm. Let me think...*Nothing*." I rolled my eyes. "The flow of information with Ridge is decidedly one-way. He needs to know every time I fart, but all he told me was that he had some shit to take care of in Florida. Something about a funeral."

"Your brother's protective."

"He's a control freak."

"It's possible to be both, you know," Steele said with a grin.

"Maybe." I turned my head to give him a hard look. "But I wouldn't suggest trying it."

He chuckled. "Duly noted."

"So the funeral?" I prompted. "That's how you... inherited this place?"

He sighed. "Short version is, we all knew a guy named Charlie... in a professional capacity, you might say."

"So he was a criminal," I surmised.

He grinned. "Yeah."

"And?"

"*And...* somehow, he had an attack of conscience right before he died. I don't know why or how. I mean, we weren't besties, and he hadn't exactly stayed in touch. He left us a bunch of shit to do, like I mentioned yesterday. Assignments."

"You called them crusades last night," I pointed out. We hit the second-floor landing and kept climbing.

"I'm starting to think maybe they are," he said seriously. "At first I thought... well, I dunno what I thought. Charlie didn't exactly give us the opportunity to decline his invitation. He has dirt on all of us, so it was more like, *sign up or hang.* So I wasn't real *kumbaya* about getting involved. But if the other assignments are like this one? Taking down assholes like *Senator John Harlan?* Sign me up. I hate bullies."

I snorted. "Let me guess, you were protecting the nerds back in... wherever you went to high school? Somewhere in the south, I'm guessing."

"Charlton County High School in Folkston, Georgia. Smack between the Okefenokee Swamp and the Florida border."

"So you're a redneck?" I teased.

"American by birth, Southern by the grace of God," he agreed. "And I was a scrawny out gay Cuban kid who couldn't even speak Spanish. I was protecting *myself* against bullies anyway, jus' seemed neighborly to extend that protection to the other victims of the social hierarchy."

I grinned. "How does a chivalrous, redneck swamp-man suddenly become a criminal? One who gets blackmailed by another criminal into joining a crusade?"

We hit the third-floor landing, where a hallway ran left-to-right. At the left end, a large wooden door stood closed, but we headed right, toward the sound of voices.

"That's a long story for another time," Steele said, rubbing the back of his neck while he led me into the room, his other hand snug at the small of my back. "But I'm not technically a criminal. Ain't never been charged with anything."

"*Finally,*" Ridge said when we walked into the room. He looked me up and down suspiciously, like he wondered if we'd maybe stopped for a quickie along the way. "Chat on your own time, Alvarez. We have shit to do."

Honestly. I was gonna kill him, and any court on Earth would acquit me.

"Relax, Pfeiffer," Steele said.

The room was snug compared to the other living areas in this monstrosity of a house, and I liked it. Three big, deep brown sofas arranged in a horseshoe shape faced a giant monitor. A small wet bar, complete with popcorn maker stood against the far wall...not that anyone was making popcorn right now. The carpet was thick and plush, and even the walls were covered in some kind of fabric. Whether for acoustics or atmosphere, I wasn't sure, but I could tell from the impressions in the carpet that the sofas had once been arranged in three rows and had only recently been moved.

Ridge sat in the seat closest to me, at the end of the horse-shoe closest to the door, dressed all in black like he was going to a funeral... or out on a job.

On the other end of the horseshoe was Wes, the redhead I'd met last night, wearing a T-shirt that looked like a Star Trek uniform. He didn't look up from whatever he was typing on his phone as we entered.

Two other guys, who hadn't been around when we got in yesterday evening, sat on the middle sofa. They glanced suspiciously from Ridge's face to mine, and back again, like identical twins were some strange voodoo they didn't understand.

Steele slid his palm down over my hip and grabbed my hand. The gesture was supportive, as if he was reminding these guys that I was the victim here. It was also blatantly proprietary. Not normally my thing, but from this Steele, I dug it.

Like, a lot.

Meanwhile, I could practically hear Ridge's teeth grinding, but I ignored him. He'd been simmering since yesterday morning—longer than that, probably; since whenever he'd seen the pictures—and he was spoiling for a fight. I was in the mood to give it to him.

He *knew* I was no virgin. Hell, he'd been the first person I'd told when I slept with Jake Montero back in high school, just like Ridge had told me when he'd fucked Monica Selms...and Pete Burkett (though sadly, not at the same time.) But we weren't in high school anymore. I knew he hadn't been celibate since the day he'd dropped me off in D.C., but I accepted that it was none of my damn business who he'd slept with unless he chose to share. I don't know why he thought it was any of *his* business to police my sex life, either my personal one *or* my professional one.

I wasn't a naïve idiot either. It was like the man forgot that he'd had help sneaking around Alamosa in our formative years, providing alibis and distractions as needed. I had solid instincts for people—not something I expected the other guys to believe, given the little matter of Snow White, but something *Ridge* should have known—and they told me that Steele was trustworthy. Besides, I wasn't exactly jumping into the guy's bed. It was only a harmless flirtation, a thing I hadn't known I needed.

At least for now.

"Leo Shook," the older man said, standing up and coming forward to shake my hand.

"Hey. Breck," I introduced myself. "Nice to meet you." I almost added *Officer*. Guy was obviously some kind of law enforcement. Strange to see him in this crowd.

He nodded.

The other man, who seemed to be trying to blend into the sofa with his brown hair, brown eyes, and generic looks, lifted his chin. "Carson Grieves."

His voice was vaguely accented—not quite American, but not quite anything else either. British, maybe, or halfway in between.

I nodded politely.

"Okay. Let's get this party started," Wes said, looking up finally and tossing a smile to both Steele and me.

Steele motioned to the empty corner between Leo and Ridge, and I led the way, taking the seat closer to Leo and leaving Steele to sit closer to my brother.

"John Harlan, Senior Senator from the great state of Florida," Wes said, pushing a button that made Snow White's face appear in living color on the giant screen. His eyes looked soulless enough in real life, but enlarged they were ten times worse.

"He's a Floridian?" Leo asked, shaking his head sadly. "I really should've made time to vote in the last election."

I laughed. The guy was cute, in a silver fox kinda way.

"You really should have," Carson agreed. "It's people like you who ruin things for the rest of us."

Leo turned his head, narrowing his eyes at Carson. "The rest of you? You mean convicted felons who can't vote?"

"Convicted felon," Carson sniffed, clearly offended. "I meant people who live in other states, *obviously*. I'll have you know, I've never been convicted of anything in my life."

I noted he didn't say he hadn't committed the *crimes*, however.

"Besides," Wes said. "You can vote again as soon as you're off parole." All eyes in the room turned to look at him, and he shrugged, his brown eyes dancing. "Best criminal's an informed criminal."

"True," Carson said. "Much like Senator Harlan, everyone's favorite John?" He pointed at the Senator's picture on the screen, and I laughed, catching the joke.

"Sorry, but he was not *my* favorite john," I corrected. "I had lots of others I liked better."

Steele snickered and put his hand on my thigh, squeezing appreciatively.

"Exactly like Harlan," Wes agreed. "Get this. Former fucking pastor of a church up near Marianna." A picture of a large, brick church appeared on screen, with Harlan and his family standing in front of it.

"He's a pastor?" That was possibly the most horrifying piece of information I could learn about the guy. "He only wanted boys who looked young."

"Oh, not just the ones who looked young, Other-Pfeiffer," Wes said. He pressed something else on his remote, and pictures floated up onto the screen. A couple of boys who looked just like Danny. One who looked just like Ridge and me.

I felt like I might be sick.

"Duncan Schaeffer's parents made a complaint to the Board of the church that Harlan had inappropriate contact with him. So did Jamie Carmichael's," Wes said.

"And lemme guess, nothing happened," Leo surmised.

"Depends on what you mean by nothing," Wes said, an obvious thread of anger in his voice. "Both families made sizeable down payments on houses shortly after their complaints. Carmichael's dad scored a job in the church, too."

"Fuck," I breathed. That was so much worse than anything that had happened to me. I'd been attacked, yeah, but I'd made choices that led me there. And I'd never imagined Snow White was a person I could trust. Unlike these boys, who'd had no way of knowing.

Steele's fingers squeezed my leg again in support.

"Marcus Diamond's family was the only one who contacted the police and made a formal complaint," Wes said, pulling up a picture of a police report. "Of course, this record doesn't officially exist, and no charges were ever filed."

Leo leaned forward, elbows on his knees. "Dirty cops?" he growled.

"Or true believers. Who's to say?" Wes said. "Either way, they did wrong by this kid. Parents moved out of town a couple years later."

"Least they got him out of there," I said.

"Nah," Wes said softly. "They didn't. Marcus Diamond killed himself a year after this report was made."

A cold tingle snaked up my back and raced down my arms. John Harlan was a *monster*.

"He's dead," Steele rumbled. "One way or another."

Carson was staring at the screen, at the picture of Marcus Diamond's brown curls and elfin features. "But first, we take away everything. His money, his power, his friends, his *legacy*. We leave him with *nothing*." He looked at me. "Vengeance."

I nodded. "It won't be easy. Guys like him don't get where they are just because they have money or prestige. He's got insurance policies."

"Like what?" Leo asked, turning toward me. The force of his attention pinned me to my seat.

"Like..." I swallowed and let myself feel the weight of Steele's hand on me, let it soothe me. "He has these legendary parties. I know people who've been to them. He invites his friends to hang with him and hires a bunch of boys and girls to entertain everyone. But the deal is, he tells the hookers to make sure they get his friends in certain positions and hands out bonuses if they do. The other boys figured it was part of his kink, right? Snow White *always* tapes his own encounters, so maybe he likes watching his friends getting it on, too? But I figured it was blackmail. That's why Cisco didn't cancel him as a client, even after what happened with Danny. That's why no one ever even breathed his real name."

Wes shook his head, disgusted, but Carson shrugged. "It's what I'd do. Get leverage like that on someone, and you've bought their silence. Best case scenario, if one of his victims talked, would be mutual destruction," he mused. He looked around the room at each of us in turn. "Which is why we need to turn the game back around on him."

"My man," Wes said, pointing a finger at him approvingly. "What do we need to do?"

"We identify his weak spots, and we target them without mercy," Carson said without inflection, and I reassessed my opinion of him. Fucker wasn't bland, he was scary. In a good way. "Who are his major donors?"

Wes pulled a keyboard out of thin air, and his fingers flew as he punched the buttons. A list appeared on the screen: names, addresses, and amounts so staggering I blinked, making sure I was reading correctly.

Leo whistled under his breath. "Asshole was making a mint."

"How can he be that popular?" I asked, horrified.

"He's not." Steele's fingers rubbed a soothing circle just above my knee. "He's not just holding that leverage over people's heads so they can't tattle on him, he's making people pay through the nose to ensure his silence."

"Not for long," Carson said with a satisfied smile. To Wes, he said, "Number twenty-three on the list."

"J. B. Waters, Pharmaceuticals?" Wes said, clicking the name. "From Pittsburgh, P-A. What's so special about it?"

Carson's smile widened. "I own it."

"The fuck you do," Ridge said, half-doubt and half-hope. "How?"

"By being Benjamin Waters, heir to the Waters fortune, of course." Carson brushed an imaginary piece of lint off his immaculate button-down shirt.

Leo sat back. "You do understand you can't hope to impersonate a real person like that. His picture will have been in the media, stockholders will have seen him in person."

Carson rolled his eyes. "You're adorable, Leo." To Wes, he said, "Go on, pull up the Board of Directors."

Wes gave him a skeptical glance but did as he asked.

And honest to God, Carson appeared on screen, along with half a dozen other white men. His hair was different in the photo - slicked back and thinner, somehow, but it was unmistakably him.

"So... that's your real name, then?" I wondered.

Carson smiled. "You're adorable too. What does *real* mean? Legally, I'm Ben Waters. I have his driver's license, courtesy of the Commonwealth of Pennsylvania. But then... the State of Arizona says I'm Carson Grieves. I also bear a striking resemblance to Peter Nobocook of Ketchikan, Alaska." He looked at Leo and winked. "Not that our association can be proven."

"Of course not," Leo said drily. "I wouldn't dream of trying."

"Back up the bus," Ridge said, because it wasn't enough for him to be my personal No Fun Police, he had to rain on everyone else too. "You're telling me you. Ben Waters, or whoever you are. You donate money to John Harlan's election campaign? You bankroll this fucker?"

I had to admit, had was a valid reason to be angry.

"That is pretty low," Leo said, shaking his head.

Carson shrugged, unconcerned. "Keep your friends close, but your enemies closer. And if at all possible, gentlemen, keep them *on your payroll*." He clapped his hands once. "If we want to figure out his weaknesses, we need to get close.

And it's time for John-Boy to pony up some of the goodwill that Ben Waters' donations have purchased. Senator Harlan is about to get a new BFF."

I smiled up at Steele. This was a decent start.

"Enough! That's... that's *enough*," Ridge yelled, and everyone turned to look at him. But he was looking at Steele.

"What?" Steele demanded.

"You, you keep *touching* him," he said, nodding towards me. "Your hands are all over him, and you've been eye-fucking each other the entire time!"

I blinked, stunned and, well, a little embarrassed. I tried to move my leg away from Steele's hand, but he clamped down firmly on my knee.

I could feel the change in Steele's demeanor, from his easy going, gentle humor to something way darker and more volatile. "What crawled up your asshole, Pfeiffer?" he growled, voice warning Ridge to think carefully before he answered.

Ridge ignored the threat. "He's *vulnerable*, you overgrown toddler." He jumped out of his seat and glared down at Steele, clearly not processing just how much bigger Steele was than him. "He's been *abused*. He's a fucking *victim*. And you're sitting there just taking advantage of him!"

At first, I didn't really get what Ridge was saying. Who was vulnerable? Who was a victim? But as I watched the emotions play over Ridge's face—guilt and anger, sorrow and confusion—I realized he meant *me*.

Because being beaten meant I was weak, and choosing to be a sex worker meant I was vulnerable? Anger stole my breath and made my nose tingle, but if I cried right now, that would be the final humiliation.

Steele looked stricken by Ridge's accusation. "No," he started to say. "I'm not—" He tried to pull his hand away.

"Stop." I grabbed his hand in both of mine, trapping it against my leg.

The others looked at me like I might either explode or shatter, but they didn't have to worry. I wasn't a danger to anyone in the room, except fucking Ridge, who *still wouldn't look at me at all*. As if I were contaminated.

I pulled Steele's hand off my leg, and he nodded acceptance, twisting slightly like he was trying to put some space between us. Then in one smooth movement, I lifted myself bodily into his lap. The shock in his eyes was a beautiful thing, and so was the way his arm immediately braced against my back, supporting me.

I threaded my hands into the hair on either side of his head, holding the wiry curls like reins.

"Steele?" I whispered against his lips. "Honey? Am I taking advantage of you?"

Steele's gaze drifted up to the ceiling, and he pursed his lips like he was searching his memories for any transgression I had enacted upon his body. Bless him. He shook his head slowly. "No, sir," he answered finally. "No, you are not." His smile said it was a damn shame, too.

"Thank goodness," I cooed. "And I can say for certain that you've never taken advantage of me. Crisis averted. You can sit down now, Ridge."

"But..."

Sweet baby Jesus and all the little angels too. He was so fucking stubborn.

"Ridge. Ryder. Pfeiffer." I let my voice go subarctic, but I didn't raise it at all. Later, there'd be time for yelling, but for now, we had bigger fish to fry. "Sit down, or I swear to God I will tell everyone what happened the time you stole the Shaggin' Wagon."

"The... but you *promised*," he hissed, not moving.

I looked at him, like I was staring into my own eyes. "Once upon a time, there was a green Nissan Vanette that belonged to one of the fine, upstanding citizens of Alamosa, Colorado," I began. "It had curtains all around the interior. And Ridge thought it would be *hilarious* to steal it off the street and park it in the middle of our high school football field."

"Enough," Ridge said, gritting his teeth.

But it wasn't enough. Not if he was still standing there looking at me like that.

"So he broke into it," I said, still holding his gaze. "While I went to go pick the lock on the gate around the field." I twisted on Steele's lap, looking around the room at the others. "Since I was his very willing accomplice."

"Breck Mason Pfeiffer," Ridge warned.

Ooh. We were both pulling out the middle names now. Shit was getting ugly.

I was undeterred. "Sure enough, the van comes along, right on time, only it *tears* through the gate, up over the pavement and out onto the field. Like, I expected flashing lights or demons from hell to be chasing him. And then Ridge jumps out, bow-legged, and ran off. I thought he'd injured himself." I smirked. "But no, it turns out what happened is that my brother, the great thief Ridge Pfeiffer, stole a car that people were *fucking in*."

"Oh my God," Steele breathed, staring at Ridge.

"Uh huh. A couple of stoner lovebirds, communing behind the curtains. Only Ridge didn't realize it at the time. He thought the bumping of the car meant it needed new shocks."

"A mistake anyone could have made," Ridge bit off tightly, folding his arms over his chest.

"Sure, bro. But then, just as Ridge was turning into the high school parking lot, the woman climaxed. She started screaming, 'Oh, God! Oh, my fucking God!'"

"I thought someone was being murdered!" Ridge said defensively, daring me with his eyes to continue. But I would. Oh, I would.

"I like to think the motion of the van helped give the woman the ride of her life," I said solemnly. "But alas, Ridge had an unfortunate reaction to being so startled."

I glanced back around at the others again. Wes looked confused.

"He shat himself," I clarified.

Stunned silence filled the room.

"You... in the middle of... really?" Leo asked, halfway between horror and laughter.

"I've heard worse," Steele said soothingly. "Hell, I've done worse."

But Steele's words only made Ridge madder. "Don't patronize me," he spat. He shook his head at me, slowly. "I don't know what the hell you thought you were accomplishing by embarrassing me."

"What? Do you feel victimized?" I taunted. "Weak and vulnerable? Need me to protect you, bro?"

"No. I feel pissed," he said. "And like I want to kick your ass."

I nodded. "Yes," I whispered. "Yes, Ridge, exactly. And that's exactly how I feel too. I'm not weak or vulnerable. I'm a little bit embarrassed. But mostly, I want to see this fucker burn. Get it now?"

Ridge seemed startled for a second, then he frowned like he wasn't quite sure I was being honest. But finally, he sat down, and I told myself that was a victory. For now.

I cleared my throat and rearranged myself so I was sitting back in my own spot on the sofa, though quite a bit closer to Steele than I had been. "Sorry," I said. "For the theatrics. You were saying, Carson?"

Carson smiled at me, slow and real. "I, for one, appreciate some good theatrics." He sighed. "But about Senator Harlan. I would suggest that we wait and see where he's going to be, and work around that. I'll call him and set up a dinner."

"He'll be in D.C. on Saturday," I told them. "He's throwing a party. He, uh, wanted Danny and me to attend."

"That works," Carson said. "I can meet with him there."

"Better idea!" Wes interjected, pulling something else up on the screen. "Looks like Harlan's going to be right in our back yard on Wednesday, as keynote speaker for a Faith Fundamentals dinner." He looked up. "What's the over-under on him having an after party for his besties?"

"No doubt whatsoever," I said. "He's absolutely arrogant enough to have a sex party after a religious gathering. Probably gets off on it."

"Hmmm," Leo said, looking at Carson.

Carson looked back warily. "Hmm? I don't know if I like that *hmmm*."

"Oh, you definitely won't," Leo said. "Never fun being the bait."

"Christ," Carson said wearily. "I'm gonna go get my ass videotaped, aren't I?"

"Luckily, it's your best side." Leo smiled.

Steele and Ridge groaned.

Carson sighed from the depth of his lungs. He threw himself against the back of the chair, waving a hand gracefully yet somehow dismissively, in the air. "Fine. I *guess* I can sleep with some cute little thing in the name of the greater good. If I can find any one at *all* amusing in the middle of *Florida*. I mean, if I *have* to." He sounded exactly like the kind of bored trust-fund baby any crooked politician would love to have a hold over.

He caught me staring at him and winked, then sat straight up, resting his elbows on his knees. "That will work." He was all business now, all traces of the spoiled rich kid gone. "Ben Waters already has a bit of a reputation as a playboy."

"Good. And I'll also plant some lovely little articles from the Pittsburgh newspaper," Wesley added. "Nothing too obvious, of course. Maybe some grumblings from your Board of Directors?"

"Hey!" I waved my hand, feeling like I'd lost the plot sometime between them deciding to send Carson to the dinner and him getting his ass taped. "Explain it again for those of us who don't speak fluent con?"

Carson turned to me. "The best way to get close to Harlan, to get him to trust me, is to let him get info on me the way he does with his other marks. To make him think he has something he can hold over me."

"If he thinks Carson... er, *Ben Waters* is in his pocket, he'll be more likely to relax," Steele explained, "knowing there's that whole mutually assured destruction thing happening."

"In other words, Ben wouldn't be able to take Harlan down without exposing his own indiscretions," Leo said. "And with as many people as Harlan has in his pocket, there's no question whose word would be believed, if it came to that."

"And to sweeten the trap, Wes is going to plant some news articles online to make it look like Ben's been caught being naughty before and can't risk the scandal of being caught again," Ridge added.

Wes nodded. "Nothing makes an asshole like Harlan feel friendlier than knowing he has someone by the short and curlies."

"Which works out fine," Carson said, his jaw set tight. "Since nothing pisses me off more than someone who thinks a position of power means he can take whatever he wants." He stood up from the couch. He nodded at everyone. "I'm off to make some calls."

Wes hit a button on his laptop, and John Harlan's face disappeared from the screen. "I'm gonna go get creative with the news," he said.

"Hey," Leo warned. "Nothing too terrible. I feel like Carson's... *attached*... to this ID."

Wes saluted on his way out. "You got it, chief."

"Pfeiffer," Leo said to Ridge, "come chat with me for a minute."

Ridge looked at me, then back to Leo. "Later," he said.

"Now. I have questions about that incident in Malaga." Leo stood and walked toward Ridge.

Ridge's attention was caught. "What incident in Malaga?"

"The one with the Matisse."

"Oh! That was beautiful! But it wasn't me," Ridge said sadly.

"No, but I have a theory about how it was done," Leo said, wrapping an arm around Ridge's shoulder. "Let's talk."

Ridge looked at me and shook his head once, almost apologetically. "Yeah," he told Leo. "Yeah, okay."

They left, and Steele and I were alone in the room. I puffed out my cheeks and sighed. "Sorry about my brother," I said to Steele. "God. It's like he can't even stand to look at me, he's so disgusted."

AGAINST MY BETTER JUDGMENT, I didn't pull Breck back onto my lap. That really would've been taking advantage of him. I settled for putting my arm around him. He settled against my side with a sigh, his head resting on my shoulder. "I don't think Ridge is disgusted by you."

"No? You think it was a sign of respect when he called me a whore? When he couldn't make eye contact? Or was it the way he called me an idiot for giving money to our mother?"

The ache in his voice fucking killed me.

"I don't have any brothers, but it looked to me like he was feeling guilty."

"What does *he* have to feel guilty about?"

"Maybe letting you get into this mess?" I tried to speak confidently, though I really had no idea what Ridge was feeling. I hadn't known any of these guys for very long, and maybe I was just projecting what I would be feeling onto Ridge.

Breck pulled away from me, and I missed the warmth and the feel of his body immediately. He shifted on the big leather couch, tucking one leg under the other and turning toward me, a scowl on his face. "See, that's the thing!" He poked me with his index finger hard as he emphasized his point. "He didn't *let* me do anything. *I* chose to be an escort. I made this decision, and you know what? I'm okay with it! You wanna know the shameful, slutty truth? I even *like* it sometimes. Not every john is a creeper like Snow White. Sometimes the sex can be really hot, and I get off on it. How disgusted do you think Ridge would be if he knew that?"

I didn't know how Ridge would feel about it, given that Breck was his brother, but I thought it was pretty hot, too. Sitting next to Breck on the plane yesterday, I'd decided I'd pay good money just to see him and Danny get it on while I watched. I thought it would be better not to say that.

"I know that. I know you're a grown-ass man. But Breck, you almost got killed. It's not crazy for your brother to be worried."

"I could get killed crossing the street," he said emphatically, giving me another poke. "Life is risky."

"Tell me about it. But people always use that expression to justify doing *really* risky things, when the truth is, life is dangerous enough without doing stupid shit that you don't need to be doing."

"Says the man who, *what*, takes bullets for a living?" He shot off the couch, prowling around the room as if sitting still was driving him crazy.

We'd never talked about the shit I'd done, but his guess was pretty accurate. I watched him as he paced the room ranting and waving his arms. He was so gorgeous and so passionate, I didn't think I'd ever be able to look away from him.

I understood where Breck was coming from, but I also understood Ridge a little better. Breck made me want to wrap him up in a blanket and keep him safe, and I'd only known him a few days. It had been a long time since I'd felt so personally protective of someone. If I could, I would do pretty much what Ridge had done. Set Breck up in a safe place, with a financial cushion so he didn't have to be a rent boy, and send him to school so he could have a good life.

Crime didn't pay. Not in the long run. Sure, Charlie had died rich, but he still had died young. The longer you were in this life, the harder it was to get out. An education would give Breck more choices than I'd had, either when I joined the military or when I'd gotten out.

Joining the Army had seemed like an easy choice. Lord knew, my mama didn't have any money set aside for college. Daily survival had been touch-and-go at times. But I damn sure wasn't going to spend my life shooting swamp rats and living off the bounty, either.

Once I had joined up, it was as if every part of me had jumped up and down screaming, *Yes. This is what you're looking for. This is what you need.* Nothing would do but for me to get into Special Forces, to take the most dangerous assignments. If I was going to be a soldier, I was going to be the best soldier I could.

After years living like that in places sane people avoided, what was I supposed to do when I got out? Become an accountant? Write poetry?

Like Breck had said so boldly, so bravely, about being a hooker, I liked my job.

And it wasn't something people talked about in polite company, but, yeah, I liked being *good* at my job, too. I fucking loved the adrenaline rush that came with it. Whether it was from fear, excitement, terror, or relief, the feeling was addicting. Laying your life on the line every mission, living on the edge every day, was like a drug.

But after a while, it had become impossible to tell the difference between feeling scared, thrilled, and murderous. That was when I'd known it was time for me to get out.

The transition hadn't been easy. Chasing that high had led me into some seriously dark places and had given me even more demons to deal with. I'd found there weren't a lot of legal ways to get that feeling in the civilian world, but luckily, some semi-legal occupations offered a taste of it. I was trying really hard to stay walking right on that edge without falling over into some dark place.

So instead of going out and shooting the bad guys no matter how much they deserved it, I tried to focus on protecting the good guys. And Breck was definitely one of the good guys.

I must've been quiet for too long, because Breck was staring at me, his head tilted like a dog that's just been asked a question it can't answer. "Protecting people, even taking bullets for them, is something I need to be doing," I said.

"So is this." His gaze challenged me to refute him. "Even if my having sex for money disgusts Ridge."

"I think he's angrier at you for not coming to him when you needed money, and disappointed in himself for not paying better attention, rather than disgusted by what you're doing. Ridge is no choir boy."

"I think he can be disgusted at the same time," Breck said. "He's multitalented that way."

God, he was even more adorable when he was being stubborn. "Well, if he is, I think it's more about what you did with the money he gave you than what you're doing to earn it back. Judging from the little bit of conversation I heard, that really wasn't your money to give away, was it?"

"You know, I didn't ask him to give me that money," Breck said, blue eyes blazing. "I tried to refuse it a hundred times. I *knew* it came with strings, no matter what Ridge said, and I didn't want this fucking expectation between us, like he was investing in me, and I owed him some kinda return on his money!"

I frowned. "Jesus, Breck. It's not about strings! He's worried about you getting hurt. Hurt by your mom." I paused and looked at him significantly. "Hurt by a client."

"Screw you. Now you're on his side?" He crossed his arms over his chest and glared at me.

"No." I leaned back against the couch, trying to look as nonthreatening as possible. "I'm not on anybody's side but my own. I'm just saying you might want to cut him a little slack. Because it sounds like he went to a lot of trouble to get you a shit ton of money so you could make a better life for yourself. And you just turned around and gave it to your mama, who doesn't sound like the most fiscally responsible person in the world."

"Don't act like you know anything about my mother."

"Not *your* mother, specifically, but I know a lot about addicts, kid. And I know whenever they come around asking for a lot of money, it's not because they're collecting for Toys for Tots."

"No shit! But you know what? I didn't give her the money because I'm an idiot, okay? I gave it to her because... well, because I *had* to. And I don't have to defend my choices to you or to him. This is my life. I'm a grown man, the exact same age as he is! If I wanna risk my life, I will. If I want to have sex with someone for money, I will." He crossed the room, locking eyes with me the entire time. I didn't stop him as he climbed back onto my lap. "And if I want to have sex with somebody not for money, I will."

I set my hands on the back of the couch, trying not to touch him. "Breck."

"What? I want you, Steele. And I know you want me."

That obvious, huh? "For right now, I work with your brother. Your very protective brother, who doesn't want anyone taking advantage of you. You and me... that would make things complicated."

His reply was succinct. "Fuck Ridge."

"He's not the boss of you?" I asked, trying to lighten the mood.

He put his hands on my shoulders and leaned in and spoke directly into my ear. "No one is the boss of me."

Goddamn. I had no doubt that was true. And it was going to make protecting him very difficult.

He would hate being packed away like a princess in a tower no matter how angelic and delicate he appeared. Since I couldn't do that, I'd have to do the next best thing. Stay close to him at all times. That wouldn't be hard, but right now, in this room at this moment, the thing he needed protection from the most was me.

Despite all my flirting and the come-ons, I was actually a little frightened of the idea of sleeping with Breck. One of the reasons I knew about addictive personalities so well was that I was one. I could tell that with one taste of Breck I could become addicted to him as easy as sliding into a warm bath. I didn't know if that was an addiction I'd ever be able to break. I already loved the way he felt straddling me, and it was taking all my self-control not to grab him, pull him against me, and kiss him until we both lost our minds.

But Breck didn't belong in my life, he didn't belong in this house. And he certainly didn't belong in the bed of some douchebag senator. He belonged someplace better with good kids doing good things that would make the world a better place.

I wasn't sure how to convince him of any of those things, though, without coming off as pushy and overprotective as Ridge had.

Breck's lips touched my ear, and I shivered. I reached for his hips to push him off, I swear, but apparently my body had other plans. My fingers tightened around him, my thumbs slipping into the grooves of his hipbones as if those delicate hollows had been carved just to fit me.

He nipped at my earlobe, his fingers tugging at my hair, and my cock jerked. I could feel him smirking against my skin.

"Senator Harlan," I blurted.

Understandably, Breck leaned back, not accidentally grinding his ass against my growing hardness. "Wow. Way to kill the mood. What about him?"

"We have to stop him."

"No shit. That's why I'm trapped in a mosquito-infested state with my judgypants brother and his psycho group of Super-frenemies. Can we at least fuck before we fire up the jet and take down the bad guys?"

I slid my hands under the hem of his shirt. Damn, his skin was soft and the muscles under it were sleek and strong. He was gorgeous and fiery, and I wanted to protect him more than I'd ever wanted to protect anyone. The best way I knew to do that was to eliminate the threat.

Breck leaned in to kiss me, and I let him for a long second. I'm only human. But before things could get too heavy, I pushed him away gently. "Sweetcheeks, we can't do this."

"Yeah, we totally can." Breck settled heavily in my lap, shifting so he dragged his ass across the erection pressing painfully against the seam of my cargo shorts. He groaned softly. "We absolutely should do this. Ridge can fuck himself."

"That, right there, is a reason why we shouldn't," I said firmly. "I'm not into you using me to score points against your brother." My totally not-virtuous dick, meanwhile, was screaming *use me, please use me*.

Breck shook his head. "Ridge isn't here right now." He reached down and popped the button on my shorts with a quick flick of his wrist. "Hello, beautiful," he said as he rubbed his thumb over the head of my cock.

"Fuck, Breck, you're going to kill me."

"Well, we can't have that now, can we? If you die, who will protect me?"

"I thought you didn't need protection?"

"Hmm." He slid his hands down my shorts, cupping his palm against my cock. "Damn, you're a big boy. I tell you what, you let me get my mouth around this delectable cock, and I might let you protect me."

"Fucking hell." I was trying to hold on, but I'd been half hard around Breck since yesterday morning, and it had been months since I'd been with anybody. My encounters tended to be quick, anonymous, and basically forgettable. I didn't think anything with Breck would be forgettable.

Breck laughed at me, and I broke.

Wrapping my arms around him, I pushed him down to the couch with a growl. He laughed again, wrapping his arms around me and grabbing onto my shirt with both hands. "You want this?" I rested on my elbows and searched his face— his bright blue eyes, his pink lips—for the truth.

"Fuck you. Yes, I want this. What else do I have to do? Send you an engraved invitation? Because I will. I bet Josie knows where to find one." He struggled underneath me, as if trying to get away. I pressed my weight down, grinding our cocks together in a way that rode the border between pleasure and pain.

"Oh, god, *yes*. Kiss me," Breck said.

With one massive exception, I had never been one to disobey a direct order. I kissed him. His soft lips parted beneath mine, and he wrapped his legs around my waist as best he could. His mouth was hot, and the small whimpers he made as I tongue-fucked him were even hotter.

I fucking loved kissing, and it had been a long while since I'd been able to take my time and learn the taste and feel of a man's mouth.

Breck's hands were all over me slipping under my shirt as far as he could reach. His nails dragged lines down my back. The leather squeaked under us as we dry humped like teenagers.

Breck moaned into my mouth, his fingers slipping under the leg openings of my shorts and digging into my thighs.

"Jesus, Steele," he panted. "Please, let me blow you. I have to blow you. Please, please. I'll make you lose your mind. Fucking let me get my mouth on you."

My entire body shuddered, my balls pulled up tight as the combination of begging and ordering pushed me right to the edge of orgasm. I dropped my head to the curve of his shoulder and bit gently on the cords of his neck. *Holy shit.* We still had all our clothes on. What would it be like when I had him alone to myself for hours in a private room? I might not survive that.

Breck laughed, loud and incredulously. "Goddamn, you feel fucking amazing."

Suddenly, I remembered I'd never heard the door close after everyone left. With a feeling of dread, I pushed myself up high enough to look over the back of the couch. Sure enough, the door stood halfway open. "Shit."

"What?" Breck asked, even as he grabbed the front of my shirt to pull me back down.

"Door's open. Anyone could've walked in or heard us from outside."

"Good. I hope Ridge got an eyeful." Breck's mouth and chin were red from kissing and stubble burn. A flush of arousal tinted his cheeks pink, the rosy glow disappearing into the neck of his T-shirt.

Okay. I had to stop. With one last kiss, I pushed myself reluctantly off Breck. I fell back against the arm of the couch.

"What the hell?" Breck pushed himself up on his elbows, his hard cock tenting the front of his shorts. "You can't just fucking stop."

"Not like this," I said.

"Like what, then? Do you want to go to my room?"

"No. I think we should stop."

"Why in the hell would we stop now?"

"Because, when we do this, if we do this, I want to know that you want me for me. And that it has nothing to do with proving something to your brother or to yourself."

"Huh," Breck said. "Is that so?"

"It's for the best. For us, and for the mission."

Breck nodded. "For the mission." He popped the button at his waistband and unzipped his fly slowly. Licking his lips, he pushed his shorts down to reveal a cock just as pretty as he was. He had a thin happy trail leading to a nicely trimmed nest of gold curls. His cock was long and hard, pink shading to dark red at the top. He wrapped his hand around it, and his eyes fluttered shut as he dragged his hand slowly from bottom to the top.

"Oh, Sweetcheeks, what are you doing to me?"

"This isn't for you, and this isn't about my brother. This is for me."

I couldn't help myself. I leaned forward, crawling over to him. He stopped me with a hand to my chest. His other hand didn't stop moving on his cock.

"No. Stay still or leave."

My cock was so hard, it hurt. Obediently, I sat back so that I wasn't touching any part of him. Gorgeous bastard made a show of it. Caressing himself slowly, breathing heavily and groaning. The whole time, he kept telling me how good it felt, how much he loved it. His hand moved faster and louder until the slap of flesh against flesh was so loud, they must've heard it downstairs. I didn't care if they did.

I bit back the *don't stop* that desperately tried to force its way out. I was panting as hard and as loudly as he was. I kept my hands clenched on the back of the sofa, so hard my knuckles turned white.

Breck's chest heaved, and I could tell he was close. The tips of his ears, the skin over the bridge of his nose, and the delicate curves of his cheekbones flushed dark pink, and his thighs trembled.

Eyes locked on mine, he reached under his shirt and pinched his nipples harder than I would have dared. "Oh, fuck," he groaned, his hand speeding up on his cock. "Oh, fuck." He shoved his fist into his mouth to muffle his shout, and his back arched up off the sofa as he came, shooting onto the glorious, smooth skin of his stomach.

I clenched my teeth together so hard, I thought I heard something crack. Lust stabbed sharply into my gut as my balls tightened painfully. Biting my lip against a yell, I pressed my hand against my cock and came, shooting hard and seemingly endlessly into my briefs.

Breck ran the finger through the pearly streaks on his chest and then sucked it clean.

My body trembled with a huge aftershock as I watched his eyes close in bliss.

I had been right. I was addicted to him; his taste, his sounds, his laughter, his eyes, and his spirit. And I hadn't even had to touch him to feel the high.

"We're going to get this guy," I said as my breathing evened out and my heart rate settled back to normal.

"I know you will."

I clamped my lips shut against the need to say more, to make promises about what would happen once the mission was complete. That was exactly the kind of thing I was trying to avoid.

We had just pulled ourselves together when Josie knocked quietly on the door.

"Lunch time," she said in her sweet southern voice. "If you boys are hungry."

Josie wasn't old, but she was still the kind of woman who would call every man under the age of ninety *"boys."*

"We'll be right down, Josie," I said. "Thank you."

As we walked down the stairs, not touching but completely aware of each other, I swore I would bring Harlan's world crashing down around him. He had to be stopped.

I'd met many men like him in my line of work. They were like wild tigers that had gotten their first taste of human flesh and had to have more. Harlan wouldn't stop. The power of having someone else's life in your hands had turned stronger men than him into monsters. If he got away with hurting Breck and Danny, there would be more lives ruined in his wake.

"HEY," Danny said, knocking gently on my open door. "You up for a swim?"

I had been lying on my stomach in the middle of my big, four-poster double bed, idly scrolling through Tumblr on the secure, encrypted tablet Josie had given me to replace my possibly-traceable phone, but I looked up at Danny's knock.

Damn, but the sun had done good things for him. He was wearing another tight little Speedo—he seemed to have an endless supply of them—and every inch of his visible skin was golden brown and glowing.

Last week, I would have salivated over him. Right now, all I could think about was one particular jerk who'd refused to lay a hand on me, even after I'd literally begged him, and had avoided me like a contagious rash ever since.

I rolled over, flopping on my back like a starfish. "Nah," I told Danny. "I'm good." I was exhausted and enervated at once, and not even the delightful men of Tumblr could hold my attention.

"You sure?" he asked. "I'd love the company."

I looked over at him again, more closely this time. Though he looked healthier than ever, his eyes were troubled and more haunted than they'd been yesterday. Maybe he was freaked out about tonight's mission, where Carson—*aka, Ben Waters*—was going to infiltrate Senator Harlan's house.

I knew I was.

"Yeah," I said, sighing deeply. Maybe some exercise would be good for me. "Okay. I'll get changed and meet you down there."

He nodded, then disappeared down the hall while I put the tablet on my nightstand and levered myself off the bed.

All but the one small duffle bag of stuff I'd brought to Chad's house was in storage back in D.C., so I had to knock on Ridge's door to beg for a bathing suit. I wasn't sure if I was relieved or disappointed when I opened the door a second later and found the room empty. Ridge and I hadn't spoken since our showdown in the media room, and the standoff was gnawing at me.

The shitty part about being stuck here with no distractions was that I couldn't stop thinking about the shit Steele had said, that Ridge might be feeling guilty rather than judgmental, and worried rather than controlling. And annoyingly enough, the more I thought about it, the more I started to think he might have been right.

It had always been Ridge and me against the world, literally since the womb, and we'd fallen into roles over the years, without ever thinking about it. I had been the distraction, keeping kindly store cashiers engaged in helping me "find my Mommy," while Ridge stuffed his jacket full of bread and Skippy, and snuck outside.

Then, later, I was the one who'd taken tests for both of us and gotten all of our homework done so the school would stay off our backs, while Ridge had been in charge of keeping the rent paid and the lights turned on. I was the one who'd taken care of our mother when she was high as a kite or, worse, coming down off something, while Ridge was the one making sure her fucking dealer didn't come after us when she got in too deep. All the while, we'd been a team.

The older we got, though, the deeper Ridge seemed to sink into this criminal world, and the more he pulled away from me. He went after bigger scores with bigger paydays, trying to build something up so we wouldn't be living hand to mouth all the time. And he encouraged me to focus on school, to do extracurricular activities like a "regular" kid.

"Please, Brekkie. That's one less thing I have to worry about, yeah?" I hadn't exactly protested – I think I knew even then that Ridge was trying to live his "regular" teen life vicariously through me, and I was doing it for both of us. But I don't think I got until this week just how fucked up our roles had become.

Somehow, he'd given himself over to darkness and put me on a pedestal. He'd decided he was corrupt and I was incorruptible. He'd convinced himself I needed the protection neither one of us had ever gotten as kids... and to be fair, thinking of the way I *adored* the protection and comfort Steele offered, maybe Ridge wasn't too wrong about that.

But I didn't need it from *him*. He wasn't being fair to either of us.

I kicked my shorts into the pile of dirty laundry on Ridge's floor and stole a cute pair of boy-short trunks from his drawer. I also liberated a teal polo I was pretty sure would look better on me—Ridge was way too grumpy to pull off teal—and another pair of cotton shorts for after my swim. Then I closed Ridge's door behind me.

I had intended to head for the pool, but somehow after dropping my stolen clothes in my room, I found myself walking in the opposite direction, upstairs instead of down. I wondered if Ridge would be up there with Wes, manning the comms in the media room.

But when I got there, Wes was watching the giant screen at the front of the room, alone.

"S'up?" he said when I wandered in. He was sitting all the way at the back of the room near the popcorn machine, where he'd set up some kind of command center—a huge terminal with two keyboards, two monitors, and an endless number of peripherals. I could only see from his neck to his cap of red hair.

"Nothing," I said. "Bored."

"Rifling through Ridge's shit got old, so you decided to look for fun up here?" he asked, sounding amused.

I flicked a suspicious glance at him, and he lifted his chin at the big screen, which he switched to show security footage of the hallway outside Ridge's room.

"You have cameras in the halls?" I demanded. "Do you have them in the rooms, too?"

"Nah. Chill out," he said easily. "I didn't install these, Charlie had 'em before we got here, and I just took over his system. Even *I* know cameras in the rooms would be a breach of privacy. Hallways are fair game though, so keep your naked sexcapades away from public spaces." He waggled his eyebrows. "Or don't."

I snorted. "Sorry to disappoint, but no sexcapades here," I said. I added under my breath, "Not for lack of trying."

"Aw. Steele's playing the gentleman and shutting you down, huh?"

"He told you?" I said. I wasn't sure why I'd find that so surprising, but I did.

"Nope. Just an educated guess based on the fact that he's been grumpy and distracted as hell for the last two days." Wes grabbed a tablet and walked forward, taking a seat on the sofa across from mine. "I figure if my boy had been gettin' any, he'd be less grumpy...though probably be just as distracted, as long as you're around."

"What's that supposed to mean?"

Wes's gaze met mine, and he smiled slightly. "I worked with Steele in the past. A couple of times, actually. Me behind the scenes, and him out front."

I nodded.

"Steele takes pride in being mission-focused. You go into a planning room with him, and you can be sure you have one hundred percent of his attention. He's not thinking about the football game, or the errands he has to run, or the ass he got the night before. He almost gets..." Wes hesitated. "I don't know how to describe it except to say he's *manic*. Like he's pulled so tight, he vibrates. And then as soon as it's go time, and he's off the leash?" He snapped his fingers. "Instant relaxation, like he's absorbed all the adrenaline and turned it into fuel. That's why he's the best in the business." Wes shook his head fondly. "He's a machine. Nothing gets past him. And he has no fear."

"I can see that," I said softly. I knew what it felt like to have that focus turned on me, how it burned me up from the inside out.

"Well, this time things are a little different," Wes said wryly, and I frowned.

"How?"

"He's been stomping around like a bull in heat, distracted as fuck." Wes grinned, setting the tablet on the arm of the sofa. "Yesterday, we went over the details for tonight, right? Carson heard back from the senator, and everything was a go for the public event, plus he got invited back for the private after-party. All going according to plan."

Wes steepled his fingers and flared his eyes like a cartoon villain. "Leo says, 'Okay, Steele's going to act as personal security for Ben Waters, I'm gonna act as driver, Wes will man the comms, and Ridge is gonna stay back in the van in case we need exfil.' We all think this is a solid plan, and Steele nods along with us, right? Totally on board."

"Yeah, and?"

"*And* we go through the whole plan, the timing, the new communication devices I developed, which are kick*ass* and totally undetectable, if I do say so myself. We're *ready*." Wes chuckled softly. "Then, just as we're about to all put our hands in a stack and do the whole One-Two-Three-*Go-Team!* thing? Steele shakes his head like he's just waking up and says, 'Okay, this is great, but who's with Carson?'" Wes laughed out loud.

I didn't find it funny, I found it horrifying. "You're saying that he's out there right now, distracted? Because of me? What if he makes a mistake? What if he gets caught?"

Wes snorted and shook his head. "Oh, baby. You really don't know who you're dealing with, do you?"

Well, of course I didn't. I'd known Steele approximately three fucking days. Less if you counted the fact that he'd barely spoken to me in the last twenty-four hours. What was shocking was how badly I *wanted to know*. He was fascinating to me, this combination of danger and protection all twisted into one package. And he looked at me like he really *saw* me. Not as some perfect paragon, the way my brother did, but as a smart, competent person, someone worth knowing. It was something I hadn't known I needed until I got it from him.

And I wanted more of it.

Wes gestured to the screen again and tapped something on his mystical, magical tablet. The image changed from the empty hallway in the Bat Cave, to another hallway, in another house. This one was decorated in dark terracotta with heavy wood wainscoting.

Wes tapped something in his ear. "What up, Superman?"

A strangled cough came through the speakers. "You know I hate that name, right?" The voice was unmistakably

Steele's, though the words were garbled just slightly, like he was trying to speak without moving his lips.

"Dude, it's the best code name ever. Man of Steele, you know?" Wes laughed. "*Hilarity.*"

"Yeah? You know what would be even funnier, Mighty Mouse?" Steele began hotly.

But before he could finish the threat, Leo interrupted from wherever he was. "What would be great is if both of you could keep the chatter down. Remember Carson's looped in and you don't need to distract him."

"Right," Wes agreed cheerily. "Status, Steele?"

Steele sighed. "All good," he said in that same soft, garbled voice. "Harlan brought Ben back to his playroom. Had plenty of boys and ladies there, ready to party. Drugs, booze, you name it."

Someone, maybe Ridge, whistled. "And he just brought in a near perfect stranger and offered him blow? Like you're at a buffet, and he's all, *'Try the creampuffs! And while you're at it, here's a hooker!'*?"

"Mmhmm." Steele agreed. "Arrogant beyond fucking belief."

It didn't surprise me, but then again I'd become used to men like John Harlan. They were so smug, so confident of their position and power. Taking him down would be more satisfying than any sex I'd ever had.

Yet, my brain added. Any sex you've had *yet*.

Leo's voice echoed my thoughts. "You'd be arrogant too, if you had the kind of insurance policies this guy has."

"No shit," Steele said. "Speaking of, Ben's been in a private room with the boy of his choice for, like, thirty minutes now."

Huh. I hadn't gotten a gay vibe from Carson. Then again, I really hadn't gotten much vibe from him at all. Carson seemed to have his shit locked down tighter than anyone I'd ever met. I wondered if, after playing so many different people over the years, he even remembered who he was anymore.

"There a reason to be worried?" Leo asked, a thread of concern in his voice.

I didn't really get Leo either. He had a definite cop edge to him, but he seemed committed to this weird band of thieves, like now that he considered these guys teammates, he'd throw down if Carson was in trouble. It shocked me that Ridge, who barely trusted *me* for fuck's sake, had cast his lot in with these guys.

"For him?" Steele snickered. "Nah. Worry about *me*. I'm standing in the hall guarding the door, and my virgin ears haven't heard squealing like this since I was eight and my neighbor butchered a hog."

"Ohhhh," Wes said, his eyes gleaming. He tapped a key, and Carson's muffled voice came over the speakers, accompanied by unmistakable wet, slurping noises.

"*Yes!* Just there. Harder now. That's it! Oh, good heavens! Oh, merciful *lord*!"

Wes and I looked at each other and burst out laughing.

Carson was doing the bored, affected rich-guy voice he'd done during the meeting the other night. *While his dick was in some guy's mouth.*

"That's dedication," I muttered, shaking my head.

"It's something," Wes said, looking shocked and impressed at once. "I kinda wanna keep listening to see if he orgasms in character."

"Turn it off, Bond," Leo said dryly. "There's some information we really don't need to know about each other."

I privately agreed. Dude was a fucking identity crisis waiting to happen.

"Oh, sure," Steele muttered after Wes restored the comms to their previous settings. "Lucky you, you get to shut it off. Some of us are stuck here. Not even getting paid."

"Don't whine, Alvarez," Ridge said. "At least you didn't spend two hours sweating in the back of a limo with Captain America. Man won't let me turn on the radio or the a/c. You know how I feel about a/c."

I knew how we both felt. Growing up in arid Colorado, we couldn't survive on the east coast without it.

"Driver gets to make the call," Leo said mildly. "Besides, we servants of the rich and famous don't get to waste gas while our betters live it up."

Steele grunted, a laugh in disguise. "Where are you now?"

"Leo's still with the car, but I'm doing my Birdman thing, perched in a tree," Ridge said happily. "Spying and enjoying the fresh air."

Wes looked at me. "Hey, Steele," he said over the comms. "How many guards are posted?"

"Nine confirmed," Steele answered promptly. "Two in the guard house with security feed, two on the front door, two at the entrance to the back room, and one particularly ugly guy who stays with Harlan. Two at the back entrance."

"Where are his cameras located?" Wes said, still looking pointedly in my direction.

"Exterior is covered, unsure of possible blind spots. Interior, every public room has cameras mounted. Party room has cameras hidden in the grandfather clock and a brass sextant on the mantle. Mics in the potpourri bowl on the side table – who the fuck has potpourri? – and likely others, but I didn't get to make a thorough search."

"And the mics you planted?" Wes demanded.

"Doorframe next to the entrance to the party room, to catch chatter from the guards. One under the back edge of the telephone table where Ben pretended to drop his drink. And Ben took the third." Steele sounded amused. "He has access to things I don't have."

"Thanks, Steele," Wes said cheerily.

"No problem."

Wes hit a button in his ear, like he was muting his next words. "You see what I mean? You don't have to worry about Steele being distracted. He's compartmentalized, so he's fine. But watch out when he comes home tonight. The adrenaline plays havoc with a man's libido, and I'm not sure if he'll feel like playing the gentleman." Wes smirked. "Unless, of course, that's what you're going for."

My heart skipped a beat, and I swallowed. That was definitely what I was going for, though I wouldn't wanna take advantage of Steele either.

"So, you two worked together in the past?" I said, changing the subject slightly. "You saw him after jobs in the past?"

Wes's smirk grew. "I did. And honey, you are cute as a puppy right now. But as amusing as it is to watch your little junior high crush come to fruition, I'm not telling you anything more about Steele. He has a past. We all do." Wes's expression darkened. "If he trusts you, he'll tell you."

"And what about me?" I demanded, stung by the dead-on-target accuracy of Wes's snarky comments. "Are you telling Steele everything I do?" I nodded toward the monitors.

"If he asks," Wes said. "I'm not gonna lie."

I nodded stiffly and stood. "Have a good night," I told him.

He smiled and gave me a quick salute, and I wandered back down to find Danny.

Danny was swimming laps across the broad expanse of the pool, but he stopped as soon as he saw me and pulled himself up to sit on the side. The underwater lights set the planes of his face in weird relief.

"Hey," he said, wiping a hand over his face. "You get lost on your way down here?"

"You might say that," I said morosely. I'd gotten lost at some point, anyhow. I had no idea which way was up anymore. I knew Steele was attracted to me, and I was pretty sure he liked me, too. But he was too focused on the mission to act on it, and I couldn't decide whether he'd be pleased or pissed if I stepped in and made him reconsider his priorities.

I wandered over to sit down on the edge of the pool next to Danny, dangling my feet in the water, and he leaned forward, peering at my face curiously.

"Ahhh," he said, nodding to himself. He leaned back, resting his hands on the stone pavers behind him.

"Ah, what?" I demanded, all affronted.

"*Ah*, you're thinking about the delectable *Señor Alvarez*," Danny said, snickering. "It's cute."

"It is not," I argued. "It's awful."

"You're right," he agreed sadly. "So awful. Having a guy so hot he could be a body double for Jason Momoa stare at you whenever you're in the room and scowl whenever you're not, like he can't relax without you there, is a terrible, terrible fate. I feel like, as a friend, I should offer to take this burden from you. No, no," he protested, laying a hand on my chest. "I insist."

"Shut *up*," I said, whacking him in the stomach with the back of my hand. "It's not like that. He's focused on the thing with the Senator."

"Oh, right right right! The truly terrible thing is that he's trying to avenge you like a knight in shining armor. Like that doesn't get my dick hard *at all*." He snorted. "You poor creature."

I chuckled weakly. "I guess, when you put it like that." I shook my head. "It's just. I kinda want him to want me more than he wants that? Or as much, at least. I want to be a part of getting the vengeance, so I'm not a distraction but, like, a partner." It sounded dumb when I said it out loud, but Danny nodded.

"You want respect," he said sagely. "You don't wanna be the princess in the tower who never gets found. You want the Pretty Woman fantasy. You wanna rescue him right back."

"Maybe," I said, turning my head to look at him. I ran a hand through my hair, messing up the curls. "Maybe that's it."

We sat in silence for a minute, staring at the lights reflected in the water and the ripples we made with just the smallest movements of our feet.

"Breck," Danny said suddenly, then stopped. He turned to look at me. "It's so weird calling you that."

I'd dropped the whole Rocky pretense as soon as we got on the plane, considering Ridge couldn't seem to remember to call me by my alias.

I laughed. "I know. But good weird. I kinda like that you know my name now. That I can trust you." I shrugged. "It's like my life was fake for a long time, pretending to be this mild-mannered college student by day and a rent boy at night. Both of them were *me*, but neither of them was *completely* me."

"You can't keep up a lie indefinitely," Danny whispered.

"Exactly. But I wasn't really thinking about the future. It was kind of day to day thing."

And I was treating this thing with Steele the same way, I realized. Maybe it didn't matter if we fucked today or tomorrow. Maybe there was a long game in there that I hadn't considered. Not a commitment, though I was kind of weirdly not freaked out by the idea of that with him, but a way that not everything had to happen today. That we could wait and let things develop, after I'd helped him bring down the senator and shown him just how formidable I could be.

"Breck," Danny said again, and I looked at him, distracted.

"Yeah?"

"I did something bad. Two somethings, really." His voice was barely audible, and he looked so terrified, my heart picked up speed.

"What?" I demanded. "What are you talking about, Danny? What did you do?"

"That night," he breathed, his eyes huge. "With Snow White? I was terrified."

"I know," I said, putting my arm around his neck and pulling him in for a wet hug. "Honey, we both were. But he can't hurt us now. Like you said this morning. He can't hurt us ever again."

I pulled back and put my hands on both his cheeks. "Listen, I know Ridge. And I'm pretty sure I know Steele too. We can stay here as long as we want, no matter how pissy Ridge is with me. It's gonna be okay."

Danny shook his head tearfully. "But it won't, though. Listen, Breck, that night, after you passed out? He beat me for *hours*. I didn't..." He sobbed and pressed the side of his knuckles against his mouth. "I didn't know if I was gonna live. And I...I wanted people to *know* he'd done it. You know? I didn't want him to frame it as some kind of overdose or hit and run. So after he passed out, I... I took his pinkie ring. The antique one he wears all the time. A-and I swallowed it."

I stared at him in disbelief for five seconds, ten, and then I exploded. "You did *what*?"

"I swallowed it," he repeated miserably. "I imagined them doing an autopsy, like in one of those police shows, and them finding the ring in my stomach, like a clue." He shook his head. "All I can tell you is that it seemed like a good idea at the time and I... I did it."

"And what happened?" I demanded. "Do you... did you..." I made a vague gesture at his abdomen.

"About three days after," he confirmed. He swiped a hand across his eyes. "But I wasn't thinking at all, Breck. The guy has a fucking *videotape* of me doing it. If he noticed the ring was gone and wanted to find it, all he had to do was check the tape. Now he knows I have something of his."

Something that might be persuasive proof if Danny went to the authorities about who had beaten him, sure. But I was pretty sure a guy like Harlan would fucking *hate* thinking that a whore had taken something that belonged to him. His ego couldn't handle it. He'd come looking for it.

"Do you have it with you?" I asked. "Maybe we can get it back to him somehow. Maybe he hasn't even realized it's missing."

"Oh, he realized it," Danny said. "He texted me last night."

"Texted you? But Steele took our phones!"

"I gave Steele my burner," Danny admitted. "The one you used to reach me. The number Cisco has. But I have another one, an older one."

"What for?"

"My sister has that number," Danny said, his eyes filling with tears again. "She texts me sometimes, when something happens with the family. Just to keep me in the loop."

My stomach flipped, and I put both arms around Danny this time, pulling him into me and rubbing comforting circles into the chilled skin of his back.

"Okay. Alright, we can take care of this," I told him.

"How?" he wailed. "Breck, if he found that number, that means he knows my real name. That means he knows who *my sister is*. And he texted me—" He broke off, crying quietly.

"What did he say?" I prompted.

"He said if I don't give the ring back by Saturday, they'll kill me."

They'd likely try to kill him even if he *did* give the ring back. Hell, they might kill both of us, just for being in the room at the time.

It's funny the things you notice when you realize how fucked you are. Night frogs and insects called to each other from the bushes and tall grass. The gulf rolled softly against the shoreline. A light breeze blew the thin clouds slowly across the face of the moon.

My mind whirled. The *right* course of action was to bring this directly to Ridge and Steele, to let their little band of criminal masterminds find Danny a way out of this mess without risking his sister.

But I knew exactly what would happen if I did; they'd take the information, pat me on the head, and send me out to work on my tan while the grownups handled the mess, exactly as they'd been doing from the minute they showed up at Chad's place. And would they worry about what happened to Danny and his sister if it interfered with their plan for revenge? I honestly didn't know.

I wasn't stupid. I knew Danny and I couldn't handle the Senator on our own. But I really, really wanted a seat at that planning table next to Ridge and Steele. More than that, I wanted a lead role in taking the Senator down. I wanted John Harlan to see my face and know it was *me* who'd beaten him in the end.

"Danny, do you trust me?" I asked, pulling away from him slightly.

He nodded.

"Okay, come to my room. I have an idea."

"OKAY, *Birdman, I think we're good. You can come down now.*" Wesley's voice sounded inside my head like some sort of freaky telepathy.

I wasn't sure I was ever going to get used to hearing voices in my head. Wesley had designed his own all-in-one earpiece and microphone that fit over our back teeth like a crown. He claimed the mouthpiece translated sound waves into vibrations through the bones of our heads and sent them to the inner ear, which then translated it back to sound.

Sound, I repeat, that felt like it was coming from inside your head rather than outside. It was freaky as shit. The microphone could pick up the quietest whisper no matter what the outside conditions were. He'd had us talk to each other while we were in the showers to prove it.

Separate showers, naturally.

Wes said his version was an improvement over similar existing devices because it used the human body as an energy source and didn't require any external antenna at all. I was going to take his word for it.

"*Caw, caw, motherfuckers,*" Ridge replied from his perch in a tree outside of Harlan's Florida mansion. It had been his idea to photograph the faces and license plates of everyone coming to the house so Wes could work his magic later.

Considering the senator had almost killed Breck, and given that Ridge looked exactly like Breck, I thought it was too dangerous for him to be anywhere near the place. If the senator caught a glimpse of that face...well, I didn't know what would happen, but it would be nothing good.

Ridge had sworn he wouldn't get caught and then proved it by hiding in a tree on Charlie's property for three hours without any of us finding him.

"One thing you learn in my profession is how not to be seen," he'd said when he'd jumped down on the driveway, almost giving Josie a heart attack. "I can sit still for hours."

It had worked out anyway. We hadn't been able to find any kind of guest list, so we'd had to go in blind. At least this way we could do some investigating after the party.

Oh, yes, just like that, beautiful boy, Carson purred in my ear a split second before the sound came through the door I was guarding. *Fuck my life.*

It wasn't bad enough to know Carson was in there getting his rocks off with one of Harlan's hired prostitutes, I had to have the soundtrack pumped directly into my ear too. It had been way too long since I'd been in his position, pun completely intended, and I hoped the way I had my hands crossed in front of my crotch said *bad-ass bodyguard* and not *hard-up loser trying to hide a woody*.

To get Carson back for getting off, I started to recite some Bible verses I'd been forced to memorize as a kid under my breath, subvocalizing the way Wesley had taught us. Maybe a little bit of the good book would ruin Carson's blow job. Personally, I'd always found hell and damnation a bit of a boner-killer.

Senator Harlan, the man himself, sauntered up to me. "Sounds like your employer is having a good time."

I didn't answer, but I did press my tongue against the mouthpiece the way Wes had said would enable it to pick up all conversation around me so that we could all hear it. I hoped my button-cam recorder was picking up the video. A button camera felt so old-school, and I knew for a fact he'd ordered them off Amazon, but I trusted Wes. If he said it would work, it would work.

Senator Harlan wasn't as ugly as he had looked in the photos. He was pushing sixty and overly-tanned, of course, and you would have thought all that tax-free money he'd gotten from fleecing the desperate true believers of his church could have bought him better hair transplants, but he was broad-shouldered and trim and wore a suit well. Too bad everything about him set my bad-guy senses tingling. Make no mistake, this man was a predator. We'd be stupid to underestimate him.

"You know, there is, ah, *entertainment* provided for you, as well, if you're interested," the senator said with a grin. "There are some lovely ladies outside at the pool. I know you men work 'round the clock, and you deserve some downtime, too. I promise you, your boy is in good hands."

"Oh, yeah, suck harder," Carson moaned from behind the door.

Harlan smirked. "Or should I say good mouths?"

I kept silent.

"Does it bother you that Mr. Waters is in there with another man?"

Why was this douchebag talking to me? Men like him usually never deigned to notice the help.

I shifted my weight, crossing my hands behind my back. My semi had disappeared the moment Harlan had stepped into my personal space. "No, sir," I told him. "That doesn't bother me at all."

"Nice suit," he said, stepping closer and rubbing the material between his fingers. "Handmade?"

"Men's Wearhouse," I answered with a straight face. "Clearance sale."

"Hmmm," Harlan purred, like he was appreciating the fine texture of the cheap-ass polyester blend fabric. "I like you. You know, if you're ever looking for another employer, I could use a good-looking man such as yourself. Makes the ladies happy when I have big, strapping men around, right?" And then he actually touched me. I grabbed my coin tightly to stop myself from punching him.

"Oh my god, he's hitting on you," Ridge said.

Fuck. He was. He was feeling me up. I added that to my list of reasons why I was going to kill him. But as much as I hated thinking about it, it could work to my advantage.

I let my professional veneer crack a little. I glanced nervously at the door, then checked the hallway to see if we were alone. We were, except for Harlan's bodyguard standing discreetly a few feet away. A big ugly guy, the man seemed distracted and uncomfortable with the sounds coming from the bedroom.

Carson, ham it up, I subvocalized. *It's pissing off Harlan's bodyguard.*

It's making me horny, Wes said. *Can't you get us some video, too, Carson?*

Less chatter, more listening, Leo snapped from inside the car. I think he hated having to wait outside, but we needed to keep him out of sight until the next part of the plan.

"I'm listening," I said out loud to the senator.

"What's your name?"

"Gonzales. Mickey Gonzales."

"Well, Mickey Gonzales." He gave me a card. "This is my personal number. Call me, and we'll talk. Are you sure you don't want to take a break? Your boss is booked for another half an hour. Trust me, he won't notice if you leave. Arthur can watch the door for you, right Arthur?" he asked without raising his voice, confirming my suspicions that the senator was also wired into his team.

I tucked the card in my jacket. It felt thick, and I fully expected to find a bug between the layers of heavy card-stock. I found it best to assume I was being recorded any time, any place. Any schmoe with a smart phone could do it. Hell, I had an app on my phone that detected hidden cameras and recorders and one that automatically recorded all my calls. I got them both for free from Google Play.

When we'd entered the house, they'd let us keep our weapons but confiscated all the phones. That showed which was more dangerous to these guys. A gun could only kill, while a video or audio recording could fuck you and your entire family over. Knowledge was power after all, and information had always been the most valuable currency, in war and peace. Wes had assured me that our new phones were uncrackable, but I'd left mine in the car anyway. Not like anyone was going to call me.

Given that blackmail seemed to be the coin of the realm around these parts, I wondered how Harlan felt safe having hookers in his home. "Aren't you worried about your, ah, entertainers letting information slip?" I asked him.

"I have some people who specially procure the men and women for people such as myself. Of course, the cream of the crop is in Washington. Those D.C. boys know the meaning of discretion. I'm always on the market for *discreet* professionals."

I tilted my head towards the door. "I'm sure Mr. Waters can attest to my discretion."

He moved closer to me. I clenched my teeth against the urge to back up or strangle him. "Well, somebody is talking who shouldn't be. I've heard some rumors about his preferences and the trouble he's gotten into."

"That's why he hired me. I'm good at making people not talk."

"And you're willing to get your hands a little dirty?"

"For the right price." I leaned into his personal space. "And for the right person."

He motioned with his head for me to step away from the door. I nodded, clearing my throat to cover me, telling Carson I was stepping away. I figured he wasn't paying too much attention to his comms right now.

Harlan put his hand on my back, between my shoulder blades. It felt like a spider, I tensed, already feeling a phantom blade in my back.

"So, I might have an opening on my security team. My real team, back in D.C. Not these locals." I glanced over my shoulder in time to catch Arthur's scowl. "I've been using one of the big guys, all former SEALs and SpecOps guys. Which one are you?"

I sensed in him that urge to play soldier that so many male politicians seemed to have. He was one of those guys who just knew he would be the big hero if he'd ever had the chance. Fuck this guy. I wasn't going to add anything more to his jerk-off material. I pulled my boyhood accent out and turned it to eleven. "I'm just a good ole boy from Georgia, sir. Got strong wrasslin' gators."

"Sure, of course," he said with a pat to my back that turned into a totally no-homo, just dudes being bros, shoulder squeeze. "Well, anyway, like I was saying, I use these guys for my close protection, and I like them well enough. But I'd feel a lot better with someone like you for my *close* protection. Someone I could trust."

"I'm flattered, sir, but you've just met me. How do you know you can trust me?"

"Let me ask you a question, son, were you raised in the church?"

"Yessir, washed in the blood. South Georgia Church of God."

"You know I was blessed enough to be a pastor for the Assemblies of God? Sadly, I chose to step down when I got into politics. Do you still go?"

His hand was still on my shoulder, fingers tightening and loosening. "Not in a long while. The church and I see differently on a few things." I looked pointedly at the door to the room Carson was in and thanked the universe when it started to open.

Harlan's hand dropped like I had burst into flames, and he backed up quickly.

"Gonzales," Carson snapped from the doorway. I guess he had been listening. "When I say stay by the door, I mean *by* the door, not in the general vicinity of the door."

"I'm afraid that's my fault, Ben. I needed your man's expert advice on a few things." He walked to Carson without a backward look at me. I watched him turn back into the party host, offering his guests all kinds of things that would get them in trouble.

Harlan's arrogance was going to be his downfall, the fate of many a once-powerful man. He'd grown careless, assuming he was untouchable. I was going to enjoy taking him down.

Leo wanted to pull our crew as soon as possible, and normally I would have agreed with him, but there was no way I was leaving without knowing the working boys and girls had gotten out of that house safely. I'd warn them to stay away from men like Harlan, but I knew they'd never listen. One girl, a woman a few years older than the majority, stopped to chat with me.

"You watching them leave?" she asked, lighting a cigarette.

"Yeah."

"Everyone accounted for?"

I nodded, and she echoed the movement. "Thanks for looking out for the kids. Most people don't care." She took a long drag of her cigarette and looked back at the house. "I got a bad vibe from this place. Don't think I'll be back. Whadda you know about this guy?"

"Let's just say, I recommend going with your gut." I usually advised people to do that. I read shit, I knew things. Our guts have what some people call a second brain, the enteric nervous system. More people should listen to their guts, it knows shit our brains don't.

"About time," Leo grumped as I slid into the back seat on the passenger's side. I ignored him.

Ridge was on his phone the entire ride home, texting with someone.

My whole body was tense. I hadn't cared this much about a job since I'd gotten out of the army. "Tell me again why I can't just shoot him? Wipe him off the Earth like the shit-stain he is?"

Surprisingly, it was Carson who answered. "Because this is about more than just Harlan damaging individual lives. The anti-LGBT and anti-immigration policies Harlan sponsors have done a lot of damage, and he's just getting started. If he gets killed, someone else will take up his mantle. If it comes out that he was murdered, they may even be able to spin his death into some kind of PR event. Use him as a rallying point."

"A martyr for the cause."

"Exactly. So what we need to do is expose his hypocrisy and that of all his scumbag backers."

"Except for Ben Waters."

"Yes. Quite," he said dryly. "But if we expose Harlan, discredit him, we destroy him *and* them. The true believers won't care, but they're nobodies. People in power will know they've lost him as a tool. His career will be ruined. His family will be ruined."

I knew that. Rationally, I understood the plan and agreed with it. I still wanted to go back on my no-kill policy. For him, I was willing to make an exception.

"So all we have to do now," Leo said from the front of the limo, "is get invited to the 'party' on Saturday, get into Harlan's house, get copies of all the blackmail material he has and tapes of him beat—" He glanced over at Ridge in the passenger's seat. Practically vibrating with rage, the kid had his fists clenched so tightly, I wouldn't be surprised to see blood on his palms. "Get the video of the senator abusing Breck and Danny, so we can get him charged as well. Then get out without being caught."

"Piece of cake," Wesley said over the comms. "I've got blueprints with wiring diagrams, and I've been talking to Breck and Danny about what they remember of the house. We can discuss the specifics later, but we need to move the show up to D.C. in time for the senator's party Saturday. Do a thorough sneak and peek while Ben Waters plays nice. Maybe one of us can get in earlier somehow."

"Yes," Carson agreed. "And I'll reach out to some of my contacts, see if they can help with anything."

"I'll try to find out who does his close protection up there. These guys were nobodies. Local tough guys. If he has the same level in D.C., I'd be thrilled. But for all we know, he's got G4S guys surrounding him day and night."

"Seems like overkill," Leo said. "You really think he'd go to that trouble?"

I shrugged. Guys hired close protection—bodyguards—for different reasons. Some because of legitimate threat of danger to them or their families. Some guys did it for ego and appearances. Those guys tended to hire way more than they needed. G4S was the biggest of the big in the government world. I wouldn't put it past Harlan to have them around his house in slickers with the company logo on it.

Then again, Harlan was high on his own self-importance. Maybe he kept his shit protected with a friendly golden retriever and a padlock.

"We'll find out."

"I want to get that Cisco guy, too," Ridge said. "Even if we give him the benefit of the doubt, say he didn't know what kind of scum Snow White was the first time, he damn sure knows now. And he's sending Breck and Danny back into that torture chamber."

Cisco. One of Harlan's *procurers* and Breck's pimp. "Don't worry," I said. "We'll take him down, too."

Leo met my eyes in the rearview mirror, looking like he wanted to say something. Wisely, he kept his thoughts to himself.

Back at the house, Ridge headed straight for his room. I'd expected him to go talk to Breck. They had to talk, sooner rather than later, but his loss was my gain.

My brain knew Breck was safe in the house, but after dealing with Harlan all evening, feeling his filthy hands on me, my heart wasn't so sure. I'd feel better once I saw him.

I could admit I'd been avoiding him. I'd told myself I needed space to concentrate on the job, and that was partly true. But more than that, the guy scared me. Made me wanna rip the senator's head off and break the hands of every guy who'd ever laid a finger on him in anger. I was taking the mission personally for the first time in a while.

Once the job was over, we'd see what, if anything, we could have. A good time at the very least.

"Where's Breck?" I asked Wesley when I dropped off my tech for him to check out.

"Am I his keeper?" he asked, mock-offended.

I raised my eyebrows and looked deliberately at the monitor on his desk that was very clearly displaying video feeds from inside the house.

"Okay, fine. He's in his room with Danny."

"What are they doing?" I took a step toward the monitor as if I could control the cameras with my mind.

Wesley shrugged. "Dunno. There aren't cameras in the bedroom, at least none that I've found yet. Believe me, if there was one in there with them, I'd be watching."

"You're such a fucking horn dog, Bond. I had no idea."

"I'm a healthy young man with healthy appetites, Alvarez."

I slapped him on the back so hard, his chair rolled forward. "That you are. Just keep them away from Breck."

"And Danny?"

I wanted to tell him to keep away from Danny, too, if only because the kid was so young and obviously had had some trauma in his life before his run-in with Senator Douchebag, but Danny was an adult, legally. Besides, I'd keep an eye on them. "Danny can make his own decisions, but I'd be cautious if I were you. Kid's been through a lot."

Wesley leaned back in his chair. "Yeah, he has. I'd love to get his story."

"Well, take him out to dinner or something when all this BS is done."

Wesley snorted. I left him to it.

I told myself there was nothing going on between Breck and Danny, but I'd seen evidence with my own eyes that they'd shared a bed before. I'd been ignoring Breck, so it would make sense for him to turn to the only person he knew here besides his brother. And, like Wesley said, he was a healthy young man with healthy appetites.

I wouldn't blame him. That would be fine. It wasn't like we were dating or anything.

Yeah, like fuck it would be fine.

By the time I hit the hall outside Breck's room, I was not quite running, but I would have placed in a speed-walking race for sure.

Knock or barge in? Knock or barge in? My brain argued with my body, and in a surprising turn of events, my brain won. I knocked. Like a normal person.

"Come in," Breck called.

I did.

To my great relief, both guys were fully-dressed and watching a show on Breck's iPad. Well, Danny wasn't quite *dressed* but as covered as I've ever seen him. His shorts actually hit the tops of his thighs. No shirt though. I could tell by his tan he'd been making the most of his time here. Something of my relief must have shown in my face, because Breck smiled at me like he was amused and turned on at the same time.

Danny rolled off the bed. "That's my cue to leave."

"You don't have to leave," I lied. "I don't want to interrupt your movie."

"Yeah, no. Hot as it would be to have a three-way with you guys, I have a feeling I would be something way beyond a third wheel here. Of course later, if you want a third, you know where to find me." He winked and flounced out of the room.

Breck set the tablet aside and patted the bed next to him. "How'd it go?"

"I'm going to kill him," I said. "Harlan. He's dead."

I stood next to the bed, staring down at the gorgeous man.

"For me?" Breck swung his feet off the bed and sat up, looking directly into my eyes.

"For you."

He stood, sliding up against my body. My arms wrapped around him, and my mind short-circuited.

Fuck whatever objections Ridge had and whatever stupid part of my brain had been holding me back. I needed to hold him, I needed to feel Breck whole in my arms.

"Think we can take him down?" Breck molded to my body, his arm reaching around my waist.

"Yeah. I do. I wasn't sure at first, but I think it's gonna work. I gotta say, Charlie pulled a good team together. He knew what he was doing."

"Yeah?"

"I trust these guys. I mean, not with my life or anything. But they're not fuck ups, you know?"

"Even Ridge?"

"Let me tell you, your brother can be a scary guy."

"Yeah. I like that about him."

"Me, too."

"Are you scared of him?" Breck asked me.

"I'm more scared of you," I admitted.

Steele's entire body tensed against mine with his words, like he'd just confessed some deep, dark secret. Maybe for him, it was. But for me, his words were more like a magic spell, an incantation that took away all of my own worries and hesitations.

I'd known from the first day that Steele wanted me —I'd seen his eyes heat and felt his cock thicken against me often enough that I didn't doubt he was attracted—but *wanting* was common as dirt. If Steele wanted to get his rocks off, he could find a willing partner anywhere. Hell, he wouldn't even have to leave the house, if the admiring glances I'd seen Leo throw him were any indication. He could get in, get off, get out, and get on his way without a single complication.

Meanwhile, between us was a veritable complication *minefield*.

A sick-as-fuck senator was threatening Danny and me, my overprotective brother kept inserting himself into my business like the chaperone at an eighth-grade dance, and Steele's own moral code seemed determined to make him step back every time he got close to me. Steele wasn't even aware of what Danny and I had been planning before he came in tonight, which was just as well, since it might make his head explode.

What he *did* know was enough to make any guy run away screaming.

But instead, Steele had come to me. He'd sought me out so he could tell me about the operation they'd run tonight, because somehow he'd *known* I'd find it comforting. He'd practically slammed the door shut behind Danny, even after Danny had made it clear he'd be down for a threesome—an offer other guys would have (and *had*) paid big bucks for. Steele wasn't just here for the sex, and neither was I.

It should have been scary as fuck. It *was* scary as fuck, for a guy who'd never felt anything more than lust and, if I was lucky, simple affection, for the guys I'd taken to bed. Whatever this *more-than-lust* thing growing between Steele and me was, I'd never felt anything like it before, and I wasn't sure I could trust it.

But I knew I didn't want to walk away from it, and I didn't want him to walk away either.

"You scare the shit out of me, too," I whispered.

He flinched.

Not exactly the reaction I'd been hoping for.

I pulled back from his embrace and found his dark eyes wide.

"Sweetcheeks, I really don't want to hurt you. And I don't mean physically, although obviously, that too. It's just..." He hesitated. "I don't want anyone to take advantage of you or force you to do anything. Including me."

I narrowed my eyes at him. "Right, and...?" I did not like where this was going at all.

"And, well, I think we should wait. Before we..." He gestured back and forth between us. "Just until things are done with Harlan. Once you're safe—and I swear to Christ, Breck, I'll make that happen no matter what I have to do—then when you have all the facts, you can decide if you really want me." He shrugged. "No pressure. No expectations. No feeling like you owe me or anyone else."

Is that what he was torturing himself with? He was adorable, he really was.

"Steele?" I lifted up on my tiptoes and interrupted him by pressing a kiss to the stubbled underside of his jaw.

He swallowed. "Yeah?"

"Do you want me?" I whispered in his ear.

"Oh, God. S*ofuckingmuch*," he said in a rush, like the words had been sitting there dying to break free. His hands came up, almost involuntarily to grasp my hips. But then he cleared his throat and pushed me away, just slightly. "But that has nothing to do with anything. The circumstances are..."

I couldn't help grinning. "The circumstances are absolute shit," I agreed. "But just so I understand, this isn't about you needing to focus, right? And it's not about you trying to let me down easy?"

He let out a chuckle that turned into a moan when I licked his earlobe with the tip of my tongue. His hips kicked toward mine involuntarily, providing very welcome friction to my half-hard dick. "I should be focusing. I told myself I wanted to wait so I could focus. But my self-control is for shit where you're concerned."

I should not have been so excited to hear that.

"Are you worried about Harlan? Or about my damn brother?" I demanded. I let my hands drift up his chest and pressed my torso to his.

"Not Harlan. I told you, our team is solid. And your brother is too professional to let personal shit interfere. But Ridge, ah... oh, *fuck me*," he growled as I flicked my nails over his nipples. "That's just not fair."

"Continue," I demanded.

Steele let out a shaking breath. "Ridge makes a...*fuck*." He tilted his head to the side to allow me better access as I licked and sucked at the smooth, salty skin of his neck. "You really need to stop doing that," he said.

The lust in his voice was so palpable, my cock gave an answering throb.

"Uh, no." My breath brushed over his damp skin, and he shivered. "I'm pretty sure I need to do this *more*. A lot more." I moved to lick his Adam's apple, and my fingers drifted to unbutton the top few buttons of his shirt. The stupid things wouldn't open. It was like the buttons were too big. "Fuck it." I grabbed two handfuls of shirt, sending buttons flying.

"Wait," Steele mumbled as my hands mapped his chest. "Wesley put a..." Whatever he was trying to say dissolved into a moan as I pinched both his nipples.

Steele whimpered, his hands clenched in fists at his side. "I'm tryin' to do the right thing here, Breck. Be the gentleman I was raised to be, for once. Ridge wants to protect you, and maybe he has a point."

"God save me from overprotective alpha males," I muttered. I grabbed his head in both my hands and forced his eyes to meet mine. "You listen to me, Castille Alvarez. I am a fully-grown man."

"I'm aware," he said, more than a little breathless. His fists came to rest on my hips, and he was holding himself so tightly, he was practically vibrating. "I'm really, really aware."

"*Excellent.* So I'm sure you'll understand that as an adult, I make choices about my own life." I took a step forward, forcing him back a pace. "If I choose not to go back to college, that's my business. If I choose to have sex with every fucking senator and all four-hundred-thirty-five Congress-people too, that's my call."

"Right, yes, I know. It's just right now..."

"And after I make those decisions? I don't need to justify them. Not to you, not to Ridge. I should not have to convince anyone that I was in the perfect frame of mind for decision-making, I shouldn't have to get my primary care physician and a notary public to sign off on me being capable of making a choice, Steele." I let go of his head and braced my hands on his chest, pushing him back another pace.

"Breck, I'm not saying that you're not capable of deciding any of that shit. Just…"

"Just *what*? Just talk to Ridge and make sure he gives us his blessing? Gives you two cows and a donkey, and you sign a marriage contract? Hmm? Just *wait* until some arbitrary time when *you've* decided that I should have recovered from the level of trauma *you* think I should feel?"

"I… that's not… no! I just want to…"

"Protect me?" I demanded. I pushed him again, harder this time, and he landed on my bed with a plop. "Yes, so you said." I shoved his shoulders until he was lying flat on the bed, all six and a half feet of muscle sprawled on the white coverlet. He seemed stunned to find himself there.

"The thing is, Steele, I like that you want to protect me. I do. Makes me *allllll* warm and gushy in the best kind of way. But right now?" I put one knee on the bed next to his. "At this exact moment?" I pulled my other knee up to straddle his legs. "Your protection is the *last* thing I want." I braced my hand on his sternum. "Do you understand?"

His smile bloomed across his face, warm like sunshine. "I think I'm beginning to."

"Right now," I continued, pulling open the remaining buttons on his shirt with absolutely no care whatsoever. "There are no expectations and none of the other bullshit you said earlier."

"Okay." Steele stacked his hands behind his head and watched me, grinning.

"There is no one and nothing in this bed but us. No old men to trouble us, no ghosts of Breck's questionable decisions to haunt us." I rolled my eyes. "And for the love of Adam Rippon, no Ridge." I bent down to place a kiss in the center of his chest and looked up to meet his eyes. "Because twincest is only hot in fiction."

He pressed his lips together and nodded. "Understood."

I sat up and spread the two halves of his shirt wide. The man was a fucking miracle, every muscle lovingly sculpted from marble and covered in warm, smooth flesh. I wanted to take my time, to taste every millimeter of that skin with my tongue. And I would, as soon as I made sure we were both on the same page.

I sat back, just a little, just enough to slide my ass along his cock. "Right now, Steele, I'm just a boy, kneeling on top of a boy, begging him to fuck me."

He laughed, deep and full. "Jesus Christ." He lifted his hands to knit his fingers in my hair. "You are beautiful, you know that? Beautiful and crazy."

"Possibly," I agreed. "But crazy in a very, very sane sort of way. So what I want to know, Steele, is *are you going to say yes?*"

He bit his lip, and his black eyes danced up at me. He curled up from his abs with zero effort, then paused when his lips were directly in front of mine. "I don't know how the fuck I could say no to you."

He kissed me, and his lips tasted like laughter.

He rolled us both over, still cradling my head in his hands, and didn't stop until he was totally on top of me. He paused for a second to take all of the pillows off the bed and throw them on the floor.

"What the heck was that for?" I said, watching the incredibly expensive, memory-foam wonders go flying into the window and then crash to the floor.

"We won't be needing them," Steele said matter-of-factly.

I snickered. "Oh, is that so? Are you psychic? Or is there a script I wasn't given?"

"Oh, there's a script," he confirmed. He braced his elbows by my shoulders, pinning my arms, and rolled himself against me, rubbing his hard cock back and forth against mine.

Holy fuck.

I should not be as primed as I was. I had crazy stamina, for God's sake. I had fucking technique.

"I made it up yesterday morning in the shower," he continued. "I tweaked it last night in bed, twice, and then did the final revisions this morning." He leered down at me. "Also in the shower."

If I thought too hard about Steele bringing himself off in the shower, and his bed, my brain would break or liquefy. So instead of begging him to tell me every last detail, which was pretty much what I wanted to do, I gave him an exaggerated pout instead. "Awww. That's so sad for you. All that creativity and effort going to waste."

"And why is that?" he challenged.

"Because I have a script, too," I said. I bit my lip and let my eyes go hot as I gazed up at him, tracing my fingers over every inch of his naked stomach that I could reach with my elbows pinned. "I worked on my script in the shower, too, but I didn't *finish it.*"

His eyes glittered. "You didn't?"

I shook my head. "No. I realized I hadn't worked hard enough? You need to work on these things really, really hard," I told him earnestly.

He swallowed and stared at my mouth.

"I tried again in bed last night, but I couldn't quite finish then either. It was the last thing I did before I went to sleep and the first thing I *worked on* this morning." I sighed dramatically. "I brought myself right to the edge of *finishing* so many times."

"And did you?" His voice was gritty, an octave lower than usual.

"No," I whispered, blinking up innocently. "I figured I should wait for you to help me."

He thrust his hips again, and we both groaned out, "*Fuck!*" simultaneously.

His dark eyes bore into mine, and he was breathing hard, but he grinned broadly. "Only one thing to do," he said, his voice coated with the thick, syrupy southern drawl I'd only heard him use once or twice.

"Let me have my way?"

"Nope. We'll settle this the old-fashioned way. We'll wrestle."

I blinked. He'd said *wrestle* like *wrassle,* and holy shit it was adorable. I would do a lot of truly sordid things for that grin, but. "We can't *wrassle*, King Kong! You're like seventy-seven times my weight. You could pin me in a second."

He pursed his lips thoughtfully, and I wanted to kiss him senseless. His hard cock was still rubbing against mine, but languidly, like he was hardly even aware of it. Hardly even aware he was driving me batshit.

He shrugged, as if he'd exhausted every possible solution to the dilemma. "I guess that means I win, then," he said brightly. He did another of those crazy ab contractions and brought his knees up to straddle me in one swift movement, keeping my elbows pinned to my sides. "So lemme tell you what I'm gonna do to you first."

Oh, fuck that. I narrowed my eyes and dug my fingers into his rib cage.

He screamed like he'd been electrocuted and arched away from me.

"Whatsamatter, Castille? The big, strong protector-man can't handle a little tickling?"

He flopped down on the bed next to me and curled in on himself, folding his hands over his chest, but I surged to my knees and followed him.

"Stop!" he laughed. "Fucking stop! There's a whole section in the Geneva Convention about this!"

"Whose script are we following? Whose?" I couldn't even remember what the fuck I was talking about, but I'd be damned if I let him win. This was the most fun I'd had in ages. Maybe the most fun I'd had ever.

"Mine," he insisted through his laughter. "Mine, mine, mine." A flash of triumphant glee in his eyes was my only warning. He grabbed both of my hands and rolled over on top of me again, pinning me down in the same spot where I'd been a minute ago.

Then, like the most gloating gloater who ever gloated, he dipped his head and licked a broad stripe up my cheek. He leaned back, smiling, like he was waiting to see my reaction. Christ, his smile did things to me.

"Ew," I complained, even though what I felt wasn't even in the same universe as disgust. "Doesn't the Geneva Convention have rules against that?"

He shook his head seriously. "You should really know better, Pfeiffer. Never start a land war in Asia, and never, never start a tickle fight with the Charlton High School All-Scholastic Wrestling Champion." He pressed my wrists more firmly to the mattress, and his eyes gleamed. "Unless you want to be at his mercy."

The accent. Oh, God. *At his merrrseee.*

Then he waggled his eyebrows at me and bit his lip, cramming decades worth of sexy thoughts into one lava-hot glance, and I was done for.

Kill me now.

Dead.

I'd packed a lifetime of sexual experiences into six months... or so I'd thought. I knew of every kink and had tried most of them. But if you'd told me it was possible to balance on a razor's edge between outraged laughter and premature ejaculation, I would have called you a liar. For all that I'd seen and done in the last six months, humor had never entered the equation, not once. But all of a sudden here I was, with my cock throbbing and joy bubbling in my chest, and it was everything I hadn't known I needed.

"Well, maybe I wanna be at your mercy," I told him, only it came out different than I'd intended, not arch and teasing, but low and serious. Honest.

And just when I started to worry that I'd fucked something up, he let go of one of my wrists to cup my cheek and leaned down to press the sweetest, softest kiss to my lips.

It took about two-point-four seconds for us to shuck our clothes after that. I remember exactly *nothing* about the process except that one minute his suit pants and my trunks were there, and the next they were gone, and I was so fucking relieved that finally there was nothing between us.

I wanted to lean back and look at him. I wanted to paint my name on his chest with my tongue. I wanted to finally, finally get my mouth on his cock. But every technique I knew had somehow flown out the window into the Florida night. Every practiced move, every nuanced glance I'd honed had decamped to some other part of my brain. Now that we were finally naked and pressed against each other, all I could do was *feel*.

His thumbs stroking my hipbones were the most erotic sensation ever. The heat of his chest against mine spread through every part of me, and for once in my air-condition-ing-loving-life, I welcomed the heat. I wanted the nip of his teeth at my jaw, my ribs, my belly button, and the chafe of his leg hair against mine as he moved down my body.

He took my cock to the back of his throat in one smooth motion, and my hips bucked off the bed.

"Jesus, *fuck*," I yelled. I hadn't been kidding about the edging earlier, and between that and everything that had happened tonight, I was poised at a precipice. "Fuck, fuck, fuck. Warn a guy!"

The vibration of his chuckle around me, and the hard weight of his hands holding my hips against the mattress were his only response.

It was gorgeous, and the noises I made were mortifyingly loud, but I couldn't stop them any more than I could stop the tears that kept building up behind my eyes. Everything about this night was so intense, even more so than I'd imagined it would be when I'd fantasized about it earlier. And not just physically. Steele was drawing all these emotions out of me, joy and anxiety and protectiveness and caring, and I had no clue how to handle them.

When he finally pulled off and crawled back up my body, I was pretty sure he could read all this shit, clear as day on my face. I wished I were half the liar Ridge was.

"You okay?" he asked, brushing one thumb over my cheek.

I nodded and threw my forearm over my eyes. "It's just been a minute since I picked someone to be intimate with, that's all. Been a minute since I *wanted* to." Such a fucking sap. "Just, like, ignore me. Or give me a second."

But Steele didn't pull away or take this marvelous opportunity to question whether I was *really really really sure* I wanted this, or whatever. He just cupped my cheek the way he had earlier. "I've got all the minutes you need."

"Ugh," I groaned, moving my arm away. "Disgusting. Stop being so nice. I can't handle it."

He grinned. "Awww, whatsamatter, Brekkie? *Hot little ass* can't handle a little *tender*?"

"Asshole."

He reached down and wrapped his huge hand around my cock, then tugged gently.

Shiiit.

"Pardon?" he said.

"Nothing. *Nothing*," I squeaked.

"That's what I thought," he said, satisfied. "How do you want it, then? Hmm?" He braced on his elbow and reached up to gently yank one of my curls. "Want it rough? Want it gentle?"

"I thought this was your script?"

"It is." He grinned. "This was the script. Me, giving you exactly what you want."

Damn.

"Then yeah," I agreed. "I want it hard." Hard and fast and rough enough to burn out all this other stuff, all this shit that made me *way* too fucking sappy about something that, despite the serious attraction between us and the way he made me laugh my ass off, was really still just sex.

Steele tossed me a wink and climbed off the bed, then opened the nightstand drawer. He threw a tube of lube on the coverlet beside me and kept rummaging.

"Uh, Breck?" he asked curiously. "There are like three toys and four kinds of lube, but I'm not seeing your condoms, babe."

Oh. *Oh, shit.*

I sat up in bed and stared at him. "Fuck, I didn't even think. I don't have any," I told him.

"You don't?" I got why he was stunned, given my line of work, but...

"No," I wailed. I ran a hand through my hair. "I don't. I mean, I use them religiously when I have sex. It's just that I don't have sex when I'm not, you know, with a client." I met his eyes. "I didn't expect this. I didn't expect...you."

The look he gave me was complicated. Surprise, but hotter. Amazement, but sweeter.

"Should I go get some?" I asked ready to literally run to the fucking store.

Steele he shook his head. "I've got this." He found his suit pants under my swim shorts on the floor and dug out his wallet and the condom inside. He held it up between his fingers and grinned. "You were saying?"

Oh, God. "Hard and fast," I demanded, pulling my legs up to my chest. "And I don't need prep. I'm already set." My toys had gotten an extensive workout earlier in the day.

Of course, he had to fucking verify that himself, running the pads of his fingers over my rim to tease me before dipping a well-lubed finger inside.

"You see?" I panted when he'd braced himself above me. "I told you."

"Oh, I see," he agreed. He withdrew his finger and quickly shoved two more inside, hitting my prostate and setting off a white-lightning chain reaction up and down my spine. Then the fucker smiled at me, all slow and knowing, and did it again.

This was what I'd been afraid of. This, exactly. This stupid *connection* that was irrational and likely a fucking figment of my imagination. I didn't know how to trust it or him or myself.

Steele sucked in a ragged breath, His eyes were way too bright, and he looked sick, or stoned, or both.

"Fuck, Breck," he said. "Just. I wanted to but I can't."

"What?" I demanded. "You can't what?"

"I can't wait."

"No shit. This is what I've been *saying*," I told him, and he laughed. A quick puff of sound that seemed to be pulled from him.

I grabbed the condom he'd thrown on the bed earlier and ripped it open, then turned on my side and grabbed his fucking beautiful cock. "I want this. Now."

He nodded.

I rolled the condom down his length and added a thick coating of lube. I was prepped but his dick was in proportion to the rest of his body, and there was no way this was going to happen without a little burn.

I found myself flat on my back the next instant, with Steele leaning above me, poised at my entrance. "I wanted this to start slow," he laughed. "Make it special." He shook his head. "I am constantly underestimating my powers of self-control with you."

Jesus, the man had no idea. If this got any more special, I was going to spontaneously combust, leaving behind nothing but a cloud of dust.

Steele was practically trembling with want as he pushed inside me, and it was humbling.

God, seriously, I was disgusted with myself. I knew better than to make sex, even really hot sex between people who liked each other a lot, into a hearts and rainbows affair. But there was something special about wanting a man who wanted me back in equal measure, a kind of parity I'd never experienced before.

I was used to guys lusting after me because of my face or my body or what I could do to them. I'd never had anyone look at me like I was this precious thing. Not like I was fragile, but as if I might fly out of his grasp at any moment. I was used to that illusory feeling of being detached and in control that I'd had with my clients. I'd let myself believe that control meant safety, and I'd found out just how wrong I was. But this, right here, was the real deal.

The way he moved inside me, the joy and total absorption on his face, were potent. I barely had to reach down and touch myself before I was coming all over my chest. A second later, he pulled out and whipped the condom off so he could splatter his release on me, too. My dick gave a tired twitch at the sight.

"That was..t was..." *Magical. Transcendent. Mind-altering.* "Good," I panted as he collapsed half on top of me. "Really good."

He rolled to one side and gasped out a chuckle. "See, now I *want* to take that as a compliment, baby. But considering you were fucking a lot of old, white grandfather-types, I just don't know."

I pulled away and stared at him in disbelief. "Was that...is that a prostitute joke? Really, Castille?"

"Too soon?" he asked with fake solicitousness.

I smacked him in the gut, hard. "Your come is still on my chest," I pointed out.

"Yeah," he sighed sleepily, clearly pleased as fuck. "That was hot."

I rolled my eyes. "No. Etiquette. Whatsoever."

He chuckled and rolled on me more firmly, knocking the breath out of my lungs. But I kinda liked it anyway. "Oh, son. If you wanted some refined asshole, you're screwed." He forced my legs apart with his own and rested his head on my chest. My stomach was being glued to his chest, but he didn't seem to care, and fuck if I cared either. "You've got yourself a swamp rat, instead."

He sighed heavily and relaxed on to me. Oh, damn. Steele Alvarez, the smart-mouthed giant, the military-honed badass. was a full-body cuddler. And he wasn't treating me like I was breakable. He wanted to be on top, and he trusted me to tell him if it was too much.

That was a hundred times more dangerous than some whack-job senator.

But instead of running, instead of kicking Steele out of my bed with a wink that promised more casual fun tomorrow, I lay as still as I possibly could so I wouldn't disturb him and wondered how long my swamp rat might want to stick around.

I SHOULD HAVE BEEN THINKING about ways to crush Senator John Harlan so completely, his slimy buddies could snort him. What I was doing was wondering how long Breck would keep me around before telling me to get lost. Eventually, inevitably, he'd go back to his college life and I'd go back to doing what I did. But my plan was simple: I'd follow him to George Washington and anywhere else until he kicked me to the curb.

Early morning sun beat down on my naked chest as I stretched out on one of the teak loungers on the patio near the pool. A few more days in Florida, and I'd be as tanned as a Mr. Universe contestant. I was going to give a medal to whoever had decided to have this meeting by the pool.

Leo occupied another lounge chair, hiding from the sun under the shadow of the upper balcony. In sunglasses and a white T-shirt, the Fed stared intently at the printouts of several of Harlan's offshore accounts. *Following the money*, as the old saying went. Forensic accounting had taken down more bad guys than guns ever could.

Carson sat next to Leo, frowning and tapping angrily into his phone.

Wesley sat on the edge of the pool in Star Wars-themed swim shorts, dangling his feet in the water and watching the show. His head swiveled from right to left as Danny floated past on an inflatable raft shaped like a giant pink flamingo, wearing nothing but miles of tan skin and a bright blue banana hammock smaller than most of my underwear. Tragically, as much as I appreciated Danny's God-given beauty, I couldn't stop searching the patio for the man who occupied ninety percent of my attention lately.

I jumped as a shadow fell over me and cold water drops rained onto my face and chest.

"Enjoying the view?" Breck asked, leaning over the back of my lounge chair. He shook his head and more droplets flew from his curls onto my body. He was shirtless, and the turquoise bathing suit he wore, while marginally larger than Danny's in that it covered his entire ass, barely reached the top of his pubes.

"Fuck yeah," I said, reaching for him. He laughed and dodged easily out of the way.

A gust of wind sent Danny's bird raft bumping into the side of the pool. "He looks so peaceful," Breck said, watching his friend. "I have the strongest urge to jump on him."

"Me, too." I wiggled my eyebrows teasingly. Breck punched my arm, and I laughed. "Hey! You're invited, of course."

"As a third?"

I nodded. "Or you could just watch, if you'd rather."

Breck snorted. "You wish, old man. No way you could handle me and Danny together."

Laughing, I pulled him onto my lap. He was probably right. God, he felt so good in my arms that I couldn't even care about the glare Ridge was giving his brother and me. In my opinion, his glare was growing weak, becoming more for appearance's sake than any actual animosity he felt for me. He seemed to be growing resigned to the thought of Breck and I hooking up.

The sound of metal wheels rolling over cement drew all eyes. Josie rolled a cart loaded with glass pitchers filled with frosty drinks in unnatural colors. Today's outfit was a high-waisted nautical-themed bathing suit right off a Betty Grable poster and candy-apple red platform sandals. She rang a small bell, like the world's most alcoholic ice cream man, and obediently we converged on the glass-topped table.

"Drink up, boys. I'm trying a new rum from Barbados that Charlie never let me touch before. But I figure, there's not much he can do about it now."

Leo took a pink drink garnished with spears of pineapple and maraschino cherries. "Remind me never to get on your bad side, Josie."

She scoffed. "You just do what Charlie needed you to do, and we'll get along just fine."

Danny joined the group, leaving wet footprints in his wake. Wesley trailed behind, eyes locked on Danny's ass so hard, he bumped into the kid when he stopped walking. He caught Danny by the shoulders. "Sorry!"

Danny frowned at him, reached for the blue drink with orange slices, and took a step away. Ooh, Wesley was going to have to up his game.

"We'll get the job done. Don't worry, Miss Josie," I said. "Piece of cake."

It really should be. So far, Harlan had stuck to the basic bad-guy plan. An email had arrived this morning asking for another 'campaign contribution.' When Ben-slash-Carson had refused, a second email had come from an 'anonymous source' with a lovely little montage of Carson and his fuck buddy from the party along with a boilerplate blackmail letter straight out of bad-guy school asking for a few thousands dollars 'campaign contribution.'

"Easy for you to say," Carson grumbled. "It's not your money we're spending."

"Not yours either," Leo reminded him. "You'll get reimbursed by Miranda when all of this is over."

I grabbed an orange slushy beverage and pulled up a chair. "So how's it work? You just pay him through PayPal or something?"

"No. He set up a 'dark wallet' type transaction," Carson said. He and Leo exchanged looks.

"Big deal," Wesley mocked. "I could install that on my grandmother's computer, and she still has an AOL email address."

"Your grandmother was probably hacking systems with a toy whistle and a landline thirty years ago," Carson said.

Wesley wagged a finger at him. "Allegedly. And she was never convicted. This is barely a step up from that."

"Still," Cason said, "it makes it very hard to track."

"But not impossible," Leo said.

"What am I missing?" I asked. Computers were not my strong point.

"Well, there's no proof yet," Wesley said, "but it seems like the senator is into more than just run-of-the-mill blackmail. You don't need this level of encryption and trace hiding for that. Most people getting blackmailed are other criminals and aren't going to run to the police." He waved at their little group. "Case in point. Dark Wallet is the kind of thing used by the big boys."

"I fucking hate these people. They're why I stay out of cybercrimes. Dark Wallet? Who names these things? Four-teen-year-old boys?" Leo scowled.

"Maybe the same people who called a boat Boaty McBoat-face," Breck offered.

"The real question," Ridge reminded everyone, "is how are we going to take him down now that he thinks he's got Carson bent over a table?" He shot Carson a smirk. "Liter-ally and figuratively."

"Hilarious," Breck said, rolling his eyes at his brother's joke. "But seriously, what *is* the plan from here on?" He folded his hands on the table and stared at each of us expectantly.

I sighed at Breck's eager expression and frowned, almost as much as Ridge had when Breck and I had shown up at breakfast together. Finalizing the plan *was* the point of this meeting, after all.

Once Carson-as-Ben had agreed to the senator's second demand for cash, Harlan had invited Carson to a party this weekend at his home outside D.C. and had even instructed him to bring a rich, like-minded friend, because being a blackmail victim was so much more fun when your friends could play too. Logically, I knew Breck had to be part of the planning because he and Danny were the only two who had seen the inside of the senator's home, but I didn't have to like it.

"The real question is," Carson said, "Where and how do I file my receipt for reimbursement?"

"You have more than one multi-million-dollar corporation, Grieves. Suck it up." Miranda walked out the door from the living room, her high-heels clicking against the cement, and sat gracefully in a free chair. She reached for the nearest unclaimed frosty cocktail, and Josie watched as she took a sip.

With a white blouse tucked into a dark blue pencil skirt and her hair pulled back into a tight bun, Miranda looked like the kind of lawyer who could steal your company right out from under you and you would thank her for it. I was glad she was on our side.

"Very nice," Miranda said, smiling at Josie. "Is that the Barbados rum?"

Josie cackled. "You know it! I told Charlie it was a crying shame to leave it languishing in the cabinet."

Miranda raised one eyebrow. "He never listened to anyone, did he?" Her eyes softened as she looked at Josie.

Josie gave her a soft smile in return. "No, he did not." She lifted her cup. "To Charlie and his posthumous hospitality. May he be in some afterlife with a bar, a band, and beautiful men to watch."

"Is everyone here gay?" Danny blurted out, sounding almost exasperated.

I'd been wondering that myself.

"I am," Leo said.

"So am I," Josie chimed in, reaching forward to clink glasses with Leo.

"Me, too." I grabbed Breck by the waist. "Ask him."

Breck nodded. "It's true. Well, at least he really likes—" I slapped my hand over his mouth before Ridge lost his mind.

"I think I'm bi," Danny said shyly. "But I've never really dated anybody."

"Me, too," Wesley added quickly. "I mean, I know I am. Pan, really, I guess."

"What about you, Carson?" Leo asked curiously.

"I'm whatever I need to be." Carson's posh accent was back in full force, and he gave what I imagined was supposed to be an enigmatic look over the edge of his glass.

"Oh, please. All of Sarasota knows you like the D, Grieves," I said. "You're a loud one."

"You should talk," Carson said.

Ridge looked like he'd bitten into a lemon. "Can we change the subject?"

Breck slid off me and into his own chair. Reaching over, I grabbed the arm and dragged him closer to me with an awful screech of metal on concrete. "Sorry."

"Excellent idea." Miranda angled her chair so the shadow of the umbrella covered her a bit more. Not that it made much of a difference in a hundred and fifty percent humidity, but it would slow down getting a sunburn. "So gentlemen, do we have a plan?"

Carson and I exchanged an amused glance. It was *we*, now that the planning was well underway?

"Yeah, as much of one as we could come up with. And for whatever it's worth," Leo said.

Miranda smiled, acknowledging the truth of the statement.

No matter how much planning you did for even the smallest operation, the only thing we could count on was that something would go wrong. We'd done as much prep as we could while still being in Florida.

We really needed to get inside the senator's house and get a look at the security systems and the layout, but we hadn't figured out a way to make that happen. Danny and Breck only remembered a few rooms, and that there was an entrance from the garage. Google gave us limited info, since the place was behind a huge gate and surrounded by trees that blocked the view from above. All we knew was that the house was big and situated on a river, possibly with a huge boat moored at the dock. Not particularly helpful.

The lack of hackable security cameras frustrated Wesley. I knew because he hadn't stopped ranting about it.

"What kind of maniac doesn't have networked cameras? My seventy-six-year-old aunt can see her front and back door cameras from her laptop." He threw himself back in his chair in disgust. "This guy...there's no feed. Nothing. I don't get it. I need to be close enough to control his wi-fi and use it to hack into his devices, make them do some spying for me. I could watch him from the camera in his laptop, listen to his conversations through his smart TV... and if the man has one of those home-control devices that you talk to, we are *set*. Those things are freakishly sensitive. I'll be able to hear *everything*."

"You can do that?" I asked. That just seemed wrong.

"Yeah, I can do that."

"Legally?" Danny asked. Wesley gave him a look.

I'd called the senator to see if he'd be interested in hiring me, but he'd proven elusive. So we were going in almost blind. Not anyone's favorite situation.

My phone rang, vibrating against the glass table top and startling us all. I picked it up. "It's Harlan."

"Answer it," Miranda said.

Danny moved closer to Breck, and Breck reached for his hand. The kid looked pale, like Harlan could somehow sense him over the phone.

"Gonzales," I barked into the phone, putting it on speaker so the others could hear.

"Mr. Gonzales, it's Senator John Harlan. We met at an event at my Florida home."

"I remember, Senator. I've left a few messages for you on the number you gave me."

"Yes, well, I've been busy. As a matter of fact, I don't have much time right now." Harlan sounded annoyed. "I'm finding myself in a bit of predicament."

"How can I help?" I glanced at Wesley to see if he knew what was going on. He shrugged. Leo, however, looked smug even behind the douchey sunglasses he and every other FBI agent, special or not, wore everywhere.

I could *hear* Harlan frowning. "It seems the head of my security team has been arrested, and I've received information that makes me believe the rest of them may have been taking bribes or otherwise been compromised."

"Really?" I asked as Leo grinned. He leaned back in his chair and finished off his alcoholic slushy. "Arrested for what?"

"As far as I can tell, failure to appear for some traffic offenses? I'm not sure, but neither his lawyers nor mine have been able to spring him. There seems to be more going on than I can tell. It doesn't matter. The reason I am calling is that I am having an important gathering at my home outside D.C. this weekend."

"Yes, sir. I had been planning on accompanying Mr. Waters as his close protection." I was improvising. I hoped Carson would play along. Miranda nodded approvingly.

"Had been?" There was a moment of silence.

"We've had a parting of the ways."

"So you're available?"

"I am."

"Excellent."

After a bit of back and forth, we agreed that I would meet the senator tomorrow, which was the day before the party, to go over some basics and get a feel for what I would be doing.

Everyone exhaled when I ended the call.

"Well, that is a break!" Josie said. "I think that calls for another round of drinks." She started to stand up.

"Josie." Miranda laid her hand over Josie's. She shook her head slightly. I noticed she didn't move her hand once Josie sat back down.

"Yes," Carson said. "That was extremely convenient. Leo, you didn't seem surprised."

Leo exhaled. "I didn't want to say anything in case it didn't work out. I had a few friends pull some strings, fake some paperwork. They won't be able to hold the guard longer than a day or two, but that's all we need."

A small part of the worry lifted from me. I would have been at the house, no matter what, but now, as a direct employee of the senator, I would have free access to the house and to his security system.

Truthfully, I didn't give a fuck about the other people Harlan was blackmailing. I wanted vengeance for Breck, pure and simple.

"How does this affect the plan?" Miranda asked. I thought I saw a drop of sweat on her forehead. The air was getting stuffier by the minute. The afternoon thunderstorms were coming early today. The quiet splash of the low surf sounded muffled.

"It's going to make life a whole lot easier," I said. "We've got your basic get in, get the files, set a virus to destroy his hard drive and any copies on the cloud, and get out. Piece of cake."

Leo snorted.

"Carson as Ben will be keeping Harlan occupied and doing some general intel gathering. Leo is there as his *like-minded friend* and newest recruit. Since he's obviously a Fed, we're going to stick close to the truth. He's under investigation by the Bureau, there's bad blood, yadda yadda," I explained.

None of us knew exactly what was going on with Leo, so I wasn't sure how close that actually was to the truth. Wesley might, but if he did, he wasn't saying. We had an unspoken agreement not to pry into each other's lives any more than necessary. I was more than fine with that.

"I'll find out as much information as I can about the place tomorrow, and we can adapt," I said.

"We're operating on the assumption that he keeps all his files together," Ridge said. "There are just so many unknowns here. I'm not thrilled with it. We don't even really know what we're looking for."

Wesley nodded. "Hard as it is to imagine, Harlan might have files sitting on some computer with no Internet connection. He may have a hard drive sitting in a safe. We just don't know. We have to get inside."

"And we will, especially now that I'm going to be running security for the party." I reached over to touch Breck again. I couldn't help it. If he was within touching distance, I was going to touch him as much as I could.

Miranda picked up her glass, swirling the dregs of her drink.

"Wes is going to monitor everything from nearby. Ridge will be Wesley's main eyes inside."

"Oh?" Miranda's lifted eyebrows showed that she wasn't sure about that part of the plan. I hadn't been either, at first. The fact that Ridge looked *exactly* like the guy Harlan was planning to kill would be a dead giveaway... *if* Ridge got caught.

"It will be fine, Miranda," Ridge promised. "I'm very good at hiding and blending in. And now Steele can find me a safe place to hide. I plan on getting in hours before the party. If all goes well, I should have the locations of safes, computers, and file cabinets before the party starts. The reason I'm here is because I'm very good at stealing things and not getting caught."

"And worse comes to worst," Wesley added, "if he gets spotted, Harlan will probably think he's Breck, since Harlan's been strong-arming Breck's pimp into forcing Breck to be there."

"So Breck is expected to be at this party?" Miranda asked.

I couldn't help it. I crossed my arms over my chest and scowled. Next to me, Breck sighed.

Just thinking about that asshole hurting Breck and Danny made me want to change the plan to taking him out with one well-placed sniper bullet. I knew all the reasons why we couldn't, but it still felt like it would be satisfying, and it would keep Breck well out of his way. Ignoring his squawk of protest, I hauled Breck out of his chair and back onto my lap.

Maybe if I waited until after Harlan was politically and financially destroyed, I could kill him. Face to face would be so much more satisfying than a bullet in the back of the head. I was sure Breck and Danny would want to get a little payback. Danny seemed like a babe in the woods, a minnow in a shark tank, but I knew he wasn't. You didn't end up selling your ass in D.C. without some kind of tragic back story.

"What's the worst that can happen?" Breck asked. "You'll be there, right? And Leo and Ridge and Carson? I'll be safe. And I want to look in Harlan's face when he realizes he's just fucked himself. I want him to know I helped bring him down."

"And how will he realize that?" Miranda asked.

"Wesley has a plan," Danny said, sounding a little impressed.

Wesley's cheeks pinked. "It was Carson's idea," he admitted. "I just figured out how to do it."

Miranda turned to him.

"Men like Harlan have to be humiliated in public. Their public image is the most important thing to them. Photograph, videos, audio recordings, they can all be faked. In order to crush him, there have to be witnesses and incontrovertible proof of his...indiscretions."

"You're going to cause a scene." Miranda was pleased.

"We're going to cause a scene." Carson's smile echoed hers.

"And I am going to be there." Breck's voice was firm.

"Me, too." Danny sounded a little less sure of the wisdom of that decision. Smart kid.

"He wants to kill you." I'd gone over it a hundred times. I couldn't think of any other reason the asshole would want them there. To have a pleasant chat? They'd promise not to tell and he'd let them go? I didn't think so.

"He won't," Breck said, scoffing. "We'll be fine."

He was naïve if he thought young boys didn't get killed by powerful men all the time in every corner of the world. Sometimes right in front of you. My fingers tightened around his arms. "No."

"No?" Breck lifted one eyebrow and peered up at me challengingly. "What do you mean no?"

"No," I repeated. "It's not happening." I looked around the table. "We need to think of another plan. One that doesn't involve Breck and Danny."

"The senator is expecting me to be there, remember? I told Emilio I'd be at the party. I *want* to be at the party."

"Well, the senator's going to be fucking disappointed, then. And so are you."

Breck struggled to get off my lap. I tightened my grip around his waist. No fucking way was I letting him go. It wasn't safe. Sweat started pouring down my forehead. How was it getting fucking hotter?

"I need to be there," Breck said, wrenching out of my arms.

"No!" I lunged out of the chair. I knew I was overreacting. Part of me knew, at least. But another part of me, the part that was in charge, that part of my mind was somewhere else. Thousands of miles away on another mission with a boy who didn't survive.

Breck dodged out of my way.

"This is personal for me, Steele! You don't get to decide what I do! It's not up to you!"

I shook the gritty feeling of sand out of my eyes, and the smell of hot metal and blood was somehow in my nose. "It's too dangerous. He wants the both of you dead."

"My whole life has been dangerous, and so has yours. I want this. I need it. I'm not a child."

But he was. He was just a child who didn't deserve any of this. And I was going to get him out. I'd promised. I was fast, quicker than most people expected from someone my size. I lunged, grabbing him with both hands.

"Steele!" someone yelled. Someone else grabbed my hand and tried to pry Breck away from me.

"No! You can't be there. You can't. I won't be able to do my job."

"Don't you put that on me. I can take care of myself. I was doing it way before you came around. I managed for years. Me and Ridge."

I shook him, hard. "Yeah? Yeah? Where was he when you and Danny were almost killed? I'm not using you for bait. I'm not. I can't. I can't do it again, I can't risk that again."

With that, the past crashed over me, washing away the present. I was back where I'd never wanted to be. So I did what I always did. I ran.

I STARED at the spot where Steele had been long after he'd run away. Ridge, who'd been holding Steele back, stood staring, too, and I'm pretty sure the shock on his face was mirrored on mine.

"What the fuck was that?" Leo demanded.

"That was a man reaching his breaking point," Wes said. He shook his head and looked at me. "Congrats, Blondie. You broke him. I didn't think it was possible."

"That's not..." I began, but then I swallowed. My eyes filled with tears.

What was I gonna say? I hadn't *meant* for that to happen? Hadn't meant to push so hard, he'd had to run away? Sure, that's not what I'd intended to happen, but my intentions didn't count for shit when I was hurting someone I cared about. I knew how protective Steele was, and I'd pushed anyway, demanding he let me put myself in danger. All because of my pride.

When my back was against the wall, when shit got real, my pride made me push back.

When my mom had come to me threatening Ridge, I'd given her all the money in the account Ridge had set up for me. I'd told myself I was protecting Ridge by keeping the truth from him, but really, I'd been protecting my pride. And I'd decided to earn back the money the fastest way I could, so he never had to learn the truth. Pride again. And when that had failed *spectacularly*, and he'd come to help me, I'd pushed and pushed, too proud to accept that he had a right to worry about me.

The question now was, what was I going to do about it?

"I'll just go... make sure he's okay," Josie said into the silence. She half-rose from her seat.

"No," Danny said, standing and holding out a hand to stop her. "No, Breck should go."

Wes snorted. "Breck's the last person Steele wants to see right now."

"*Au contraire.* Breck is the *only* one Steele wants to see," Danny retorted.

"And you know this, how? Breck's the one who caused this whole..."

"*No*," Danny said, talking over him. "He didn't." He glared at Wes. "I don't know what your issue is, Geek Boy. Maybe you've been staring at a screen so long, it's made you incapable of being a decent human, so let me school you a little bit. *We* are *people*. That means we don't have circuits that follow straight paths, it means we don't always make logical decisions, and it means we all have our own motivations for

the shit we do, which don't always follow the prime direc-
tive." He paused. "That was a Star Trek reference, there.
I'm tryna get on your level."

Wes blinked at him. "Are you... are you for real right now?
You don't know the first fucking thing about..."

"About Steele's past? About your secrets?" Danny
demanded. "Nope. Not the first thing. And I don't give two
shits either. But I know you have 'em, just like I have mine.
And they make us have knee-jerk reactions when people
scare the crap out of us." He looked at me. "And both Breck
and Steele look like they're scared to death. So that means
this... *mission*, or whatever the fuck you're calling it, can
just sit the fuck down and shut the fuck up."

"I, uh, think you might be mixing your metaphors a little,
sweetie," Josie told Danny in an audible whisper. But then
she nodded firmly and raised her voice. "But I agree with
you in spirit. This mission can shut the fuck up for a minute
while Steele and Breck have a talk."

"Josie, maybe that can wait until..." Miranda began, but
Josie gave her a stern glare, and Miranda held up her hands.
"Alright, alright. It's like The Bachelor: Gay Edition over
here. Go get your man, Pfeiffer," she told me.

I hesitated. What was I supposed to say? How could I make
this better? Even now, my mind screamed for me to push, to
insist, to convince Steele that I was right and that I needed
to do things for myself.

Surprisingly, it was my brother who stepped forward, his
face solemn. "Danny's right, Breck. Steele needs you." He
jerked his head in the direction Steele had headed. "Go talk
to him."

"But I don't know..." How to do this. How to care so much for someone without being a total pushover. How to play any role but my mother's... or my own.

Ridge seemed to read my mind. "You care about him, don't you?"

I shot him a look.

"Right. And any idiot can see he cares about you," Ridge continued.

"Apparently, if you finally figured it out," Leo joked.

"So you'll find a way to work shit out, Brekkie." He gave me a small smile. "Have confidence in yourself. You were always the smarter of the two of us when it came to shit like that, after all."

"Shit like that?" I repeated.

"Emotional stuff. Caring stuff." He shrugged.

I frowned. "I'm beginning to wonder if that's true," I told him honestly. I'd always imagined myself as being more in touch with my emotions, more open and available, but that was surface stuff. The really deep shit made me want to vomit. "I'm starting to think you've been better at it than I have, in some ways."

Ridge made an exaggerated expression of shock. "Wait, I'm sorry. Did you just admit that I was better at something than you are? Did you just actually come out and say it in so many words?" He turned to Wes. "Do we have anything recording this right now?"

I rolled my eyes and punched him in the gut—his very, very solid gut. "And this is why we can't have nice moments," I told him.

One side of his mouth turned up. "We'll have our nice moment later. For now..."

"Yeah, yeah," I sighed, staring at the beach. "For now, I'm gonna get my man."

I took a deep breath and straightened my shoulders.

"Jesus, I've seen men face down gun-toting assassins with less of a pep talk than this," Wes bitched. "Can you just go find Steele and screw like bunnies so we can all move on with our lives?"

I chuckled and Ridge shook his head.

"Such a charmer," Danny said. "Tell me, have you been laid in this millennium?"

Wes's jaw hardened. "I have no problem pulling, thank you very much."

Danny folded his lean arms over his chest and glared down at Wesley. "When you say pulling, do you mean..." He made a wanking motion with his fist, and Wes turned red.

"I don't need to have sex every day, like some people. It's not my fucking career," Wes snapped, pushing his chair back with a scrape. He seemed to realize what he'd said the next minute, and his face blanked. "Not that..."

"Not that there's anything wrong with that?" Danny retorted. "You know, I so appreciate it when you, a near total stranger, give me your implicit blessing on my life choices." He patted me on the arm. "Go take care of Steele, honey." His voice hardened. "I'm going to take care of this asshole."

Lucky Wes. I found myself smiling, in spite of everything, because Danny was somehow in his element now, not the scared, fragile man he'd been just a couple of days ago. And I knew that I had these people – Leo and Carson, Ridge and Steele, Josie and Miranda, and even Wesley... maybe *especially* Wesley – to thank for it.

I grabbed a towel I'd draped over a chair and wrapped it around my waist as I walked around the pool and down to the beach. *I could do this.* Somehow. And if I didn't, what was the worst that could happen?

Well, Steele could walk away from me, or I could give in when I really didn't want to, losing my self-respect.

Both of those prospects were legitimately terrible, so that wasn't comforting at all.

The tide was high when I reached the beach, and the white sand was nearly deserted except for a few lonely souls splashing around on a sandbar down toward the public access area in the distance. It was easy enough to find Steele, a lone figure standing in calf-deep water, staring out at the horizon. His skin glowed like copper in the sunlight.

I approached him quietly, still unsure of what to say or how to begin. I stood next to him, maybe a foot away, and fixed my gaze on the same spot he was watching so intently.

"I'm sorry," he said without preamble. "I freaked out. Did I... hurt you? Physically, I mean?"

I turned my head to look at him and found his profile, instead. "What? No. Of course not."

"I was holding you tightly. Too tightly." He laughed once, without humor. "I should know better."

"You weren't," I insisted.

He nodded, but his face was stony, unreadable in a way I hadn't seen it before. And it was weird that after knowing him for such a short time, I could say that an expression was strange or looked wrong on him, but it was true. Everything about Steele was heat and vitality. He'd warmed me inside and out from the first moment I'd met him.

"His name was Asadi," Steele said, his dark eyes still focused on the water. And though his voice was even, like he'd recited this story before, the pain just beneath the surface of those few simple words made my heart ache.

"He was twelve when I met him. He wanted to be a doctor or possibly a superhero when he grew up." His jaw moved back and forth for a moment. "But he didn't grow up."

I took a step closer, crossing the distance between us, and laid my head against Steele's arm. He didn't acknowledge my touch at first, but then a shudder moved through him and his body relaxed a fraction.

"We were on a mission in Sar-e Pol in northwest Afghanistan to take out Haji Khan. Khan was a local crime boss who'd been on our radar for years as a drug trafficker who hid his illegal activities by claiming he ran a kind of halfway house for underprivileged kids, teaching them job skills. But then he got greedy. He started expanding his opium empire into actual terrorist activities, which took him from a low-level threat to a situation that needed to be dealt with. We weren't sure if he was tied to the Islamic State or the Taliban...hell, it could have been both for all we knew...

but Khan was no true believer, and the locals knew it. He was a sick fucker with a taste for power and a craving for young boys."

Oh, God. I closed my eyes.

"The Powers That Be wanted him taken out, but quietly. No cluster bombs lighting up the mountain, you know? And that's where my team came in." Steele blew out a slow breath.

"Our plan was to make his death look like a targeted hit from a rival, the kind of thing that wouldn't arouse much suspicion. But the problem was, the guy was fucking *surrounded* by children. Always a kid in the house, a kid sitting *right* beside him in his fucking car, a kid standing in front of him like body armor when he walked through town."

He shook his head. "Fucking frustrating, but the guys upstairs were determined that this was the way to play it. *Minimal* civilian casualties, they said. Not *none*, just minimal." His voice was bitter. "The guys on my team are fucking professionals, dedicated to the mission, but there was no way any of us was taking out a kid. That wasn't acceptable to any of us."

"Of course," I whispered. I could see where this was going, felt the horror waiting for me, ready to steel my breath. How did Steele live with the things he'd seen and done? How did he get over it? Could he?

Maybe the problem was, he hadn't.

"We'd been boots on the ground for a little over a week, keeping an eye on some of our undercover guys. We'd clocked Asadi in our surveillance, of course. He was one of Khan's favorites. He always, just...had his fucking hands all over that kid. And the sounds. Jesus." Steele's voice was starting to shake, and he sighed from the bottom of his soul, rubbing his hands across his eyes as if he could erase the sights and sounds from his memory.

"So one night, we're tucked away in our fucking hidey hole, and the kid just comes strolling into our camp, leading a couple of goats." Steele chuckled, like he was reliving it, and maybe he was.

"He just *appeared* out of the desert night, right in front of our fire. Like a fucking tiny djinn. We're SpecOps. We're supposed to be secret. But there he was. And the kid says *he* can help *us*. Told us Khan knew we were watching him, but he could get us the intel we needed to take Khan down."

Steele shook his head. "I didn't trust him at first, you know? How the hell had he found us?" He paused. "Cutest fucking kid. So underfed, man. I thought he was eight. Ten at the most. Reminded me of myself at that age."

I nodded, imagining Steele's forceful personality contained in a slightly smaller frame – condensed and concentrated. The kid must have been a force of nature.

"Over there...you can't be sure. You can never be sure. Lots of kids are tools, weapons, something to be used. A weakness in us that they can exploit. And the kids, they don't know what the fuck is going on, right? They just...do what they've been told."

"But then Asadi tells us..." Steele paused and swallowed hard. "He tells us how Khan took him from his family, from his home, when he was only seven. Threatened to kill them all if Asadi tried to escape. Told him he was too beautiful for a boy and how his beauty tempted men. And I could see that some part of the kid thought it was true, even though he hated Khan and knew he was evil. I believed Asadi then," Steele whispered. "I believed him."

I pressed my hand gently against the small of Steele's back, afraid of startling him the way I'd be afraid of waking a sleepwalker. Steele was so caught up in the memory, it almost felt like the same thing.

Steele cleared his throat. "Some of the other guys weren't as sure. *Check twice*, you know? But then Asadi showed us how Khan had marked him, branded him on his shoulder like he was an animal." His voice cracked. "I think that was enough for everyone."

"God." I leaned more of my weight into Steele's side, a slight pressure I hoped conveyed my sympathy, since I knew literally nothing I could say would be enough to take away his pain.

"We promised. We fucking promised we'd keep him safe, get him back home."

Steele drifted off, staring at the horizon while whitecaps lapped at our legs, sucking our feet further into the seabed as they retreated. Gulls screamed and cawed. The sky was so blue it almost hurt, and the sun beat down on us, breaking into golden splinters on the water. I knew Steele wasn't seeing any of it, though. He was gone far away, across the ocean and through time.

One wave, larger than the rest, broke against us, splashing my thighs and plastering thick seaweed around Steele's knees.

Steele shook his head as if coming out of a trance, then bent down and scooped up a handful of salty water. He splashed his shoulders and chest with it, cooling himself down.

"So, anyway. The kid started hanging around more and more, right? Whenever it was safe for him to get away. I taught him how play solitaire, and the other guys gave him the dessert from their MREs. He was like a mascot, the little brother we'd never known we needed." Steele paused, then continued after a moment. "And he was fucking *useful*. Determined. Brave. Told us Asadi was Urdu for *lion*, and that's what he wanted to be."

Steele swallowed hard again, and when he continued, his voice was barely a whisper in the warm breeze. "He started feeding us information, a little at a time. We were able to intercept a couple major transports, one of drugs and one of weapons. But what we really needed to do was take this fucker out, and the brass was getting impatient. Then Asadi told us Khan had a major meeting planned, something big enough that he'd be sending the boys away for nearly twenty-four hours. Meanwhile, chatter from our intelligence experts suggested that a Taliban power player was moving into the area. It all seemed to fit. We planned a raid for late that night. When Asadi was out of the house and it would be *safe*."

"*Oh, fuck*," I breathed. I pulled back to look up at Steele's face and almost wished I hadn't. His eyes were *haunted*.

"That's about right," Steele agreed. "The op was a total clusterfuck from start to finish. Khan totally knew we were coming. There was return fire the second we came over the wall. More security than we'd ever seen in the week we'd had eyes on the place. I don't even know where the hell they'd come from. We'd had eyes on every road in and out of that fucking place. And when we breached—" He broke off and shook his head.

I wrapped my other arm around his waist, holding him securely. I wouldn't push, *wouldn't*. But every instinct said he needed to get this out, to purge it like poison, and I prayed he'd keep talking. He draped his arm around my shoulder.

"When we breached, Asadi was there," Steele finally continued. "Khan's fucking human shield. Ops was screaming in my earpiece *take the shot, take the shot, take the fucking shot, Alvarez*. But I couldn't. I *wouldn't*. One of my men screamed in Dari, '*Duck, Asadi!*' And right then Khan realized that Asadi was the one who'd betrayed him." Steele looked down at me. "I could see it in his fucking eyes. He knew it."

"The whole firefight—you've ever been in a firefight? No, of course you haven't," he said before I could answer. "They're loud, Brekkie. Fucking loud every time. And shit shows like this? Hell. Gunshots and women screaming and shit exploding. Your buddies are going down around you. Plaster's flying off the walls, dust and dirt everywhere. You can't see, you can't hear." He pressed the heel of his hand over his ear and shook his head as if to clear it. "And you're just... Your body is pumped up with adrenaline. You can feel your heart beating against your eardrums."

With my head pushed against his side, I thought I could *hear* his heart beating. I felt his chest heaving, sucking in oxygen against a threat that didn't exist. This time the silence stretched. I fought with myself. Should I urge him out of the water, out of the past, and back to the house? Or should I ask what happened? I wasn't sure I wanted to know.

No. I knew I didn't want to know. But if Steele had had to live through it, and if that brave Afghan boy had had to suffer whatever horrible fate I knew was waiting for him, I could be strong enough to listen.

I didn't know how or even *if* my hearing the end of the story would help. It couldn't change the outcome, of course. But if simply listening would in any way lessen Steele's burden, I had to do it. I would do it for Asadi. For Steele. "What happened?" I asked, knowing I would never be able to forget it, whatever it was.

"We lost," he said bitterly. "It was a slaughter. Two of my men were gone. Almost every one of Khan's guys was dead or subdued. He knew it was over for him. And then? I hear a helo coming. *Whup-whup-whup,* rotors shaking the whole fucking house. And I know it's not one of ours, it's gotta be his. His ticket out. Khan starts walking backwards to a door, Asadi held tight against him, holding him up high so we can't get a head shot, and he's got this big motherfucking knife pressed right against the kid's throat. 'I kill him,' he's screaming in English. 'I'll kill the little whore.'

"So what can we do? We follow him, eyes on him the whole time. Weapons up. And just as he jumps into the helo, the asshole slits Asadi's throat. Right in front of us, Breck. As close as that fucking sandbar is to us right now. It happened in an instant, and there wasn't a goddamn thing I could do to stop it. He killed the kid and threw his fucking body at us." Steele's nose flared, and his throat worked. "Asadi was still alive when I got to him," he whispered. "And when the life drained out of his eyes, he was looking at me like '*you promised.*'"

It was so much worse than I had imagined.

Tears ran in a torrent down Steele's cheeks, dripping into the gulf and adding more salt to the water.

I didn't try to stop my tears, either. I wasn't sure he was aware of his tears or of *me*. But after a few long minutes, he turned, wrapped his strong arms around me, and dropped his face into my hair. He shuddered.

My face was crushed against his enormous pecs, my arms clasped so tightly around him they were going numb, and Steele was clinging to me like I was necessary to his survival, like he trusted me to take his weight.

It was heartbreaking and beautiful and ridiculous all at the same time, which was pretty fitting for us... whatever *us* meant when you could count the days of your maybe-relationship on two hands and still have some fingers left over.

I'd been so worried about what to say and how to say it, when all Steele needed from me was to be *present* – to hear him, to bear this with him, and to care about him anyway.

Which was perfect, because that was exactly what I wanted to do.

I had no idea how long we stood there. I was dimly aware of a couple older ladies in visors strolling past us at the water line and the rustle of a hundred sea birds taking off from the sand all at once. None of it really touched us.

But eventually, the sky darkened as the afternoon rain clouds moved in and the wind kicked up. When the rain came, it wasn't a drizzle, but a deluge, soaking us where we stood.

"Shit," Steele said. "Come on, Sweetcheeks."

He hauled me back toward the house, and I went along reluctantly. I didn't want to see anyone else. Listening to Steele's story had left my heart raw and tender; I couldn't imagine what it had done to him. I was pretty sure I wasn't going to be capable of laughing along if the guys made sex jokes about us again.

But when we got back to the pool area, it was deserted, like maybe the rain had driven the others inside. Steele didn't head toward the patio near the house. Instead, he veered toward one of the outbuildings, opened the door, and dragged me in.

It was a gym – a treadmill, an elliptical, and a bunch of free weights lined one wall, while a couple of weight machines dominated the other. Interlocking black rubber squares covered the floor, and one entire wall was a mirror, probably so you could check your form.

Unfortunately, right now my form was pretty gross. My curls were plastered flat to my forehead, and the towel around my waist was sodden with rainwater, so I stripped it off and threw it in the corner.

The breeze from the air conditioning made me shiver – apparently, it *was* possible to have it jacked up too high. Who knew? But Steele turned around and wrapped his arms around me again, just as he had out on the beach. Even though he was as wet as I was, he was so fucking *warm*. I burrowed into him, burying my nose in his armpit.

Steele grunted. "Wait right here," he said. He walked to the back of the room, ducked around the corner, and returned a couple of minutes later with two big white towels raised triumphantly in his hands.

"Charlie thought of everything," I said as Steele draped one of the towels around my shoulders and pulled it tight, then chafed my arms through the fabric, like I might catch hypothermia from the slight chill.

"He's got a sauna back there," Steele said, frowning. "I can turn it on if you wanna warm up? Or there are showers." He took the second towel, which I'd assumed he'd gotten for himself, and tied it around my waist so I was wrapped up like a burrito.

A very warm, emotionally raw, insanely turned-on, and possibly *in love* burrito.

"I don't want a sauna, Steele. Or a shower." What I wanted for him to fuck me again. I needed it so badly I could practically imagine every detail in living color. I would be putting my fingerprints on those mirrors before the day was out.

But first, there were things we had to resolve. "We need to talk. Though, I guess you're probably pretty talked-out," I said softly. I extracted one hand from my swaddle of towels and cupped his jaw. "There are things I need to say, though."

Steele nodded woodenly and retreated a pace. "Yeah. Yeah, I figured you would. Listen, for what it's worth, I truly didn't mean to go off on you, okay? I get that I had no right to do that. I'm sorry. I feel like an idiot. And I appreciate you listening to my tale of woe out there." He hooked his thumb over his shoulder in the general direction of the beach. "I really had no right to unload that on you either."

I stepped toward him and grabbed him by the back of the neck. "You really *are* an idiot," I informed him.

He nodded again, and I shook him – all six tons of him – and forced him to look at me.

"You're an idiot... *if* you think that you freaking out about keeping me safe would make me anything but stunned and grateful that somehow the universe put you in my path! Especially now that I know where all of that fear came from."

He frowned, like he couldn't quite understand my words. It was adorable... and ridiculous. "*God*, Steele. You're amazing, you know that? But you take on so much responsibility for everyone, too much for one person. And you know that you can't control every force in the universe." I pressed my lips together. "Part of me wants to back down and let you take charge of this thing with the senator. To stay home and sew your camera button back on or whatever." I gave him a half-smile. "But I can't."

"You deserve vengeance," he said. "I get that. I do. It's just..."

"That's not it," I said. "I do want to be there. I told you that. But after everything you told me, I'd be willing to back off or at least compromise. But I can't."

"*Can't?*" His hands came up to my hips, and he held me lightly, but his dark eyes were clear now, penetrating, like something in my tone had finally broken him free from the guilt and memories that haunted him. "Why, *can't?*"

I licked my lips. "Wellllll." I cleared my throat. "It turns out that Danny wasn't completely upfront about handing over his cell phone when we got here."

Steele's eyes widened. "Jesus. Did he communicate with someone you know? Can Harlan track him here?"

"No," I said. "I don't... I don't think so." Honestly, the thought of Snow White tracking Danny here hadn't even occurred to me. *Fuck.* "But he doesn't have to. Because Danny told Harlan he and I would be at the party. At his house."

Steele froze in place, I swear he even held his breath.

"Danny took his ring," I blurted. "The night that he beat us. Danny came to for a minute, took Harlan's pinkie ring from his finger while Harlan was asleep or passed out, and.... and *swallowed* it." I shook my head. "He wasn't thinking clearly. He was out of his mind. He thought we were gonna die and that ring would be the clue that implicated Harlan when they found our bodies."

"He watches too much fucking TV," Steele spat.

"He does! Totally. But like I said, he wasn't thinking and... well, Harlan had to know it was one of us, obviously, and if he taped the encounter, which seems to be his MO, he'd have seen Danny. Which he did, also obviously, since he, uh, started texting Danny death threats if he didn't return the ring."

I was babbling now, praying that Steele didn't walk away. I'd kept this information from him, from everyone, and I was just now realizing how stupid and shortsighted and selfish I'd been. Pride, pride, pride. Damn it.

"He texted Danny death threats?" Steele said, his voice rising an octave. "And neither of you mentioned it to me? To any of us?"

"I only found out the other night," I told him. "But I... yeah. I kept it from everyone. Because I figured you or Ridge, or both of you, would want to cut me and Danny out of the plan to take down Harlan. I was annoyed at you for stopping stuff the other night up in the media room and generally treating me like a kid who didn't know what he wanted and..."

"And so you wanted to prove your maturity by keeping this from everyone on the team?"

I winced. "I'm sorry," I told him. "Honestly. I was selfish. But when Danny and I were in my room, before you came back from Harlan's party, Danny texted Harlan back on the secure tablet Josie gave us and told him we'd be there Saturday. With the ring."

Steele stared at me, his jaw clenching. Finally, he nodded. "Okay."

"O-okay?" I stammered. "Just...okay? Do you mean okay, like you'll deal with it but you hate me now? Or like, okay you accept my apology or..."

"Or, okay, I get that you didn't want to stay home *sewing my buttons*." He shook his head, but it was like he was exasperated with both of us rather than just with me. "That's not *you*. So... we'll go back to the original plan, with some modifications. And I guess I'm gonna have to work on my overprotectiveness. Because I get that you're the kind of person who really needs to feel in control of his own life."

"I'm pushy," I told him, repeating what I'd told myself over and over earlier. "And proud."

"You're resourceful," he countered, pulling me into him so that the hard plane of his stomach rubbed against mine. "And you don't back down. And those are good things, Sweetcheeks. I love those things. We're just gonna have to work on this, because going forward I am going to want to smother you in cotton wool, and if I try, you're gonna be mad. As much as I love prickly Breck, I don't actually want to make you angry."

Going. Forward.

Which meant this wasn't the end. And it also very possibly meant the whole *holy shit this feels so permanent* vibe I'd been feeling for him (and pretending I didn't feel because it was way too soon for that) was reciprocated.

Emotions I couldn't put into words clogged my throat. I opened my mouth, then closed it again. "I could promise to kick your ass if you try," I told him finally.

"I don't doubt that for a second." He hesitated. "I'm going to try to back off. But you've gotta understand, Breck. I'm not always a good guy. Not when it comes to stuff like this. So if you're there, you're going to listen to me without hesitation. When I say duck, you duck. When I say run, you do the best Usain Bolt impression anyone's ever done. Okay?"

"Yeah," I agreed. "Yes, of course."

He nodded, somewhat appeased, and I pressed a kiss right to the center of his chest. God, this guy. Protective and reasonable and logical and sensitive and hot as fucking hell. He was perfect. Perfect for *me*, anyway.

But when I tried to raise up on my tiptoes to kiss him, he held my hips tightly and stopped me. "Breck. There's one more thing you need to know."

I frowned at the thread of unease in his tone. "What's that?"

"After Asadi was killed, the higher-ups figured we were compromised, so they extracted us. They wanted to wait for Haji Khan to resurface elsewhere and find a different low-key way to take him out. But I couldn't let that happen. My men couldn't let that happen. We hunted the bastard down in Mazar-e Sharif a week later, and..."

"Killed him and every single guy who worked for him?" I finished.

He narrowed his eyes. "Did Wes tell you? Or did you see the evidence Charlie had?"

So this was the blackmail Charlie had on him. It made sense. But unless Charlie was a total asshole, I'd have been willing to bet that none of the information would have ever seen daylight, even if Steele had turned down this "job."

"No," I told Steele, my eyes staring into his unflinchingly. "Wes didn't say a word. He didn't have to. I knew because that's exactly what I'd have done. And I wouldn't spend a single minute regretting it, either."

He gave a half laugh, and his dark, serious eyes lit up. "I don't know where you came from, Breck Pfeiffer, but I'm starting to think I owe Charlie a big fucking favor."

I grinned. I couldn't agree more. Somehow I'd found the one guy on the planet who thought my biggest flaws were assets and who looked at me – the whole boiling hot mess of me – and saw something precious.

"And maybe," I whispered. "You just owe *me* a *fucking*." I lifted myself on my tiptoes, and this time he didn't stop me. I wrapped my arms around his neck and whispered in his ear, "Maybe you should make sure I know how to obey."

A shiver ran through him, and that made me shiver too. Steele's arms came around me like bands. "I'll get you warmed up," he promised, and I didn't protest even though *cold* was the last thing I felt.

I had no need to push or protest, because I trusted Steele to get us exactly where we both needed to go.

I HAD TO KISS HIM, how could I not? He'd seen the worst of me and not turned away. I'd never imagined anyone would accept me like that.

When I'd freaked out and run from him, he'd chased me down and listened and understood. He hadn't told me to calm down or that everything was going to be okay because he knew it never would be. That Asadi's death was something I was going to have to live with the rest of my life.

But if I were very, very lucky, Breck would be someone I got to live with for the rest of my life.

I lifted him up, cradling his ass in my hands. He wrapped his legs around my waist and his arms around my neck.

I could have stayed there kissing him forever, his hand cradling the back of my head and his lips firm beneath mine. He was so slender. I bench-pressed more than him every day, so it was no effort to hold him up with one hand. With one arm under his ass and the other around his back, I pulled him even more tightly against me. Any space between us was too much.

His kisses turned desperate, and he shivered. The towel around his shoulders fell to the ground. His skin was warm and smooth against me, reminding me that I was still damp and cold and I was going to give him pneumonia if I didn't stop kissing him, at least long enough to dry off. Maybe we could take this somewhere warmer, somewhere with a bed.

I could have done that, but I didn't do any of those things.

He pulled away, mouthing up my neck and licking the rainwater off my skin. "You're wet. And cold and tasty." He unwrapped his legs and tried to slide down, but I wouldn't let go. I caught a hand in the waistband of his tiny bathing suit and yanked. He ended up dangling from my arms, the towel bunched up around his waist and his naked ass hanging out.

That I had to see. I turned us so we faced the mirror. "Now that is fucking sexy."

"Put me down you Neanderthal," he said, laughing.

"Soon." I cupped his ass cheeks, kneading them and loving how they felt in my palms. His back was a smooth expanse of tan skin I wanted to map with my tongue. His mop of curly blond hair begged for my fingers.

"Stop!" He smacked me on the shoulder, not really angry. "You're cold. Put me down."

Reluctantly, I did. The way the other towel slid off his hips, leaving him completely naked, mollified me a little. Thanks to the mirror, I could see his front and back at the same time. It was glorious.

Before my body could act on its urge and sandwich him between it and the mirror, he bent down and yanked my bathing suit off too. I stepped out of it at the same time I pulled my wet shirt over my head.

"Nice coordination," he said approvingly. Grabbing one of the towels off the floor, he roughly and quickly rubbed me down from shoulders to feet. Crouched down as he was, my cock was right at his face level when he looked, and he eyed it greedily. "Hmm." With a wicked grin, he swallowed me down.

Holy fuck. The contrast between the heat of his mouth and the chill of my skin weakened my knees. I pitched forward, hands landing flat against the mirror for support.

Breck laughed around a mouthful of my cock. He pulled off with a pop, then licked a long stripe up the underside of my cock. He closed his lips over the head, dug his fingers into my ass and pulled me deep into his mouth.

"Jesus, fuck. *Fuck!*" One hand flew to the back of his head, holding him in place. I clamped the other on his shoulder. I tried to hold back; I hadn't been able to take my time the first time we'd fucked, and I wanted to remedy that. I wanted to take all the time in the world. But really, how much time did we have? How long would it be until someone came looking for us?

Breck's tongue swirled around my cock, and he sucked hard. My eyes closed against my will, and I caressed his cheek. God, this kid. This *man.* He turned me inside out. Was it wrong to fall in love in the middle of a blow job? *Was* it love? Would I even know if it were?

His hand tightened on my balls, and I gasped, my eyes flying open. Pulling off, Breck sat back on his heels and stroked his heavy erection. "Do it, babe. Fuck my mouth. Please," he begged. Arching back, he rested his head against the mirror and closed his eyes in pleasure as he pumped his hips into his fist. A dark pink flush of arousal spread down his neck to the divot of his throat.

My brain shorted out. I let him take a deep breath, then grabbed his hair and yanked him back down on my cock, pumping fast and hard into his mouth. He gagged, his hand grabbing at my hips, my ass, his nails digging into my flesh and dragging me deeper down his throat. I forgot how to breathe.

It was hotter than the sun.

Breck had one hand between his legs as he jacked his cock to the rhythm of my thrusts. "God, look at me, Breck. Look at me." I tugged on his curls, and Breck looked up, blue eyes blazing, mouth red and stretched wide over my cock. His throat worked as he tried to swallow the mix of spit and precum flooding his mouth, but it poured down his chin. His chest heaved as he tried to breathe and suck me off at same time.

With a yell I'm sure they heard in the main house, I pounded my fist against the mirror. I dragged my cock out of the heaven of his mouth, and with a pained moan I dropped to my knees. I cradled Breck's head in my hands and pulled him up for a kiss.

I love you, I love you, I thought as I kissed him hard, licking my own taste out of his mouth. But I didn't say it. With the memory of Asadi so close to the surface of my mind, I didn't feel worthy of saying it.

Breck pulled away but kept his hand on my face. I rubbed my cheek against his palm, needing the connection and the reassurance. The black of Breck's pupils almost obliterated the sky blue of his eyes. "Steele," he whispered. "Baby. I—"

"Stand up," I said, before he could finish. I wanted to be able to say it first, but I couldn't. Not yet.

When he stood up, I pulled him in for a long, deep kiss, hoping my body would convey what I couldn't say. "Turn around. Look at yourself."

He did, and I took his hands, drawing them up over his head and wrapping them around my neck. "Keep them there."

He shuddered, eyes locked on mine in the mirror.

We looked fucking amazing together. Breck's body was so much smaller and paler than mine, despite his time in the sun. His hard cock bounced, rocking with every panting breath. I wanted to do so many things to him. Unspeakable, depraved, delicious things that would please both of us. But mostly I wanted desperately to watch his beautiful face as he came apart because of *me*, because of how good *I* could make him feel.

I ran my hands up and down his body, cupping his balls, stroking his cock and pinching his nipples until he writhed against me. My cock pressed hard into the small of his back, and I couldn't stop thrusting against him.

"Fuck me, Steele," he begged. He pulled out of my arms and leaned forward, hands flat against the wall and glaring at me over his shoulder. "Come on, baby, please, just fucking *fuck me* already."

I swear on my mother's grave, the only reason I didn't plunge into him without condom, lube, or prep was because the angle was all wrong.

With a pained groan, I went to my knees again. Spreading Breck's ass with a hand on each cheek, I pushed my tongue hard against his opening, licking as broad a stroke as I could.

He yelled, his knees giving out, but I held him up by his hips. He tasted of rain and the sea. I kept up my assault, opening him up with my tongue and my fingers until he was begging and I couldn't hold him up anymore. "Please," he gasped as he collapsed to his hands and knees. "Jesus, fuck, please." His skin flushed deep pink from the tops of his ears to his nipples, and when his eyes met mine in the mirror, they were wild, wrecked, bottomless pits of desire I couldn't look away from.

"Condom," I gasped out.

"We don't have any!"

"We do. Hold on. One second." I kissed him on his tailbone and ran into the bathroom, my cock slapping against my stomach with every step. I pulled open every drawer until I found the stash of condoms and lube I'd spotted the other day after a workout.

"Ride me," I said, ripping open the condom and throwing myself on the floor, my head to the wall. "I want you to watch yourself in the mirror while you fuck me."

"Yeah. Yes. Fuck, yes." Breck grabbed the condom and had me covered and lubed before I could blink. Then he straddled me, lined my cock up, and his eyes locked on our reflection. We both groaned as he took me in with one long, smooth glide.

"You feel so fucking good." I lifted my head and shoulders off the ground so I could see my cock sliding in and out of him.

"So fucking deep," he said with a moan. "You're so big, so perfect. You fit me so good. We look so fucking amazing together."

We did. His fair, rosy skin contrasted with my dark olive-tinged tan, and his slender but strong body complemented my much larger, bulkier frame. Light and dark, thick and slim, we were a study in contrasts.

Every time I tried to change the pace, Breck ignored me. Shaking his head and slapping at my flanks, he fucked me exactly as fast or slow, as hard or as soft as he wanted to. There was no mistaking who was in charge here. He alternated between stroking his cock and caressing my torso and shoulders. Every so often, he would lean down to kiss me, letting me wrap my arms around him while his legs clamped to my sides. Trapped between our bodies, his cock rubbed against my abs with every thrust.

I cried a wordless complaint as he ripped his mouth away from mine. "God *damn*, you feel amazing." He leaned back, resting his hands against my thighs and ground his ass down against me. He moaned with the change in angle as my cock rubbed across his prostate over and over.

His legs trembled against mine, and a clear drop of nectar dripped from the tip of his cock. "Breck," I whispered, pleading for something I couldn't name. "Breck, please."

"I'm here, baby. I'm right here." He leaned forward again, bracing himself over me and looking me right in the eye. "I'm alive, and you're alive," he said without stopping the rolling of his hips. "We're going to take down a very bad man together, you and I, and you're going to protect me and keep me safe because that's what you do."

In that moment, he owned me totally. My debauched angel, riding my cock and holding my heart and soul in his hand. "I would die for you," I vowed, the words slipping past my lips without my permission.

Breck slammed down on my cock, his eyes blazing with heat. "Don't do that. I don't want that."

"What do you want?" I trembled beneath him, every cell of my body waiting for his answer even as I hovered on the edge of an orgasm I thought might kill me. *Anything.* I would do anything for him.

"I want you to live," he whispered, pushing himself to his knees as he slid up my cock with an agonizing slowness. "I want you to be happy." He stopped at the apex of his trajectory, barely holding me in. All I could do was wait. His back curved in a beautiful arc, his cock hard and shiny as he stroked it a few times, moaning softly at how good it felt. Suddenly, he dropped forward, hands landing flat on my chest. "And I want you to fuck me like you want that, too," he demanded.

So I did.

I grabbed his hips as he held himself above me, forcing me to come to him. I thrust my hips up off the ground, shoving my cock balls-deep. The sound of our bodies slapping together was almost loud enough to cover my wordless grunts and Breck's shouts of *fuck*, *baby*, and *harder*.

There was no stopping my orgasm now. My balls were pulled up so tightly into my body, they hurt. I knew I'd find my fingerprints bruised into Breck's skin in the morning. My heart pounded as pleasure bordering on pain ratcheted higher and higher in my body. "I can't...fuck...babe," was all I could get out before I slammed into him one last time. I shouted loud enough to chase the birds from the trees, and every muscle in my body locked up as I came longer and harder than I could ever remember. Light shimmered at the edges of my vision as my diaphragm refused to work and my lungs burned.

I vaguely registered Breck's yell and the feel of his hot release landing on my body, marking me as his from chin to chest.

Legs trembling, I lowered my ass slowly and carefully to the ground. Breck collapsed on top of me, his head resting on my chest. I clasped him to me, staying inside him and thrusting slowly, drawing shudders and soft moans of pleasure from both of us as long as I could.

We stayed that way, not speaking, just kissing softly, stroking as much of each other's skin as we could reach until our breathing slowed and the awareness of how sweaty, sticky, and chilled we both were registered on our sex-stupid brains.

Breck winced as he sat up, his skin peeling away from mine with a rude sound. "We're gross, baby."

I traced my thumbs over the cut of his hipbones. "Y'know, I don't think anyone but my mama's ever called me *baby*."

"Do you want me to stop?"

I thought about it for half a second. "Nah. I like it. Sounds real good coming from you."

"Good." He leaned down, carefully keeping our bodies apart, and kissed me. "Baby?"

"Yeah?"

"We're disgusting, and we need to shower."

"Yeah. But not right this second. One more kiss?"

He smiled. "One more kiss."

IT WAS STILL the middle of the night when I crept out of my room and down the hall, wearing a T-shirt and a pair of elephant-print pajama pants I'd stolen from Ridge's room a couple of days before. I tried to be as silent as possible, but I was pretty sure my growling stomach was going to wake the whole damn house.

By the time Steele and I had finally come back from the gym, freshly showered and naked under our towels, dinner had already been in full swing. We'd heard the clink of glasses and silverware from down the hall as the guys, along with Josie and maybe Miranda, communed in the kitchen. Tiptoeing through the patio door into the living room like the thieves we occasionally were, with bare feet and still-damp hair, we'd exchanged a look. *Do we really wanna go in there? How hungry are you?* Then each of us had grinned because we'd both decided we were starving. But not for food.

It was amazing to remember that I'd considered my sex drive DOA a week ago. Steele was like an electric shock from those paddles they use to restart your heart in the hospital. Suddenly, I was back, ladies and gentlemen. And apparently insatiable.

I vaguely remembered Steele trying to wake me some time after round three to see if I wanted a snack, but I'd been supremely, sublimely fucked out. I was pretty sure I didn't even fully open my eyes, let alone say anything intelligible. Now it was three o'clock in the morning, though, and my stomach was trying to digest itself, so I had no choice but to leave my comfortable bed and the even more comfortable man who seemed to love acting as my personal mattress to forage for food. At least I had high hopes that Josie's kitchen would be stocked with food, unlike the last few places I'd lived.

As I crossed the darkened living room, I glanced out the giant windows and sliding doors. The moon gilded the waves and turned the white sand silver as far as the eye could see. It was a gorgeous view, day or night. *You've come a long way from Alamosa, Colorado, Breck Pfeiffer,* I thought. I was a pretty lucky bastard, all things considered.

Tiny lights inside the glass-fronted cabinets gave the whole kitchen a golden glow. Josie had a bunch of crank-handled cereal dispensers set up along one wall, like the kind they had in the cafeteria back at school. My stomach growled encouragingly, so I grabbed a bowl and set it under the Special K when a voice called out behind me.

"There's carne asada left," Ridge offered. "I know it's your favorite. Nice pajamas, by the way."

I spun around to see my brother sitting in the breakfast nook with a variety of tinfoil-covered plates and plastic containers spread out on the table in front of him. He sported the same bed-head as I did and wore a bright-pink Palm Beach tank top, and pair of pajama pants with monkeys on them.

Ridge nudged one of the plates in front of him with his fork. "Rice and beans here, too," he said. "Grab a plate, and I'll heat some for you."

"I can do it." I swapped my bowl for a plate and approached the table cautiously. Things between Ridge and me had been so strained and shitty, I wasn't sure if he was going to yell at me more or not.

I decided I didn't care if he did. Being cut off from him was driving me crazy, especially since I'd realized how much my own pride was to blame for the distance. I wanted to fix this somehow. "What's got you up at this hour?" I asked, trying to be nonchalant. I loaded up a plate with steak, rice, and vegetables. "Didn't get enough at dinner?"

Ridge shrugged and contemplated the tortilla he'd been piling with meat, salsa, and refried beans. "I have a lot on my mind," he said. "And you know I think better when I have a full stomach."

I nodded. Of course, most of the time when we were growing up, our biggest worry was that we didn't have full stomachs. "You worried about the plan to take down Harlan?"

He put down the tortilla and licked salsa off his thumb thoughtfully. "Eh, not really. We've got a good team here, and I feel like we'll figure it out."

I frowned. "What, then?"

"Well." Ridge glanced away from me, his eyes fixing on the glass doors that led outside. He drummed his fingers lightly on the table. "It really bugged me," he said, turning his gaze back to me abruptly, "watching Danny and Wes outside earlier. Some of the things Wes said were total bullshit. He made it sound like he was judging Danny for being a prostitute."

I lifted one eyebrow. "Uh, *yeah*. That's because I'm pretty sure he was." I shrugged. "Or he was just being an asshole. That's possible, too. But most people think it's totally acceptable to have sex because you're bored, drunk, curious, guilty, lusty, greedy, or sold into a dynastic marriage so your father can rule Europe." I tapped my fork against my outspread fingers, ticking each one off. "But agree to a sexual transaction that actually could pay you money and suddenly you're a pariah."

I was getting wound up, which was the last thing I wanted, so I forced myself to take a deep breath and shrug. "I get that society still feels like sex should always be some kind of deep, absolute, committed thing, and I'll even agree that it's pretty fucking awesome when it is." I smiled, thinking of the man upstairs in my bed. For me, sex was *infinitely* better that way. "But it's not like that all the time, or for everyone, and that should be okay, too."

To my shock, Ridge nodded. "It is okay. Any kind of consensual sex is okay."

I'm pretty sure my jaw dropped. If he'd declared himself a flat-earther in that minute, I would have been less surprised. "But you...back in D.C... you said... you made it sound like..."

Ridge's mouth scrunched up. "Yeah, I know. I figured that out after the conversation today. At first, I didn't get why you were pissed at me. But then the comments that came out of Wes's mouth were pretty close to some of the things I said. But I swear, Brekkie, I wasn't passing judgment. It's none of my business how much sex you have or with who." He paused. "Okay, that's a lie. I *do* care that it's someone who's decent to you and doesn't, you know, beat the shit out of you or blackmail you into doing things."

I tilted my head from side to side like I was considering. "Yeah, okay. Granted."

"But other than concern for your basic safety, I'm in no position to judge. I literally steal other people's shit to make a living."

I pulled one of the chairs out from the table, scraping it against the tile floor, and plunked myself in it. "But then why did you say those things?"

"Because I'm pissed at myself." He bit his lip and shook his head, staring over my shoulder again. "The whole reason I left you in D.C. was because I wanted you to have a chance at something new, something better. Something where our past didn't touch you, and you could reinvent yourself into... I dunno, whatever you wanted. I didn't want you to be associated with a thief."

My stomach flipped unpleasantly, and I realized I'd never fully understood his reasons for leaving before.

"I kind of assumed you left me there because I was holding you back," I whispered.

"*What?*"

"I mean, I know you wanted me safe and happy, obviously." I waved a hand in the air dismissively. I'd never doubted that for a second. "But I figured you also wanted me out of sight and out of mind, so you could have something bigger and better. Those last few months, you never talked about your jobs with me. You never shared, when you always used to before. It felt like maybe you'd outgrown me or something. Decided to leave the naïve little dumbass to play around in college while you went on to steal the Declaration of Independence and find a treasure."

He squinted at me in disbelief. "First of all, I would never steal the Declaration of Independence. That's for Nicholas Cage movies. Remember the first rule of thieves?"

I laughed. "Never take anything you can't fence?" I ran a hand over my eyes. "Right. Duh. Silly me."

"Uh huh. And second, how could you think that I'd outgrow you? You're the best part of me, Brekkie. You and me, we're a team." He pointed his finger back and forth between the two of us, and my chest squeezed. "You're the brains of the operation. I just do the grunt work."

"Oh, fuck off!" I protested. "That's the opposite of true."

He shrugged. "Pretty true from where I'm sitting. It was my job to protect you, and instead I left you completely *un*protected."

I exhaled a cross between a groan and a sigh. "What is it with me and overprotective men?" I asked the ceiling. "Is this my lot in life?"

There were worse fates, though, and that was the truth. After spending months feeling like I was completely alone, I could verify that.

"Clearly, I didn't do such a great job of taking care of myself at the end there," I allowed. "But I'm still here. I'm still alive. And I don't want to be anyone's responsibility." I slid the food around my plate, then looked at him and spewed out everything I'd been thinking in a jumbled rush. "I'm sorry I was an ass to you before. I know you were worried about me, but I didn't want you to be. I wanted to protect you for once."

"Protect me?" Ridge pushed his plate forward, all his attention focused on me. "What's that mean?"

I sighed. Ridge was gonna lose his mind with this part. Was it too late to remove the sharp cutlery from the vicinity?

"It means that I didn't give money to Mom because she came to me with some sob story. Honestly, I'm a little insulted you even thought that. I mean, *come on.*" I leaned back in the chair and tried to lighten the situation with humor. "I've literally seen the woman force herself to vomit on a cop to convince him not to arrest her for shoplifting. I'm not exactly gonna fall for her whining about how she's a *changed woman* or whatever." I snorted. "That woman is incapable of change. Once a malicious cow, always a malicious cow."

Ridge's nostrils flared, and his jaw set. "Right. So what did happen to the money?" His voice was low, dangerous.

I swallowed. "I gave it to her. I wouldn't lie about that, Ridge. The maternal unit called me a while back. Said the cops had come to the trailer, asking her about a theft at the Denver Art Museum the night before we disappeared." I ran a hand over my mouth. "And she was gonna tell them all about how you'd come back that night and took off in a rush, how you'd supported us by pocketing shit since you were ten, how you earned the money for my tuition by stealing. She said if I gave her the money, she'd stay quiet."

"Such a bitch," he breathed.

I nodded, spreading my hands out on the table. "She is, and I'm so sorry, Ridge. I don't know why she does this shit."

"The drugs and the booze might be a clue."

"Yeah, but with her I honestly don't know which came first, the bitchiness or the addiction." I folded my hands on the tabletop and looked down at them. "And I didn't want you to find out that she was... you know..."

"A bitch?" he repeated. He let out a deep breath, then a half-chuckle. "It's no secret."

"A big enough bitch to rat you out to the cops if I didn't pay you off," I corrected. "That was kind of a surprise to me, not gonna lie."

Ridge sighed. "Well. Wouldn't matter if she did."

I frowned. "It kinda would. It might not be proof, but maybe they'd start looking and..."

He shook his head. "Nah. It's all BS, Brekkie. I've never stolen anything from the Denver Museum of Art." He tilted his head to the side. "Except maybe some food from the gift shop that time we went on the field trip, remember?"

"What? But that night, you *did* come home in a hurry. You *did* insist that we had to take off right away. And it was a big score."

"It was," he confirmed. "But it wasn't at the museum." He paused. "I stopped talking about my jobs with you because I didn't want you to ever have to lie for me, Breck. I don't want this stuff to touch you. I still don't."

My face flamed, and my stomach tumbled. "Oh my God," I whispered. "Oh my God, I'm such a fucking idiot."

Ridge shook his head. "You're not."

"Uh, I beg to differ. Jesus *fucking* Christ!" I stood up and cradled my skull in my hands as I paced the breakfast area, because otherwise I was afraid my head might actually pop off. I couldn't remember the last time I'd been so angry. And it was a good thing my mother was nowhere near me right now, because I would happily call the police and tell them about every illegal thing *she* had done in the past twenty years, even if it took all night and all day tomorrow.

And it would.

"Calm your shit, Brekkie," Ridge said mildly. Then the man actually pulled his plate closer to him, then calmly folded his tortilla and took a big bite.

I stared at him like he was a pod person.

"I think it's kinda sweet," he said around a mouth full of food. "You running interference like that."

"Sweet? Except for the part where I gave her money for *nothing*!" I reminded him. "Thousands of dollars we will never see again!"

He dipped his head in acknowledgement. "Yeah. 'Cept for that part." He took another bite of food. "But it's not about the money." He stopped himself. "Okay, I mean, it is, because that's a fuck ton of money. But I have an AmEx Centurion card now." He grinned up at me as he chewed. "You wanna go back to school, I think Charlie can set up a scholarship for you from *beyond the beyond*." He wiggled his eyebrows.

I sat back down in the chair, my legs weak. A week ago, I'd had zero options and no prospects. Now suddenly the future stretched out in front of me, full of actual possibilities. It was a little overwhelming, honestly.

"I'm not sure if I do," I told him. "I might be done with college for now." I might wanna see where Steele wanted to end up and work out something with him.

Ridge smirked knowingly. "Yeah, I figured that might be the case."

"It was more than fifty thousand," I told him bitterly. Somehow this seemed relevant, like I needed to make a full confession of my idiocy in order to move on. "That's why there were multiple withdrawals, and why there was still no money in the account, even though I'd been working for Cisco for months. She kept coming back, bleeding me dry." I winced. "Christ, you must've thought I was the worst hooker in all the land, to still have no money to show for it."

Ridge nudged my plate closer to me, a reminder to eat.

I didn't need the reminder. Now that things with Ridge seemed to be calmer, my hunger had returned with dizzying force, and I grabbed my fork to dig in.

"I'll be honest," Ridge said, brushing a hand over his curls as he watched me eat. "I might be cool with hooking from a moralistic, no-judgment perspective. But, uh, I don't spend a lot of time thinking about how successful you were at it."

I snorted around a mouthful of rice. "Fair."

"And," he said softly, "it's also not a career choice I'm gonna be thrilled about you making again. It's your choice. Fine. But it's fucking unsafe, Breck. And, be honest: you didn't do it because you were feeling sex-positive and thought it would be fun. You did it for the reason most people do it. You were desperate. You needed money. And once you got in, you couldn't get out."

I nodded slowly, taking a bite of tortilla. He wasn't wrong. "I didn't want you to have to fix things for me."

"Breck," he said, so seriously that I looked up from my plate to meet his eyes. "Have you ever considered that I took care of you because I wanted to, not because I thought you couldn't do it? Bro, making sure you're okay sometimes feels like the only decent thing I've ever done in my life." He shot me a rueful grin. "And I guess I didn't even do such a good job with that in the end, huh? Since you didn't feel like you could call and ask me for an assist when shit went bad?"

Well, damn. I had literally never thought of it that way. I'd felt like a leech, a freeloader. But it turned out Ridge's point of view had been completely different.

"Maybe from now on we can take care of each other," I suggested. Then I wrinkled my nose. "Okay, gross. That was way too sincere, even for me."

Ridge snorted. "No shit." He glanced over my shoulder again and smiled. "Besides, I'm thinking I'm gonna have some competition for that." He lifted his chin toward the doorway, and I turned to find Steele leaning back against the wall with his arms folded over his chest, watching us. He must've stopped by his room on the way down, because he was wearing a tight black T-shirt and a pair of cargo shorts that hung precariously from his hips.

I licked my lips. *God*, he was hot.

"Not competition," Steele disagreed mildly. "Help, though." He walked over to stand next to my chair and nodded at the food on my plate. "You gonna share?"

I grinned. "Maybe. With the proper incentive."

He bent over, pressing his leg against my side, and licked at my lips. "Mmm. Tasty."

Yes, he was.

When Steele stood up again, I looked over at Ridge to gauge his reaction, but he merely rolled his eyes.

"If you're sitting down, grab the key lime pie from the fridge first," he told Steele, and I smothered a smile, accepting this as the only sign of approval we were likely to get from my brother. I was okay with that.

Steele grabbed the pie, along with a big bowl of salad and a six-pack of beer. I pulled out a chair for him and stood up to get him a plate.

"So, did you guys work out the rest of the plan for Harlan's party while we were, uh, *busy?*" Steele cleared his throat as he took his seat.

"Busy screwing like rabbits, you mean?" Leo walked into the kitchen and yawned. He wore a pair of jeans and a T-shirt, and his jaw was covered with a thick layer of scruff. I'd never seen him look so mussed and human before.

"Hey," Steele warned, but Leo snorted.

"Get over yourself, Alvarez," he said, strolling across the kitchen to collect a plate from the cabinet for himself before plunking himself down in the seat next to Ridge. "Literally no one cares. Pass the rice, Breck?"

I handed it over wordlessly.

"We didn't finish planning," Leo continued, piling rice on his plate. "You're supposed to be point man, for one thing. And we couldn't finalize anything before we knew whether Breck and Danny would be involved." He glanced from me to Steele. "Did you two work it out? Can we move ahead as planned?"

Steele nodded. "Yes, we can move ahead. With modifications. Breck wants to be there, so he's coming. And Danny too, if he wants to."

"He wants to." Danny slunk into the kitchen, looking half-asleep. He scratched at his bare stomach above his boxer shorts. "Hey, are there any more of the sweet pancake things left?" he asked Leo. "I think Florida makes me peckish."

"The *molletes*? How should I know? Check the fridge," Leo demanded, his voice still gruff with sleep. "Do I look like the dessert czar?"

"You look like the asshole who ate four at dinner," Danny returned without much heat. He opened the fridge and peered inside, like he was hoping the food would jump out at him. "Whatever's left are mine."

"Uh, how do you figure that, Junior?" Leo glanced up from the veggies he was heaping on his plate. "You find them, you bring them here and we'll divide them."

"Oh, so you're the dessert czar, now?" Danny rolled his eyes and grinned in challenge. "Fuck that. I'll fight you for them."

I shared a look with Ridge, and we both snickered. Leo outweighed Danny by a solid forty pounds, even before you accounted for the extra food he was shoving in his mouth.

"I'll put twenty on Leo," Ridge said. "Sorry, Danny."

Danny squawked in protest.

"Nah," Steele said. "Smart money's on Danny. Kid's scrappy. And besides Leo will be too full."

Danny gave him a grin and a chin-lift from across the kitchen.

"It'll be a full-on Dessert Death Match," Ridge said in his best announcer voice. "There can only be one winner..."

"Hey! No one is fighting over food in my kitchen! If we're out of something, I'll make more." Josie walked through a side door near the patio doors that I hadn't noticed before, since it was designed to blend in with the cabinetry. She smacked Danny lightly on the shoulder, shooing him out of her way so that she could access the fridge.

"What are we looking for?"

"*Molletes?*" Danny begged, batting his eyelashes.

Josie grabbed a big glass dish and held it up triumphantly. "Aha. Fortunately, I plan for every contingency." She put the dish on the counter. "You want these heated up, sweetie?" she asked.

"Yes, please" Leo called from the table, and Ridge elbowed him. "What?" Leo asked around a mouthful of food. "They're fucking good."

Josie laughed. "I've got plenty for everyone."

Danny came to the table and pulled out the chair between me and Ridge. Steele pulled my chair closer to his and draped an arm over my shoulder as I tucked into a second serving of steak. It really *was* fucking good.

"Here you go, boys," Josie said a few minutes later, setting a huge platter of sauce-drenched pancakes in the center of the table. The cinnamon-sweet smell of them assaulted my nose. "You want to try some, Breck?"

I nodded and glanced up at her, then froze as I noticed her outfit for the first time. She was dressed in full-on vintage workout gear, from her high-topped pink sneakers and legwarmers to her leotard and braided purple sweatband. It was like the ghost of nineteen-eighties Jane Fonda had materialized in front of me.

"Josie, will you marry me?" I asked her.

She grinned down at me. "Well, I would, sweetie, but I always said that if I got married again, I'd make sure I was the prettiest one in the relationship." She winked. Then she looked around the table at the crew of us stuffing our faces and smiled with satisfaction. "You're all up early today."

"I'm looking for a late-night snack." Wes came wandering into the kitchen, wearing the same clothes and the same surly expression he'd worn yesterday afternoon. He looked at Josie and frowned. "Was there a Jazzercise memo I missed?"

Josie ignored this. "You take a seat over there, and I'll get you some coffee."

Wes looked at Danny, who studiously avoided looking back. "Nah," Wes said. "Really, I'd rather just have some chips and an energy drink. Gotta fuel the late-night work, you know?"

"*Energy drink.* Too much of that shit'll make your dick fall off," Josie informed him. "I read it on the Internet." She smiled guilelessly, but something about her expression told me that no matter how good these cons were at their jobs, Josie was the smartest one in the room. "Sit down," she repeated. "I'll get you an espresso strong enough, you won't close your eyes until next week. But in return, you're going to eat a plate of food along with it. And maybe I'll forget you insulted me with your energy drink comment."

Wes looked like he was going to argue, but finally held his hands up in surrender and took a seat as far away from Danny as possible, like he was determined to avoid confrontation.

Unfortunately, Danny didn't get the memo.

"Playing all those high-fantasy games with your pimple-faced gamer buddies must be *exhausting*, huh? *Help me, PussyDestroyerXXX!*" he said, all high-pitched and mocking. "*The troll has nearly breached my castle! My portcullis can't handle the onslaught without your magic!"* He gave Wes a challenging look. "Such a workout."

Wes raised one eyebrow and regarded Danny steadily. "First of all," he said, totally deadpan, "how did you get my username? Only my very closest friends call me *PussyDestroyer*."

I burst into laughter, and so did everyone else. Even Danny snorted, almost unwillingly, and shook his head.

"And second, while I truly appreciate your concern for my, uh... *portcullis*? My castle hasn't been breached in years, Danny, so I'm not worried." He smiled smoothly. "And you can take that any way you want to."

Ridge made a hooting noise.

"Oh my God, are you two still doing this mating dance?" Carson demanded. He strolled into the kitchen wearing a big burgundy quilted bathrobe, grabbed a piece of meat with his fingers, and slumped in the chair next to Wes. "You wankers need to fuck and get it over with."

Wes narrowed his eyes at Carson. "Uh, buddy? You got a little somethin'..." He brushed his fingers over his own chest and then motioned toward Carson's.

Carson looked down at the V-shaped gap at the top of his robe where a blue, rune-like symbol that hadn't been there earlier was now visible. Carson grabbed both edges of the robe and held them closed with one hand. His nails were painted black.

"Sorry," he said airily, reaching for another piece of steak. "I was on a conference call."

Ridge and I exchanged a look across the table, and I saw Leo mouth the words, *"Conference call?"* at Wes, who shrugged.

I wondered who the hell he'd been pretending to be. It seemed like a pretty kick-ass line of work, getting to take a mental vacation and become someone else for a little while. Though, leaning against the warmth of Steele's arm, Carson's life seemed less appealing now than it would have last week.

Leo cleared his throat. "So, now that we're all here." He looked at each of us in turn. "We might as well finalize what we're doing at Harlan's party?"

Steele pinched my arm lightly, and when I turned in his arm to gaze up at him, he gave me an encouraging nod.

"Uh, about that," I began. "Danny and I have a ring to return."

"A ring?" Wes repeated, looking from me to Danny and back again. "Explain."

And so I did, hesitantly at first, telling them what Danny had done to Harlan, and then what the two of us had planned.

Once I was done, I leaned back against Steele, braced for everyone's anger. But none came.

"So you pretty much *have* to show up Saturday night." Leo nodded. "We can work with this."

"Do you have the ring?" Wes asked Danny. "With you in Florida, I mean?"

Danny nodded. "Upstairs."

"I might be able to do something with it then, depending on the design. Hide a tracker inside it, maybe. Keep tabs on the asshole," he mused, like he was talking to himself as much as to any of us. "Can you get it for me?"

"Sure." Danny frowned at Wes. "But isn't this the part where you remind me how stupid I was for taking the thing in the first place? And how disloyal it was for us to email the senator behind your back?" He seemed braced for the worst.

Wes shrugged. "I don't know about anyone else, but I'm not gonna say shit. How were you supposed to be loyal to people you barely know? Fuck, I don't trust people I've known for years, let alone these fools." He waved a hand to indicate everyone at the table.

Carson nodded in agreement.

Ridge snorted. "Aw, Wessy, I'll make you love me eventually." He stacked his hands below his chin and blinked at Wes adoringly.

"Right. Try it," Wes suggested. "That'll *guarantee* I'll never trust you."

Ridge threw a tortilla at him.

"Wes is right," Leo said. He'd finally finished eating and was cradling his chin in his hands while he rubbed his index finger back and forth over his bottom lip, deep in thought. "Doesn't matter that you didn't trust us before. You're trusting us now. And I think we have everything we need to make this work."

The comfortable camaraderie around the table morphed into something electric. We all straightened in our chairs, and Ridge began stacking the dishes. It wasn't an eating area anymore, but a planning area; not a kitchen, but a war room.

"Wes, grab your laptop for me?" Leo asked. "And Josie? I think we're gonna need more coffee. I have an idea..."

"*I'M IN.*"

I exhaled softly at Ridge's voice in my ear. The kid was good. Really good. Florists, housecleaners, caterers, and waiters had been in and out of Senator Harlan's suburban mansion all day. Even though I'd been watching for him, I hadn't seen Ridge enter the house; hadn't even known he was there until he'd said my name over the comms.

At our last-minute meeting earlier in the day, I'd given him a list of places I thought he could hide and the location of every computer I'd found during my grand tour of the premises as Harlan's new head of security. There was one desktop in the office, which didn't look like it got used a lot, and the senator's laptop, which he kept in his bedroom when he wasn't using it.

The good news was that the senator didn't have any on-site security beyond me, the hired muscle guarding the VIP rooms where the hookers would be partying, and one other guy who was stationed at the front door with the woman checking the IDs of the workers coming to set up for the party. There were no foot patrols to worry about, no guy with a gun sitting at a desk watching monitors. It would have almost been too easy, if not for the really, really bad news I'd learned.

I'd been able to find a couple of Harlan's hidden blackmail cameras, and they'd been the kind that recorded on *tape*. Digital tape, sure, but it still meant that in order to take away all of Harlan's leverage over the powerful men of D.C., we'd have to find an actual, physical tape, like a needle in a goddamn haystack, as well as any copies the senator might have saved online.

Considering this house was only slightly smaller than Charlie's, with about a million bedrooms, bathrooms, closets, game rooms, and a big fucking yacht parked outside where he could hide his safe, this was kind of like climbing Everest at night in a swimsuit. I only hoped that Harlan was the kind of old-school rich guy who kept his stuff in a safe behind a picture of some long-dead relative or a knock-off Van Gogh.

That was where Ridge came in. He now had *two* jobs at tonight's party. One, insert a Wesley-provided flash drive that would not only destroy any copies of the files on Harlan's computers but apparently could somehow fly up into the cloud and destroy any backup copies there. And for the bonus round, he also had to find the senator's safe, crack it, and pray the original tapes we wanted were in there.

Though really, the idea Leo, Carson, and Wesley had come up with to get the senator to publicly incriminate himself was good enough for me. If it worked, it would scare Harlan away from Breck even if it didn't result in a jail sentence and render the senator utterly powerless.

So now we just had to make sure it fucking worked.

After scoping out the house as best I could, we'd worked out a few different plans based on the most likely scenarios. Flexibility was key in any mission.

The senator might be a moron, but he was a hypocritical, *dangerous* moron who had almost killed Breck and Danny once and almost definitely had plans to finish the job tonight. My biggest worry was that I didn't know how he planned to do it. My money was on a quiet execution in the senator's very dark, very private, soundproof wine cellar. Since the senator wasn't a man who did his own dirty work, we knew the task would fall to me. What better way to test your brand-new head of security than to make him commit a double homicide his first day on the job, right?

Harlan had questioned me several times about my loyalty and the lengths I was willing to go for an employer. I'd made up a bullshit story about being desperate for money to take care of my fictional sister, but he'd bought it a little too easily, confided in me a little too freely. I had a feeling I would end up on his *next* head of security's hit list after I'd done my job tonight.

I sighed mentally. No such thing as job security these days.

The problem, though – one of many, really – was that Breck and Danny seemed pretty sure the senator would want to have some 'fun' with them before he ordered me to shoot them. Hearing Danny relay this tidbit of information, conveniently while I'd already been at Harlan's house and unable to lose my shit, I'd ground my teeth so hard, Wesley had bitched about the feedback from my comm.

"I don't care if the info Charlie has on me goes public," I'd said to Breck earlier when we were enjoying some last minute alone time before we put the plan into motion. "As long as Harlan stays away from you. You're what I care about."

I'd thought I was being romantic. Apparently, I'd been being a dick.

Breck had practically leapt from my arms. "What?"

Much to my dismay, he'd gotten out of the nice, warm bed where I'd been hoping for some awesome pre-mission sex and paced across the carpet, yanking at his hair with both hands. His nakedness made it hard for me to take him seriously.

"So, it's okay if he beats the shit out of some other kid? Then shows up on the TV preaching about how perverted 'the gays' are? It's okay for you that he'd still have to power to change the fucking laws of the country?" His voice had risen at the end.

"No, that's not what I meant."

"These guys don't *stop*, Steele. You *know* that."

"Yeah, I know it." Give a guy like Harlan get a taste of power that comes with literally getting away with murder, and he wouldn't want to stop.

"So, as long as I'm okay, that's fine?" He'd glared at me, hands on his hips.

Part of me had wanted to say yes, but it wasn't true.

His eyes narrowed. If looks could kill, I would have been flayed to the bone. "Do you think Asadi would be happy knowing you could have stopped a man from hurting boys and you didn't?"

I flinched, the blood draining from my face. "Fuck you," I spat. It had been my turn to get out of the bed. "You ain't got no right to throw that in my face."

His eyes were huge. "I'm sorry...I didn't...I shouldn't have."

"No, you shouldn't have." I'd pulled on my shorts.

Rationally, I'd known he was lashing out in fear and anger, but guess what? I was only human. I'd been hurt and angry, and I'd known I needed to leave the room before I said or did something I couldn't take back.

Goddamn it. The last fucking thing I needed going into this was the memory of Asadi's eyes staring at me as the life bled out of him.

"Steele..." He'd sounded heartbroken. *Good.* He should.

"I have to get ready." I'd grabbed my shirt and walked out of the room.

"That's it? You're just going to leave? Fine," he'd yelled at my back. "Just leave."

So I had. It hadn't been my proudest moment.

Ridge's voice in my ear broke through my pity party. *Steele, I'm in the second bedroom now. Give me a heads up if anyone decides to come upstairs.*

Will do.

Ridge had already checked the office and one of the bedrooms, and he should be clear as long as he didn't encounter any of the cleaning staff or the senator himself. After Harlan had made sure his cameras were running, it had been fairly easy for me to put a smear of Vaseline over all the lenses. None of us wanted to be even a background extra in any of the senator's videos.

Now it was later in the evening and the guests were starting to arrive. At Harlan's request, I hovered behind him while he greeted his guests, a who's who of shady businessmen, crooked politicians, and televangelists.

I faked being nervous as Carson came through the door and introduced Leo to the senator. Harlan's grin was practically predatory at the thought of having his very own FBI agent in his pocket. As far as he was concerned, the fact that Leo was under investigation was icing on the cake. More leverage for him. I knew because he'd talked non-stop all morning about his guest list.

"Senator Harlan, thank you for inviting us to your home," Carson said as he and Leo came in. He was dressed in one of his own custom-made suits, and Leo was sporting designer threads Miranda had tailored for him overnight. Money sure did grease the wheels.

"Thank you for contributing to the cause," Harlan said. "I'm sure we can all agree that we need people in Congress speaking for the hard-working, salt of the Earth Americans who are rightfully upset at the perversions and deplorable lack of morality in our current society."

He'd given a variation of this speech to every guest, sometimes substituting 'god-fearing' for 'salt of the Earth' for the more religious guests. I'd estimated about half of the people were there for what they thought was a legitimate fundraiser. They wouldn't be making any visits to the special party rooms where the hookers waited.

Carson looked my direction and faked surprise and anger. "What is he doing here?" he asked Harlan. "I fired him, you know."

"I do," Harlan said. "Luckily for me. I was very impressed with his credentials the first time we met, and it so happened I had an opening in my staff."

Carson stepped in close to the senator. "Well, my advice? Keep your hands off his 'credentials.' He *really* doesn't care for it." He cast me a scathing grin.

It was all I could do not to laugh. Carson was going off-script.

He dropped his voice even lower. "All talk and no action, that one. *If* you know what I mean."

"Maybe he's just particular," Harlan countered. "I'm sure he and I will have a very cordial relationship."

He's had his hands all over my credentials, I subvocalized. *I'm gonna need a Silkwood shower.*

I know the feeling, Breck said, his voice hard. It was the most he had spoken to me since I'd walked out this morning.

I sobered up fast.

Carson sniffed his disbelief. "It's your money," he said, like he didn't care one way or the other. They made a little more small talk, while Leo stood silently by Carson's side, looking duly impressed by the luxury on display and more than a little envious. Then they excused themselves to go mingle.

The senator turned to greet his next guest.

God, this couldn't be over quick enough for me. Even if I hadn't known what was going on, how truly slimy some of these bastards were, I was ready to shoot half of these people. They reminded me too much of the bad guys I'd worked for.

There were only a few ethical, legitimate ways to get rich, and sometimes the difference between the bad guys and the good guys was only a matter of who was in charge. As far as I could tell, this fundraiser was nothing but a thinly-veiled excuse for rich people to congratulate themselves for their forethought in being born into wealthy families.

I noticed that the senator's own wife wasn't here this evening, which seemed to be the M.O. for most of the guests. I'd amused myself by counting the number of women who were either mistresses or paid escorts. I didn't judge *them*. We all had bills to pay and limited choices, as my boyfriend could attest. It just made the prospect of exposing Harlan for the hypocritical prick he was that much more thrilling.

It wasn't hard to pick them out, nine times out of ten. A beautiful woman over twenty years younger than her partner was either a mistress, an escort, or the guy's second (or third) wife. The male escorts were either 'nephews,' or 'family friends.' I didn't know why people were bringing their own sex toys when the senator had a whole buffet of options to choose from planned for later in the evening.

"John," a particularly oily specimen said as he shook the senator's hand. Even Harlan seemed less than thrilled with this guy. "May I introduce my niece, Clara? She starting GW in the fall, and I said I would introduce her around. Get her off on the right foot."

"*Niece*," Wesley snorted, which let me tell you was very annoying when you were hearing it through a comm that transmitted sound directly through the bones of your skull.

Wesley had set up a command center in the house next door that rivaled any war room I'd ever been in.

"How in the world did you get access to that house?" Leo had asked, his eyebrows almost disappearing into his thick, dark hair when Wes had shown us around.

"You look shook, Shook," Ridge had joked with a grin. It had been nice to see Angel-Face lightening up a bit finally. Patching shit up with Breck had gone a long way towards pulling the stick out of his ass.

"Never gets old," Danny had said, high-fiving Ridge.

"Oh, it got old in fourth grade," Leo had informed him. "Trust me."

"I've got a guy," Wes said, answering Leo's question with a total non-answer.

Leo had shaken his head ruefully. "I bet you do, Zero. How many of them are on various watch-lists worldwide?"

"We don't talk about it. It's considered bragging," Wes had answered.

Whoever Wesley's guy was, he or she had come through like a champ. From his lair next door, Wes could monitor all our communications devices and had hacked into the senator's wi-fi. "Really? The password is 1234!@#$?" he'd muttered. "Guy deserves to be hacked."

But then Wes had gone a step further and hacked into every device the senator owned that was connected to his wi-fi – devices Harlan would never have imagined could be hacked. The ease with which he had accessed the cameras and mics built into everything from televisions, to Kindles, to cell phones made me want to join the Amish or something. I'd laughed at my buddy who'd put a piece of tape over the camera on his laptop. I wanted to call him and apologize.

It wasn't paranoia if they really were watching you.

How many escorts does that make? Leo asked, pulling me back to the present. He was keeping track as well as he circulated through the party. If things went totally FUBAR, he wanted to make sure the escorts got out before the cops came.

I was really starting to wonder what Leo's story was.

Um, six, Wesley reported.

And that guy with the tie, remember? Danny said. *I recognized him.*

He and Breck were stashed at the house with Wesley until it was time for them to make their entrance. Over my many loud and rudely ignored objections, they'd gotten in touch with their pimp—ex-pimp, if I had any say in it, and given Breck's attitude this morning, I wasn't sure I *did* —and told the sleazeball they would be at the senator's house, but thankfully they'd steadfastly refused to meet with him beforehand despite his insistence.

I turned my attention back to Mr. Slimebag and his 'niece.' I'm the last one to judge family relationships, being as my whole life it was just me and my mama, but his grip on the arm of the young lady in question seemed, well, less than avuncular (I liked to read the dictionary as a kid. I was a great person to do crosswords puzzles with).

"Charmed," the senator said with a smile, taking her hand in the double-handed grip his kind used with the ladies.

I must have made a sound because Clara's eyes shifted to me.

That was one way I separated the paid companions from the mistresses-slash-trophy wives. The ones who were being paid to be there and play nice looked directly at me, assessing whether or not I was going to be a help in case stuff went to hell (which it was going to) or if I was another threat they had to keep an eye on. The gold-diggers ignored me, preferring to scope out the competition and any potential future sugar daddies.

I held the eye contact for a second, looked quickly over at her 'uncle' and dipped my chin a millimeter to let her know I had her back. Her shoulders relaxed, and her smile became a little less forced.

I followed Harlan as he worked the crowd, making promises and veiled threats as the situation called for. It took all of my professional experience to not let my revulsion show on my face. The homophobia, racism, and sexism in every casual conversation alone was enough to make me want to punch someone. Add in the obvious influence peddling going on,

278 / A.E. WASP

278 / A.E. WASP

and I was ready to beg Special Agent Shook to arrest the lot of them.

Occasionally a lone man would make his way to the back room, have a brief chat with one of the meatheads guarding the door, and come back to the party twenty or thirty minutes later, looking refreshed. I didn't know who these guys were, but I hoped somebody was keeping a list. You never knew when information could come in handy.

I have enough info for at least ten investigations, Leo said, almost silently, covering up the movement of his lips by taking a sip of his drink. "These guys are worse than you people."

Thanks? Carson said. *You can look at the tape later. Make sure to get their good sides.*

Besides the comms we wore over our teeth to talk to each other, we all had hidden recording devices on us somewhere that transmitted audio and video back to Wesley.

"Next time, you might want to remember to shut that off before you let your boyfriend rip your clothes off," Wesley had joked as I checked over my button cam. I liked the little doohickey. It had an old-school retro vibe. Made me feel like James Bond. "I've got some bad video but good audio of you two from the other night," he continued. "Or, you know, feel free to leave it on if you're into that kinda thing, just try to get a better angle. I can't see shit when the button's on the floor."

"Wesley!" Breck had shouted. "You dick!"

Ridge had moved threateningly towards the hacker before I could. "You'd better not have video of my brother, or any of us, *Bond*," he'd said.

Wes had chuckled. "I'll delete it, I promise! Nothing personal from any of you. There aren't cameras in the rooms, I swear. This stuff just showed up unexpectedly when I was checking out Steele's footage from the Florida fundraiser."

I was on hyper alert, keeping count of all the comings and goings of guests, staff, and my team. I ran over the details of the plan multiple time, visualizing our preferred outcome. I was used to a more straightforward, knock-down-the-doors-and-blow-the-bad-guys-up scenario. This circus Wesley, Carson, and Leo had cooked up was new to me.

The party in the front room was winding down, and the special, private party in the back rooms where ramping up when the moment I had been dreading arrived.

Steele, Wesley whispered just as Harlan checked a text on his phone. *Danny and Breck are headed your way*.

Shit. I wasn't ready. My ears rang with the rush of blood as my body started pumping adrenaline as quickly as it could.

Steele?

I made an affirmative noise to let Wes know I'd heard him without alerting the senator.

"Mr. Gonzales," Harlan said, "Our special guests will be arriving any moment."

I almost didn't respond to my cover name, I was so focused on the door.

The door opened, and Danny and Breck walked in like they owned the place, smiling and flirting with everyone they could. They were a fucking matched pair, and easily the two hottest men in the room. They both wore grey suits, Breck's a shade lighter than Danny's, along with light-blue silk dress shirts that were open at the collar and sported button-cams just like mine.

I wanted to pounce on Breck, and not just because he was sex on two legs. I wanted to shield him from what was about to happen with my own body.

But I knew he wouldn't appreciate that shit in the slightest. It had taken balls for him and Danny to show up here in the first place, knowing what awaited them, and even more for them to defy the senator by insisting on showing up at the front door like invited guests, rather than sneaking in the back like Cisco's other guys and girls had. Just went to show how fucking invincible the senator thought he was that he'd agreed to their demand.

Be careful, Breck, I whispered. Breck made no indication that he had heard me as he worked the party like the pro he was. Heads turned as he and Danny walked through the room. How could they not? Both of them were good looking in different ways, together they were impossible to look away from. I don't know why I'd expected them to be scared and intimidated by the assembled crowd. I'd forgotten that they'd done this before, that they'd been in this very house before.

Two hookers, I reminded myself. Two street kids who'd had sex for money. There was no one to report them missing, no one to care. If Charlie hadn't put us on the case, Breck could have been dead for weeks before even Ridge knew about it.

I wished I had worn my sunglasses to hide the fear I was sure was visible in my eyes.

Harlan greeted them by wrapping an arm around each of their shoulders, and with a jerk of his head, he motioned for me to follow them as they headed not to the back room but to the door I knew led to the downstairs wine cellar.

Bingo. But knowing I'd been right about what the senator had in mind didn't make me any less nervous for Breck.

I straightened my tie and followed the senator down the hall, keeping my expression blank.

Go time, Wesley said.

Eyes on the door downstairs, Leo confirmed. *We've got your six if needed, boys.*

Ridge? Wesley asked. *How's it going? Final countdown here, man. Don't make me start singing it.*

I got to Harlan's computer and uploaded your virus thingy.

Virus thingy. That's the technical term for it, Wes agreed. *The hard copies?*

Negative. I can't find the damn safe. I've checked everywhere. He's gonna wanna keep it close, he's gonna take it with him when he travels, so it should be here somewhere. Ridge sounded beyond frustrated. *But it's not in his bedroom, not in his office... I need fucking schematics, man. I cannot just do this shit on the fly!*

Stop complaining and find the damn thing, Pfeiffer, Leo said. *I'm having a hard time not arresting, punching or just shooting some of these people. And I think Mr. Waters is feeling the pull of temptation. His 'special friend' from the other party is here tonight.*

Don't hate, Shook, Carson said airily, *just because you can't get laid in a party full of paid companionship.*

Jesus Christ. "Focus," I snapped loud enough to make Harlan turn his head toward me. I stared him down until he turned back.

Steele, Breck said as the senator unlocked the door. We'd all practiced subvocalizing, speaking without letting actual sound past our lips. It was strange, leeched all the emotion from the words, and it was difficult to remember that we didn't have to speak out loud to be heard, but at that moment, I thanked every little strange brain cell in Wesley's head for giving it to us.

Right here, babe. I said. Our footstep echoed on the polished wood stairs. The sounds of the party faded as the door shut behind us.

I'm sorry, he said. *For earlier.*

Doesn't matter, not one bit. We'll talk when we get home. My heart pounded with each step we took.

"Where are we going?" Danny asked loudly. "Is the VIP party down here?"

When we'd reached the bottom of the steps. Danny and Breck hesitated, not willing to go further into the dark space.

"Yeah, sure," Harland snorted. "Mickey, why don't you give our guests a little encouragement to join the party?"

I was on. Taking a deep breath, I pulled my gun – my own weapon, which I'd insisted on carrying despite Harlan's protests -- and waved the boys towards the vaulted wine cellar. "Move it along, kids."

"No," Breck said, digging his heels in. Taking advantage of the situation, I pushed up next to him, grabbing him by the arm.

Danny looked terrified, way more than the script called for. He'd frozen like a deer in the headlights. And after what he'd suffered at the senator's hands, who could blame him?

Danny," Wesley said crisply in our ears. *Pull it together. Don't fuck this up.*

Fuck you, Danny said, his lips barely moving. The comms leeched the emotion from his voice but not his face. *You're not the one playing bait.*

You wanted to be part of this, Wes taunted mercilessly. *Are you punking out now?*

Danny stood straighter. His eyes shone with defiant anger. *Fuck no.*

Good, Wes said, and I'd swear he sounded just a little bit proud. *You've got this, Danny.*

"Saying your prayers, Danny-boy?" Harlan asked. "I doubt the Lord listens to slutty, thieving whores like you." Quick as the snake he was, Harlan's hand flashed out and smacked Danny across the face. Tears of anger filled the kid's eyes, but he didn't cower again. "I want my goddamn ring."

"No!" Breck yelled. By the way he grabbed my arm, the warning was meant for me, not Harlan.

I will fucking kill him, I said, and I almost didn't care if Harlan had read my lips.

Harlan pulled out a ridiculously large key to open the wrought iron grille that separated the rest of the lavish basement from the wine cellar. *Pretentious asshole.*

He grabbed Danny and practically threw him on the stone floor inside the cellar. I man-handled Breck though the door, and it banged closed behind us.

"My ring," Harlan said again, holding out his hand greedily. "Now."

Danny shoved his hand in his suit pocket and extracted the gold circlet with its enormous high-set blue stone. Wes had called it a *fucking gaudy piece of shit* when he'd worked on it last night, and he wasn't wrong. He dropped the ring into Harlan's hand without touching him.

"Ah, there now." Harlan grabbed the silk handkerchief from his breast pocket and used it to pick up the ring from his palm and put it in his pocket. "Sadly, I know where this has been," he said disgustedly.

"Kill them," Harlan instructed me, with a gleam in his eyes I'd seen before in murders and psychopaths.

Danny and Breck exchanged a panicked look that was probably only half-staged. "N-no!" he said. "I thought you said if we gave it back, you'd let us go? I thought you said we'd be even?"

"And you believed me?" Harlan laughed like he was truly amused. "God. Some people truly are too stupid to live."

"Kill? Do you really think that's necessary?" I frowned at him, giving it a good show, and hoped he wouldn't notice that my voice was a little higher-pitched than usual, per Wesley's instructions. *That's right, Harlan, look right into my little button cam and repeat your instructions.*

"Little whore stole my ring while he was sucking my dick. He deserves to die." Harlan's smile turned vicious. "And remember, Gonzalez, your fortune is tied to mine now, so you do what I say. Kill them both, dump the bodies. River out back, hiking trails a few minutes away, I don't give a shit where, and the less I know, the better. Use your imagination. But I don't want them found."

I nodded slowly. "I'll need help with that if you want it done quickly."

"Hire whoever you need. Make sure they're discreet, since it's your ass on the line if they fuck up."

I nodded again, as if this were to be expected. "If you'd given me warning, I could have had a couple guys on standby."

"Things move fast around here, handsome. You need to keep up." He stepped toward me with a come-hither smile that turned my stomach and reached down to trail his fingers *over my fucking crotch.* "But you seem like a man who'll have no problem keeping *up.*"

Breck was still pressed against my side where I was 'restraining' him, and he gave a furious gasp when Harlan's hand made contact with my pants. It was my turn to restrain *him* from tearing Harlan's arm off.

"Come find me later," Harlan whispered.

I gave him a genuine, heart-felt smile. "Oh, I will," I promised. "I definitely will."

Harlan tossed me a wink. "Do it," he instructed, moving to stand near the wrought-iron grille. No doubt blood was tricky to get out of his custom-made tuxedo.

I pushed Breck away from me, and he sprawled on the floor next to Danny.

Ready? I asked of everyone, my eyes glued to Breck's blue ones.

Ready, he said.

Danny blinked, which was as good as a nod.

"On three," Wesley said. "One."

I can't do this. My hand was shaking.

"Two."

"Do it," Harlan shouted.

It's okay, baby, Breck said. *I love you. Do it.*

"Three."

My finger jerked, and I shot the man I loved.

GOD DAMN, *those blood packs hurt when they went off.*

Wesley had purchased some kind of rig online from a special effects store, and whatever it was, it was seriously convincing. The snazzy suits Miranda had gotten for us were destroyed.

While Harlan gloated, I stayed in my sprawled position on the floor, fighting the need to twitch as the fake blood spread across the front of my chest and spilled down behind me. In the movies, they never explained how fucking *cold* the ground could feel underneath you, or how, as soon as you 'died,' your nose would start to itch *violently*, like it needed to prove to you that it was alive by sneezing right then.

Annoying, but highly preferable to actually being shot.

The senator gave a low chuckle. "Well done, Mickey." My eyes were open beneath my lashes, and I watched him move a step closer to Steele and place his wrinkly goddamn fucking *Crypt-Keeper paw* on my man's hard stomach. A shade better than caressing his dick, but barely. It was bad enough that the asshole had laid hands on *me*; I wanted to douse acid on every part of Harlan that had touched Steele and erase the feel of Steele's body from his memory banks.

Jealousy was a new emotion for me; I wasn't sure if I liked it, but it seemed I was fucking good at it.

"I think there might just be a bonus in this for you," Harlan was saying.

Wes snorted over the comms. "Yeah, right. A bonus *in his pants.*"

God. Gross. I couldn't say a damn word, not even over these sub-vocal comms, because I wouldn't risk Harlan seeing my lips move. If looks could kill, though, Snow White would be exploding in *five, four, three...*

No such luck.

Steele, you'd better move this along, man," Danny said. He'd had the forethought to land face-down when he was 'shot,' and he was better at the whole sub-vocalizing thing anyway. *Rocky's about to lose his shit.*

Danny's use of my old alias somehow brought me back to myself. Taking down Harlan, making sure he could never hurt another working guy, was way more important than my need to piss in a circle around Steele.

"Thanks, Senator," Steele said. "But I, uh... I think it'd be better for everyone if I take a rain check on the bonus right now. I'm gonna call my guys and get them to clean up the mess." He waved a hand at Danny and me.

Harlan nodded. "Good man. *Later.*"

"Oh, you know it," Steele said, repeating his words from earlier. I wondered how Harlan couldn't hear the threat in them. "It's a date."

The metal door clanged open as the senator walked out into the basement, and Steele made a show of taking his phone from his pocket and dialing a number that I was pretty sure connected to a burner phone Wes had set up. "Yeah, I'm gonna need a couple cleaners," Steele said, loud enough to carry.

The senator's footsteps echoed up the stairs, and the sounds of laughter and tinkling china floated down when he opened the door at the top.

"We clear?" Steele demanded.

We have eyes-on, Leo confirmed from above, and I allowed myself to move for the first time. *Old man's making a beeline for his secretary by the front door.*

Danny stood up and took stock of his ruined outfit while I ran a hand over my face, scratching my nose.

His secretary, Wes said. *Did we do a background on her?*

Yep. Jenny Guinn. She's inner-circle but likely not by choice, Leo said. *Single mom, no priors, worked on his rival's campaign before defecting to work for Harlan.*

"Wonder what he threatened her with," I muttered. I pushed myself up to sitting and stared at the blood-spatter all over the wood floor. Fake-death was messy.

"Do we have ears on them?" Steele demanded. He held out a hand, and I grabbed it, letting him haul me to my feet.

Negative. No listening devices near the door, Wes said. *That's where you were stationed earlier.*

Steele grunted. His dark eyes searched mine. I could *feel* his need to pull me into his arms, or maybe it was my own need to be held that I sensed. I wanted to forget our fight this morning, all the shit we'd just been through, and lose myself in his embrace.

But it was impossible for him to get any closer than he was, not when he had to go upstairs and look presentable in a few minutes, and I was standing here dripping with Carson's patented corn starch-and-food-coloring concoction.

"The metal filings are the key," Carson had told us earlier, stirring a giant pasta pot of bubbling blood in the kitchen next door, like the witch in some fucked-up kids' story standing over a cauldron. "Makes it *smell* real."

He wasn't wrong. The shit smelled fucking foul; I could practically taste the tang in my mouth.

He's handing Guinn something from his pocket. Looks like a balled-up tissue, Carson reported.

"His handkerchief, with the ring rolled up inside it," Steele said, still staring at me. "So much for keeping track of Harlan that way. Ridge, you find the safe yet?"

Oh yeah, half an hour ago, Ridge snapped. *I just decided not to tell you 'cause I'm crawling under beds for funsies now. All I've found is that the senator has a serious case of dry rot under his bathroom sink. Should I alert the authorities?"*

"Wow. Who whacked you with the snark-stick?" Danny demanded. He stripped off his suit jacket and his shirt.

"Some of us got *shot* tonight and still haven't lost our optimistic attitudes."

If you'd seen the truly disturbing porn collection in this man's nightstand drawer, Ridge began.

"Been there, honey. Posed for some of it," Danny said breezily, wiping at his chest with a clean part of his shirt. "Got the dislocated jaw to prove it."

Ridge's sigh nearly rattled my skull. *Fair enough.*

Ms. Guinn is headed upstairs, Ridge, Leo said urgently. *Look sharp.*

I'm activating the tracker in the ring right now, Wes said. *If she's taking it upstairs, maybe she's putting it with his other valuables.*

In his bedroom? Ridge breathed. *Where I am? Fuck.*

Hang tight, Wes instructed, sounding unperturbed. *Stay out of sight.*

Little tricky when I have no idea where the woman's gonna be putting the ring! Breck sounded a little frantic.

My heart beat faster than it had all night, except for the brief moment when I'd stood inches away and watched Harlan touch Steele.

Steele cupped my jaw in his huge hand. "Calm, baby," he insisted. "Ridge knows what he's doing. He's good at this shit."

I nodded. I believed that. I did. But I was overwhelmed, and seriously out of my element. There was still another whole chapter to the plan tonight, and what if... *what if...*

Steele leaned forward and pressed his lips to mine. His tongue swept into my mouth, and all my thoughts flat-lined as I was caught up in the sensation. His kiss was Xanax and caffeine all at once.

Alvarez, Leo said, and Steele broke our kiss slowly. *Five-minute warning. The senator is heading toward Carson, and he's looking way too pleased with himself. We need to start phase two before I kill this motherfucker.*

"Understood." Steele looked at me with narrowed eyes, and whatever he saw seemed to satisfy him. "You good?" he mouthed to me.

"Good." I nodded. "Let's do this."

"I'm ready for my costume change," Danny said. He was standing against one of the wine racks near the door, naked from the waist up, grinning at Steele and me as Steele finally let go of my face. "Time to go *haunt* a bitch."

Steele nodded. "I hid the bag in the downstairs bathroom, first door on the right," he said. "With the duplicate clothing for both of you that Josie gave me." He looked at me. "You need help getting dressed?"

Danny snorted and pushed off the wall to link his arm with mine. "Not from you, he doesn't. Not unless we want to add *another* naughty sex tape to Harlan's collection."

We don't, Ridge said flatly from wherever he was hiding.

"Exactly. You can head upstairs," Danny told Steele. "We'll be up in a minute, as planned."

He towed me out of the wine cellar into the carpeted floor of the basement and then into a small powder room where I stripped off my shirt as quickly as possible. Danny wiped me down with a damp cloth.

"Ridge, what about you?" Steele demanded. "You good?"

Barely. I'm currently on the dormer roof outside the Senator's bedroom window.

The fuck you are, Leo warned.

Yeah, no, just kidding. Ridge exhaled in a whoosh like he'd just jumped and landed on something. *I'm inside. The secretary left the room.*

Ring is stationary, Wes said. *She left it in there somewhere.*

Super, Ridge said with fake perkiness. *Any clue where?*

Uh... based on the blueprints, it's in the master bathroom, Wes said.

But I already checked there!

Well, check again, Wes said. *But this time do it right.*

Danny snorted, and I raised an eyebrow at him. He shrugged and reached under the vanity to extract the black nylon backpack Steele had left there.

"What?" he mouthed. "Wes is an ass, but a funny ass."

Thanks so much for the help, Wes, Ridge grumbled. *No, really. You are the MVA of this mission, buddy. That's Most Valuable Asshole, in case you're as slow on the uptake as you pretend to be.*

Wes sighed like he was thirty-two flavors of put-out. *Fine. I'm tracking you by your chip. We can play a long distance game of hot and cold.*

Oh, goody, Ridge drawled. *I love games.*

You need to get your ass downstairs, Carson insisted. *Time's wasting, and I've seen more than one old lady clutch her pearls and cover a yawn. Unless we want the only witnesses of phase two to be prostitutes and politicians, hurry the fuck up.*

In the next breath, Carson said more loudly, *Senator! You've got to tell me where you hire your staff. The drinks your bartender is serving are incredible. It's called a Brown Derby.*

"Leo," Steele said. "You have the vial?"

Leo didn't dignify this with a response, either because he wasn't in a position to subvocalize or because he thought Steele was an idiot for asking. My money was on the second option.

Danny slapped me on the shoulder, a reminder that I couldn't stand still and listen all night. I had a role to play. I pulled the clothing from the backpack, identical to the ruined suit I'd been wearing, and began dressing.

These suckers taste like grapefruit, Leo said in a jovial, outgoing way that had me and Danny exchanging a look in the bathroom mirror. *Perfect for the senator from Florida! Let me getcha one! I've had about four,* he confided.

Harlan chuckled. *Alright, twist my arm!*

Leo laughed delightedly. *See that, Ben? I always say, trust a man who can hold his liquor. Precious fucking few real men around these days, am I right?*

Carson-as-Ben made a vague sound of agreement. *You're always right, Leo.*

Hell yes, I am, Leo said. *A round for all of us! Be right back!*

Your friend seems to be enjoying the party, the senator remarked, probably to Carson.

Oh, yes, Carson said. *Loving it.*

Has he made a trip to the VIP section? Harlan sounded scary even secondhand over someone else's coms.

Not yet, Carson said. *I think he needs another drink... or maybe three. Notoriously high tolerance, you know.* He stressed the last sentence pointedly.

Ah. Thought it was something like that, Harlan said speculatively. *FBI doesn't just suspend a career man like Agent Shook for nothing.*

Quite, Carson agreed.

Here we are! Leo said, rejoining them. *One for you, Benny-Boy. And one for your lovely friend the senator. And this big one is for me. Bottoms up!*

There was a giant *slurp* over the comms that sent a shivering vibration up my spine. Not remotely comfortable.

Ooh, that's got a kick, the senator said, coughing slightly. *What did you say is in this?*

Whiskey! A man's drink, Leo told him. *Just like my daddy used to drink.*

I looked at Danny as I buttoned up my light blue shirt. I wondered if Leo was laying it on a little thick with the good-old-boy routine. I'd never heard him mention his father before.

But when Leo encouraged him to "Drink up!" we heard the vague sound of liquid and then Leo's triumphant crow of laughter. *That's the way! Yes, indeed, Senator. I knew you were a man, just like my daddy.*

The senator coughed again, and his voice sounded strangled. *Yes, well.* He cleared his throat. *Never let it be said I can't hold my liquor.*

There was a slapping sound, and I imagined Leo thumping Harlan on the back. I only wished it were harder.

Never, indeed! Well, introduce me around to your friends, Senator Harlan! These seem like my kind of guys."

I tucked my shirt into my pants and shrugged into my jacket. I wondered idly how Harlan was feeling about Leo leading him around his own party.

Didn't fucking matter though, or it wouldn't for long. Leo's job had been to lace the senator's drink with a healthy dose of Burundanga powder, more commonly known on the street as Devil's Breath or scopolamine. A couple sips of that would have turned Snow White into a zombie with almost no memory of recent events. Trust Leo to make sure the guy had taken the whole fucking drink in one go.

"Showtime!" Danny said. "Breck and I are good to go. Ridge, you ready?"

Yeah, Ridge said, sounding slightly breathless. *Wes directed me to the ring. Safe was behind a fake heating return in this bathroom linen closet. But I practically needed a U-Haul to get all the shit out of there. Papers and pictures and enough*

DNA results to put Jerry Springer out of business. Ridge paused. *Is he still in business?*

No one gives a shit, Pfeiffer, Steele said.

Right, Ridge said. *As expected, there were tapes and tapes and more fucking tapes. Wes is gonna be hard for six weeks watching them all.*

Pfft. No fucking way. Wes said, disgusted. *I'm happy to put the tapes on a system where y'all can take turns.*

I left them in Carson's car, Ridge said. *You guys can fight over them later. And I did my wardrobe change too.*

Good. Where are you now?" Steele demanded. *"I need you in the dining room to...* He broke off with a pained yelp.

I'm hee-eere, Ridge sang. Wes snickered.

Jesus fucking Christ, Steele exclaimed. *Don't sneak up on me unless you want an up-close look at your own asshole.*

Aw. That hurts, Alvarez. You don't seem to mind it when my little brother touches you," Ridge teased.

"Younger by thirteen fucking minutes," I said, because that was my expected line every time Ridge called me his little brother. "And keep your fucking hands off my boyfriend."

"Oh, *boyfriend is it?"* Ridge gloated. *"All official and shit?"*

Well, it wasn't exactly all official and shit, but...

"Yeah," Steele said. *"All official and shit."*

Alrighty, then. I grinned at Danny, who laughed silently back at me.

"In position," I said as we climbed to the top of the basement stairs and paused by the door.

"*Ready,*" Steele confirmed. "*Ridge, get going.*"

"Oh. My. *Gawd!*" Ridge said, loud enough that we could hear him through the thick wooden door as well as over the comms, though he was several rooms and dozens of people away. "Lucretia Baumgartner, your dress is *amazing!*"

Ghost-in-the-night cat-burglary aside, when you wanted a job done with zero subtlety, my brother was the man to call.

I had no idea what woman he was accosting, or if Lucretia was really her name, but it didn't matter. Ridge's job had been to make a quick scene that would be noticed by *everyone*, including the senator. Judging from the silence followed by titters of laughter, he'd accomplished that mission with perfection.

Something wrong, Senator Harlan? Carson asked in concern. *You look as though you've seen a ghost.*

No. No, I've seen a... a problem, Harlan corrected, slurring his words just slightly. *A problem that shoulda been solved already. I need Mickey. Where's Mickey?"*

Danny and I exchanged a glance. Snow White sounded loopy already. The drug was acting even more quickly than I'd thought.

Mickey? Carson repeated, so innocently I'd truly believe he had no idea what Harlan was talking about if I didn't know better. *Who's Mickey?*

Mickey, the senator insisted, louder now. *You know. Your Mickey.*

Carson hesitated. *Senator Harlan, I...I'm afraid I don't know anyone named Mickey, sir.*

Of course you fucking do, Waters, Harlan snarled. *Mickey was your man! You fired him!*

All conversation had ceased, and I imagined every eye was on the senator.

Senator, please! Let go of my shirt, Carson shouted, all affronted dignity. *It's Savile Row!*

I wished I were a fly on the wall out there, but if I went out too soon, it would ruin the plan. I could just imagine how Harlan's face looked, spittle flying out of his mouth as his face turned the same apoplectic shade of puce it had been the night he'd beaten me and Danny. The difference was, tonight *he* was the one getting fucked over.

I don't give a shit what it... what... The senator inhaled loudly. *Fuck you!* he shouted, and Carson gave a little cry like maybe Harlan had pushed him...or more likely Carson had made himself *appear* to be pushed. He was good at shit like that.

"That boy!" Harlan shouted. "The one causing the commotion. Where did he go?"

"What boy?" Leo demanded. "Senator, maybe you should sit down." He raised his voice and called out, "Does anyone know where the senator's secretary is? Or his wife?"

"Mary Lou isn't here," a woman in the crowd said, faint disapproval in her voice. "Which is *highly unusual*."

"Not so very unusual," someone else said dryly. "Not where Harlan is concerned. His entertainments aren't always appropriate for ladies."

There were more shocked gasps in the crowd, and I couldn't have stopped smiling if you paid me.

"There he is again!" Harlan said, and I assumed Ridge had made another lightning-fast appearance. "He was... where the *fuck* did he go?"

"Somebody's swear jar's filling up fast," I chortled under my breath. "Please let someone faint in horror, *please* let someone faint in horror."

Wes chuckled. *I'm just sad I had to disrupt cell service in the area so no one's live streaming this shit. No one besides me, I mean.*

"How are you even *doing* that?" I demanded. "I thought you said before that Harlan didn't have security cameras inside? Did someone plant one?"

"*Harlan did!*" Wes said happily. "*He's got a top-of-the-line smart TV from a couple years back. Only the best for our favorite senator, naturally. But of course the smug fucker didn't think to update any of his privacy settings.*" He chuckled. "*So as soon as I hacked into the wi-fi, I got myself a root shell on the TV, and now I control it. Camera, mic, and all. Eeet ees mine, alllll mine!*" he cackled like a super-villain.

"*I have no idea what a root shell is, but I'm going to get one tattooed on my ass when this is over*," Ridge promised. "*This is excellent.*"

Steele laughed. "We've got the angles right, Wes? You're not catching Ridge in the frame at all?"

"Not even a little. Kid's a pro," Wes confirmed. "Right now it looks like Harlan is flipping out at shadows."

"*Shank you*," Ridge said. "I try."

"Awesome. Danny, you're up," Steele instructed.

Danny wiggled his eyebrows at me and stepped out, closing the door most of the way behind him.

He sashayed his ass toward the living room, where all the action was taking place. When he got to the rear of the crowd, who were all pushing for a better glimpse of the senator's breakdown and not paying attention to Danny in the slightest, he stood on his tiptoes and waved wildly.

Harlan lost his mind.

"That's the other one! The other cocksucker! Right behind you!"

The crowd all turned in the direction Harlan pointed, including Danny, who managed to lose himself in the press of people.

"He was right there!" Harlan exclaimed. He walked to where Danny had been standing a few seconds before, then turned himself in a full circle, like he expected Danny to pop out at any moment. "He was supposed to be covered in blood and..." He put his hand on his head and rubbed his forehead.

The senator's secretary appeared at his side, wide-eyed.

"Senator, maybe you should lie down," she suggested. "I think you've had too much to drink. Maybe a cool compress?"

But the senator did not want to lie down. No, he wanted to run full-tilt toward his total destruction.

"I can *hold my liquor*! I'm a fucking *real man*."

"Oh, heavens," Carson groaned. "I think she's right, sir. Perhaps if you..."

"I can... I can *buy and sell you*, Ben Waters!" The senator pointed an accusing finger at Carson. "I have a tape of you and... and one of those *boys*! And don't you forget it."

Carson's jaw dropped. "Ex*cuse* me?" he demanded. "What the *hell* are you talking about?"

"Don't you... play dumb," the senator slurred, leaning on his secretary so heavily, it was a wonder she didn't collapse. "*Thass* why you're here! Because I *control you*."

Whoa. Allll the secrets were coming out now.

"I'm *here* because I was considering a campaign contribution! Which, let me tell you, you will *not* be receiving. I have *never* seen such a display." Carson looked at his audience for support.

Most of the women and several of the men were nodding, outraged. Others looked like they might vomit at any moment.

It was a pretty easy litmus test of who the senator was blackmailing, really. I imagined the only thing more nauseating than an asshole blackmailing you was a *mentally unstable* asshole blackmailing you.

"Maybe we should call an ambulance? Is it possible he's having a stroke?" Steele materialized at Harlan's side. "Sir, can you lift your arms?"

"Lift my... *I can lift my fucking arms, Mickey!* You killed them! I saw you kill them. But they didn't *stay killed!*"

Steele's face hardened. "Sir, I'm not sure who you think I am, but my name is Master Sergeant Alvarez, U.S. Army. I'm a decorated veteran who served two tours in Iraq and Afghanistan. You hired me to work security for the party tonight. Does... does any of this ring a bell?"

I almost giggled. It had been my idea to have Steele mention his service. He'd fucking *hated* the idea of referring to himself as a *decorated veteran.* But Carson had backed me up, and Leo had backed *him* up, and sure enough, we'd all been right. The crowd adored a hero, and Steele truly was one.

"Fuck you! You're... you're Mickey Gonzalez!" the senator insisted.

Steele shook his head like a sad puppy. "Does every person of Hispanic descent look the same to you, sir?"

"Senator, honestly," poor Ms. Guinn begged, nearly stumbling under Harlan's weight. "You really need to sit down. You're not well!"

"I'm calling 9-1-1 right now," a voice that sounded suspiciously like Danny's offered. "Better safe than sorry!"

"Do you know if he's taken any illegal drugs?" Steele asked Ms. Guinn anxiously, seeming to lower his voice without lowering it at all. "The paramedics will need to know if he has any narcotics in his system."

Ms. Guinn twisted her hands in worry. "I mean, from time to time he does. I... I honestly don't *know* if he's on anything right now!"

"But it's possible," Steele confirmed, his voice low and commanding.

Ms. Guinn nodded, and the crowd erupted into whispers again.

"I'm not *high*. I'm fucking *pissed*. And no one is calling anyone. You hear?" The senator knocked into his secretary, sending her sprawling into Steele's arms. "You're a *traitor*, Mickey. You and Ben Waters! And *no one* betrays John Harlan."

"Sir, I don't know who you're talking about," Steele said sadly.

"Nor do I," Carson said. His outrage was on-point, as always.

"We'll see about that," Harlan said. "We'll just see." He ran a hand over his mouth and pointed to a random man in the crowd. "You there! Jenny! Go get the tape from last week."

"Oh, dear God," the real Jenny Guinn said. She was still standing in the curve of Steele's arm like she was really comfy there.

I didn't blame her. Much.

"Sir, you don't want to do that," she told Harlan. "You truly don't."

"You remember what I can do to your sister, you little whore! Now go!" Harlan roared.

"Alright, Senator Harlan, I've seen about enough," Leo said. "I'm not going to stand idly by while you insult women and make all kinds of outrageous claims."

"You're nothing but a disgraced FBI agent whose career went down the toilet when he got lost in a bottle."

A man in the crowd came forward. "Harlan," he said urgently. "Don't you know who that is?"

Harlan's eyes narrowed. "What?"

"That's Agent *Leonard Shook*," he said pointedly. "We received a memo about his commendation weeks ago, remember? He's the one who..." He stepped closer and whispered in the senator's ear.

The senator stared at Leo, and his eyes widened. "Not. Possible."

Seriously? It was like someone changing the channel the second before the murderer was revealed. Except with no rewind.

"What the fuck did you do, Leo?" I demanded. Obviously, Leo ignored me.

"Why are we standing here and listening to this?" Steele demanded, once again taking control of the situation. "The senator's obviously disturbed, either as a result of the illegal drugs he might have taken or from some other recent traumatic incident that triggered a mental breakdown."

Wes snickered. "Oh my God! *Gray's Anatomy* is waiting for you, Doctor Alvarez. You sound so fucking competent as you make this shit up!"

Wes was right. There was nothing like a couple of multisyllable words and a confident attitude to convince people you knew what you were talking about. The partygoers were convinced they were witnessing Harlan have a psychotic break.

"Alright, fam. *My turn*," Wes said, chuckling darkly, and the lights in the house flickered out while the giant television on the wall turned *on*.

Some dramatic soul screamed, and I laughed out loud. The television blared static at first, the picture nothing but grayscale snow, and then the senator's voice and image came through loud and clear.

"*Kill them*," Harlan said, staring right at the camera. And holy shit, he looked even scarier on the video than he had in real life. His eyes were fucking *insane*.

"*Do you really think that's necessary?*" a voice on the video asked. It was Steele's voice, I knew it was, but it also wasn't. His Georgia accent was more pronounced and the tone a little higher. I doubted anyone here would recognize Steele's voice from this.

"*Little whore stole my ring while he was sucking my dick*," Crazy-Eyes-Harlan-on-the-screen said. "*He deserves to die.*"

"Oh my God!" one of the partygoers exclaimed, and it seemed to set off a chain reaction. People were gasping now, clutching one another.

"This is horrifying!" one woman shouted. "Turn it off! Can't someone turn it off?"

But Wesley was in control now, and there was no fucking way he was turning it off.

Harlan-on-the-screen continued. "*And remember, Gonzalez, your fortune is tied to mine now, so you do what I say.*

Kill them both, dump the bodies. River out back, hiking trails a few minutes away, I don't give a shit where, and the less I know, the better. Use your imagination. But I don't want them found."

Creative editing cut out the next part of the conversation that had happened downstairs, but Wes made sure to get the kill shot. The camera zoomed in on Harlan's face as he said, *"Things move fast around here, handsome. You need to keep up."* Harlan's smile became something sick and feral as he stepped toward the camera – toward Steele – and Steele angled his chest down so the button cam would capture the Senator's hand stroking over his package. *"But you seem like a man who'll have no problem keeping up."*

I wish I could say that the room exploded into pandemonium, but it didn't. Not quite. More like confusion. One woman turned to another and said, "Does that mean... John's a *gay?*"

Another cried, "I'll pray for you, John. Repent, and you'll be saved!"

Harlan had been standing in the middle of the floor, swaying from side to side, staring at the television like he was in a dream. But when Wes started replaying the feed again, the senator lost what little sanity he had left.

"Turn it off!" he yelled. "Turn this shit off!"

He grabbed a heavy tchotchke from the side table closest to him and threw it at the television, cracking the screen down the center. The picture cut off, but the sound did not. Instead, Harlan's voice saying, *"Kill them, kill them, kill them,"* sounded over and over on endless repeat.

"No!" Harlan shouted. "Nooo!"

"Aww! Boo, hiss!" Wes said, chuckling gleefully. "Haters tryna shut down my party. But now the real fun begins."

And one by one, every electronic device in the entire house capable of playback began playing the audio also. The little electronic picture frame on the mantle, the stereo in the corner, the television in the den on the far side of the dining room. It was enough to make even a sane person crazy, and John Harlan was far from sane.

"I said *enough!*" he screamed.

Steele took a deep breath and murmured sub-vocally, "If you're going to play your part, Breck, do it now."

Oh, I was so gonna do it.

The lights came back on, forcing people to shield their eyes. Harlan turned and saw Ridge strolling past the entrance to the dining room. "There!" he told Leo. "Catch that boy."

But by the time Leo turned to look, Ridge was gone. Leo looked at Harlan sadly. "Senator Harlan, based on what I saw on that tape and what I've witnessed tonight, I'm afraid I have to restrain you for your own protection." He took a step toward Harlan, but Harlan backed away.

I walked past the doorway to the kitchen, and Harlan spied me. "Him, over there!"

"He's over *there* now," Steele said skeptically. "Senator Harlan...does anyone know how long until the ambulance gets here?"

Ridge popped out of his hiding spot. Danny did too.

"Them! Him, too!" Harlan said, shouting at them.

I walked toward him. Harlan was nearly purple with rage, sweating profusely. It wouldn't be long now until he passed out completely, but before he did that, I wanted to make sure he knew exactly who he was dealing with. He wouldn't remember a fucking thing by the time the police arrived, but I needed to see recognition in his eyes right *now*.

"Are you talking about me, Senator Harlan?" I smiled sweetly. "Can I get you something? Some water, or…?"

I stepped closer to the senator and felt Steele tense as I passed him. I figured he was fighting some crazy-powerful instinct to grab me and physically put himself between me and Harlan, but he resisted.

"You," Harlan said, pointing a shaking finger at me. "I watched you die! I watched you bleed out just an hour ago!"

"Me?" I gasped, looking down at my pristine suit. "No, sir! Who did you kill?"

"You're a goddamn… goddamn *whore*," he managed to get out.

I smiled as angelically, as *sympathetically* as I could and took one last step, until I was within spitting distance of the man who'd hurt me, the man who'd practically killed Danny, the man who'd made me live in *fear*.

"I'm the goddamn whore who just helped rip your life to shreds," I whispered menacingly. "Goodbye, Senator Harlan."

Wes whistled, and the sound nearly pierced my eardrum. "And the Oscar for scariest motherfucker of the year goes to Breck Pfeiffer."

I turned to give Steele a triumphant smile, to say *Mission accomplished,* to tell him the dragon was defeated and I had a damn good idea of how we could move on with our lives.

But Harlan didn't get the memo that he was done.

The next thing I knew, I was jerked back by a bony – and fucking *shockingly strong* – hand in my hair.

"Stay back!" Harlan said. "All of you, stay back!"

Something sharp pressed into my back, and I gasped. "Knife!"

"Senator," Leo said gently. "You don't want to do this."

Harlan laughed maniacally. "You're all idiots. Every one of you." He stumbled back a pace, taking me with him, but managed to hold on to the knife and to me. "Clear a path!" he screamed. "And no fucking heroes. That goes double for you, Mickey!" he said, kicking a random man as we passed.

"I'm not *Mickey,*" the man cried, like that was really the worst thing happening here.

"Help me!" I cried, and the senator yanked my head back in retaliation.

Jesus Christ. I was going to cut every damn curl off my head when this was over.

I tried pulling away from him, elbowing him, throwing myself on the ground, but the fucker was *crazy* strong, like somehow the drug that was supposed to drop him like a sack of potatoes had given him superhuman powers, at least temporarily. Meanwhile, my brother, Danny, Leo, and the love of my life all watched me in horror, not sure how the fuck to get to me or whether it would enrage my captor further if they blew my cover by coming forward.

Harlan pulled me toward the basement stairs – the door to which I'd left *fucking open* when I'd come out of safety for my shot at vengeance. He pulled the door closed behind us.

"That will slow them down," he muttered to himself. And it would. It totally would.

Fuck.

He half-dragged me down the stairs with a strength I'd only seen in him one other time, the night he'd beaten me and Danny.

"Ridge! Get this fucking door open!" Steele bellowed. His voice was coated with panic and pain so corrosive, I felt like my own skin was being flayed by it.

"Let me go!" I begged Harlan. "Please."

I'd never gotten why people begged, in movies. I mean, the killer was hardly gonna let you go just because you'd asked him nicely. Wouldn't it be more dignified, I'd always thought, to just sorta be defiant and brave?

But there were men upstairs who loved me, and at least a couple more who liked me a fair amount. If Steele hadn't already gone into a full-fledged PTSD episode over Harlan taking me hostage, he was headed there soon. My brother would never forgive himself if anything happened to me, and Danny would probably go back to jumping at shadows.

There was more on the line here than my own life, and for *their* sakes, I'd beg.

"You're my ticket out of here." Harlan dragged me through the basement to an outside door and then through it. The damp summer air was absolutely still as we crossed a small lawn and ducked into a thick stand of trees.

"Are we heading toward the river?" I demanded, praying that Wes was still monitoring things.

"None of your fucking business," Harlan said. Then he completely confirmed my suspicion by continuing. "I'll dump your body in the water, just like Mickey was supposed to."

"You haven't killed anyone!" I reminded him, hoping that was true. "Don't start now! Remember, murder is a *sin*."

He ignored me.

My feet touched wood as he dragged me backward, and I realized that we were on the dock. It was now or never.

"You're a... you're a senator!" I told him. "You don't want this to be your legacy, do you?"

Somehow, miraculously, this seemed to reach him. Or maybe he was just getting tired of dragging me around, who knows? Whatever his reason, he threw me off the deck, into the muddy water near the shore, before he jumped into the boat.

I scrambled up the bank, back onto the grass, and sat on my ass watching the senator stumble across the deck to the captain's seat and try to get the engine started.

I thought for exactly half a second about playing superhero and jumping into the boat again, but no. There was just no way.

"You guys?" I panted, hoping my comms were still working. "I'm uh, I'm here. He let me go. I'm okay."

The boat's engine fired up and the ropes fell onto the dock with a hollow thud just as Steele, Ridge, and Leo came running across the lawn.

It was too late. The boat pulled into the river before they could reach it.

"Breck? Oh, Jesus *fuck*, Breck," Steele said, grabbing me up against him and smashing me into his chest. It was extremely uncomfortable, and I didn't care at all. Steele was practically shaking – or maybe *I* was shaking, and that was making him shake too. Either way, the only thing that made it better was by eliminating every millimeter of space between us.

"I'm sorry," I told him. "I let him get away."

"He won't get away." Leo pulled out his phone and started barking commands into it.

"You'd better be sorry, Brekkie," Ridge said, coming up next to us and laying his hand on my back. "Might not have been your fault, but I'm pretty sure you gave me a head full of gray hair tonight, and I swear to Christ, if you make me age before you do..."

Boom!

314 / A.E. WASP

The black sky flared orange like a fucking fireworks display. Steele's grip loosened, and I turned my face toward the river.

John Harlan's boat was on fire a few hundred feet from shore. We watched the senator jump into the water and flounder there.

***

"How did we not know he had a boat?" Wes asked sometime later that evening. We were sitting on the deck of the house next door, having narrowly escaped the senator's house with our spare clothes and contraband in the confusion before the police showed up and declared the whole fucking place a crime scene.

"We knew he had a boat," Leo said, tipping back his beer and stretching out his bare feet. "Fucking *Google* knew he had a boat. I just didn't think he'd try to rabbit. He had too much to lose."

Ridge sighed and propped his feet up on the railing. The light from the police boat out on the river was barely visible through the trees. "Remember this when we do the debrief," he said. "Next time, we incapacitate all modes of transportation. We remove the spark plugs. We flatten the bike tires."

Leo snorted. "Your automobile expertise is incredible."

Ridge threw a pretzel at him.

"I wonder where he thought he was going," Carson mused. He leaned his elbows on the railing and stared off into space, looking like the star of a fucking Versace ad. He was the only one of us still kitted out in his formal evening wear, and a martini glass dangled from his fingers, like he wasn't quite ready to shake his Ben Waters persona. "International waters?"

"In a boat that size?" Leo shook his head. "No way."

"Could happen! My money's on Mexico," Wes said. "That's where I'd go. Pretty senoritas. Cold margaritas... Basically all the -itas."

"Wow. Explain to me how you are, like, a savant when it comes to hacking systems and a total idiot when it comes to all other aspects of life?" Danny demanded, slapping at a mosquito that landed on his arm. He wore a pair of cutoff sweatpants and, as usual, nothing on top.

"Just part of my charm, Daniel."

"At least they caught him," I said softly. "And hopefully they'll have enough to hold him."

Steele, who was sitting beneath me on a wooden Adirondack chair, tightened his arms around me. He'd said hardly anything since he'd found me on the dock, and he hadn't let go of me for a second.

"They'll have enough when I'm done editing the video," Wes said with total confidence. "A nice highlight reel of everything we find from the tapes Ridge stole."

"Better than that, though, he lost his power." Carson turned to look at us. "You're going to email everyone on those tapes and tell them that he has no hold on them anymore, right?"

"That was the plan," Wes confirmed.

Carson nodded. "Then no one will help him. No one will pull strings. He'll be forced to step down. And I'll make it happen."

Leo frowned. "Ben Waters needs to take a long sabbatical from society," he warned. "He definitely doesn't need to get involved in this any further."

"Oh, Leo," Carson said with a grin. "You're adorable. Ben Waters won't do a damn thing. But *I* am not Ben Waters."

Steele gave a half-laugh and leaned his head back against the chair. "What I wanna know is, how the hell did the boat somehow get on fire? I thought for sure he was going to get away."

"Sometimes there are things that defy explanation, boys."

I sat up on Steele's lap and spun around to see Josie in the doorway from the deck to the house. She was wearing a sleek, black tank top and a pair of jeans, and her wet hair was slicked back into a bun.

"Josie? What are you doing here?" Leo jumped up from his seat to stare at her. I'm pretty sure we all were.

"They do let me leave Florida occasionally," she joked.

"Yes, but how did you even know where we were staying, when we..."

"I came north to visit a friend," Josie said, sidestepping his question. She stepped aside and a gorgeous blonde in a bikini appeared in the doorway beside her. "Guys, meet Greta. Greta, these are my boys."

"Why, *hello,* Greta," Wes said with a devilish grin. Danny smacked him on the back of the head.

"Hey! What the hell was that for?" Wes demanded.

Danny folded his arms over his chest and glared at him. "Let's consider it proactive punishment. You're guaranteed to do *something* dickish in the next ten minutes."

"Pleased to meet you," Greta said in halting English. Then she addressed Josie in a language that sounded like Russian. Maybe.

Josie laughed delightedly, like Greta had told a joke. "In just a minute, doll," she answered in English, putting her hand on Greta's arm.

"Boys, not sure it's a good idea for y'all to hang around here all night," Josie told us. "Not while they're searching for the folks who ruined the senator's party and set fire to his boat. A heist is only as good as the getaway."

"Nah, it's fine. None of us had anything to do with the senator's boat," Ridge told her, relaxing back in his seat again. "Not a damn thing."

"Oh, well, how nice for you," Josie retorted angrily. She set her hands on her hips and shook her head like she couldn't believe Ridge's attitude. "But *somebody* did, Ridge Pfeiffer. Somebody decent and kind and... probably really, *really* beautiful... who had only the best intentions when they did you that favor. Now, we may never know who that person is, and we certainly don't know where they are right now, but I'm confident that person would appreciate it if your ass wasn't hanging out on this porch where it would throw suspicion on them. I really think it's only fair that you consider *them* right now, Ridge."

Ridge frowned in confusion. "But, Josie, that doesn't make any sense. Wouldn't they..."

"I accept your apology for being selfish," Josie said, holding up a hand to cut Ridge off. "Say no more."

"But..."

"No need to bring it up again. You're forgiven." She clapped her hands once. "Now! It just so happens I called in a favor and got a couple unmarked police cars parked out front, ready to take us to the airport. Plus, I called ahead and told the pilot to get Charlie's plane ready for us. Who wants to be back home by sunrise? Mimosas and Bellinis on the beach?"

I couldn't deny, the idea had definite appeal. I wanted to sleep with Steele wrapped around me, I wanted to wake up in his arms, and I wanted to see the sunrise with him, tomorrow and every day.

"I'm down," I said.

"Then I am, too," Steele agreed.

"Sounds lovely," Carson said.

"Yep. Whatever." Leo tipped back the rest of his beer. "No preference."

"But, Josie, I still don't understand..." Ridge said, shaking his head.

Josie clapped her hands again and smiled broadly. "Excellent! I love it when a decision is unanimous. Now, shake a leg, boys!" She darted back into the house but paused on the threshold and swiveled to face us. "I'm really proud of you, you know. All of you. And Charlie would be, too." Then she turned back to the house and disappeared, with Greta following after her.

"What the *hell* is going on?" Ridge demanded as we all slowly vacated our seats and moved toward the door.

"I'm not entirely sure," Carson said slowly. "And my Slovenian's a little rusty. But I'm pretty sure Greta just asked Josie where to put the rest of the fireworks."

WHEN BRECK and I finally emerged from the house about eighteen hours after we'd arrived home, once I'd thoroughly examined every inch of his skin inside and out, we were greeted by applause, hoots, and hollers from the motley group of professional cons sprawled out on the Adirondack chairs around the fire pit.

Orange flames cast flickering shadows across their faces and the aromatic smoke blended with the sea scent of the night.

Breck bowed even as he blushed from the bruise marks on his neck to the ones on his ribs. (I'd done a lot of my examining with my mouth. *A lot.*)

Leo tossed me a water bottle. "You've got to be dehydrated."

I would have said something cutting if I weren't sucking down the blessedly cold liquid without stopping for air.

Breck dropped himself onto Danny's lap and motioned for Leo to toss him one, too. "The doc recommended bed rest," he said, draping an arm around Danny's neck. As usual, the kid was shirtless. I was beginning to wonder if he actually owned any shirts.

"What doctor?" Wesley asked, flicking a beer bottle cap across the blazing fire at Breck.

Danny knocked the cap out of the air with a *wa-pow* sound. "I got *mad* Ninja skills."

"I think Breck means Doctor *Luuuurve*," Josie said with a wave of her giant wine glass.

"Looking very old Hollywood, Miss Josie," I told her. Her ivory satin nightgown and feather trimmed, high-heeled sandals looked like the kind of thing the women wore in the movies my mama liked to watch. I'd bet she and Josie would get along. Maybe one day I'd get up the nerve to visit her. *Maybe.*

"Give me my boyfriend," I said to Danny.

"But he smells so nice." Danny snuffled at Breck's neck, making my boy laugh brightly. A weight had lifted off both of their shoulders, and it was really great to see them joking and laughing.

I lifted Breck and carried him over to an empty chair next to one that, to my surprise, contained a very casually dressed Miranda Bosley. "Ms. Bosley. I didn't expect to see you here."

"How could I miss the celebration of your first successful mission?" She twirled her champagne flute delicately between her fingers. "Are you going to sit down, or just stand there holding Mr. Pfeiffer all night?"

The woman flustered me. Blushing, I set Breck down in the seat. I really hoped she hadn't been around during our sex-athon. I'd been told I could be loud, and Breck wasn't shy about telling me exactly what he wanted and how he wanted it.

The sparkle in her eye told me she probably *had* been there.

I needed a drink. "Give me a beer, Bond."

Wes shook his head. "It's a whisky night, according to the bartender." He lifted his heavy tumbler in Josie's direction, and I saw her trusty bar-cart tucked next to one of the brick pillars holding up the deck.

"Sit down," Josie said. "I'll get you one."

It was a gorgeous night, and the fire added a warmth that went beyond simple heat. There was something about sitting around a campfire with friends that satisfied the deep, caveman part of my brain. We weren't quite friends, yet, but there was definitely respect and a level of trust being built up. Any of these guys would have my back against a saber-toothed tiger attack, though Josie and Miranda would probably be the ones to kill it. Without dropping their drinks.

"So what did we miss today?" I took the seat on the other side of Breck, reaching blindly for his hand. His fingers intertwined with mine.

"Well," Wes said, crossing his legs. "Against my objections, we turned the Senator's treasure-trove of blackmail material over to the individuals affected by his illicit recording activities."

"Wasn't that the plan?" Danny said.

He really was an innocent underneath the thin veneer of street dirt that covered but couldn't eliminate his innate sweetness. The only way that kid was going back to the street was over my dead body.

From the confused glares Wesley keep shooting at him, I thought I wouldn't be alone in my objections.

"Yeah, but people would have paid big bucks to get those tapes back," Ridge said with a pat on the kid's arm. "And we just handed them over with a smile."

"We're good guys, now." Wesley announced with a smile and a toast of his glass.

"Pretty sure I always was," Leo commented wryly.

"Oh, me, too," Wesley assured him sincerely.

We sat without speaking, listening to the crackle of the fire, the susurrations of the waves rolling onto the beach, and the screeching of the cicadas. The smoky whisky went down smoothly, warming me from the inside. Between the multiple orgasms over the past day and the alcohol right now, I slipped into a light daze, letting the conversation roll over me. Memories of other fires, other nights, and other friends tickled the edges of my mind with a combination of happiness and sorrow.

A soft touch to my arm pulled me back to the present.

"Mr. Alvarez, come take a walk with me." Miranda smiled and nodded toward the pool, and I stood up to follow. Miranda's fingers trailed across Josie's shoulders as she walked by her chair.

Breck watched us leave.

Miranda was barefoot, and she took a step down into the hot tub that jutted out from the main pool. I watched the shadows of the ripples dance across the bottom of the tub.

"What are you going to do now, Mr. Alvarez?" She sipped her champagne.

I sat down next to her, sighing as the warm water enveloped my feet. "Please, call me Steele."

"Will you call me Miranda?"

"Will I get the chance?"

"That's completely up to you." She kicked her feet slowly and leaned back on her hand. "Charlie loved this hot tub," she said with a small smile. "I always knew where to find him when I came by. Sometimes I still feel like he's here with me. Seeing you guys take care of his jobs helps with that, so thank you."

I narrowed my eyes. "But my part in this is done?" I didn't know what answer I wanted to hear.

"You did what Charlie needed you to do. The reports you were worried about have been taken care of. As far as the U.S. Army is concerned, the incident in Afghanistan never happened."

"I wish it never had," I admitted.

I'd expected to feel better at hearing this. All this time, I'd been waiting for the sword to fall, waiting to be called out or possibly being taken out like the loose end I was. Now, that was never going to happen.

Miranda laid a comforting hand on my knee. "Charlie understood that better than you know."

She seemed ten years younger out here under the moon than she had the first time we'd met.

"Is that why he set up all this...?" I waved a hand back to the crowd.

She laughed and drained the last of her drink. "I don't know why Charlie did anything he ever did. I don't think even *he* knew what the hell he was doing half the time. But he liked you, you know."

"What?" A bat fluttered overhead, feasting on the bugs attracted by the pool lights. "I barely spoke to him."

"The most important skill for a con man is being able to read people quickly and accurately. Charlie was the best I'd ever seen at reading people. Better than me." She shook her head as if she had thought that was impossible. "He hand-picked each of you because he saw something in you. A goodness."

I pondered that for a few minutes. "So, this is some kind of *present* from him?"

She looked pointedly at the grand mansion behind us and the luxury at our feet. Josie's laughter drifted towards us over the deeper rumble of men's voices.

"If I leave, do I get to keep the AmEx?" I asked with a grin.

"Sadly, no. But if you do chose to leave, you will be more than adequately compensated for your time." She stood up, shaking the water off her feet. "You'll be compensated 'up the wazoo,' as Charlie's will stipulates. I do hope you will consider staying, though. There is more work to do. And those men need you."

I looked up at her. "And it's all going to be like this? Bringing down the bad guys by using other bad guys?"

"I don't know any more than you do. Remember, I'm just Charlie's emissary here, making sure his instructions are carried out. But if I had to guess, I'd say it definitely involved bringing down bad guys...and maybe figuring out that none of *you* are bad guys." She rested her hand on my shoulder and gave it a strong squeeze. "The offer to stay applies to Breck, too. I'm sure we can find plenty to keep him busy as well. Think about it and tell me in the morning." She left wet footprints behind her as she walked away.

I stared up at the moon as it played hide and seek with the thin cloud cover.

I felt Breck come up behind me. He sat down, leaning against me, and I hugged him close.

"Hey." He turned his face up for a kiss, his lips still slightly swollen from all the previous kisses I'd given him. He tasted like whisky.

"So, everything good?" He kicked his feet in the warm water the same way Miranda had.

I nodded. "Yeah. Everything's taken care of."

"How does that make you feel?"

I looked up at the sky and thought about it. "I don't really know."

"I get that, believe me. I really do." He leaned against me. I wanted to stay in the moment forever and not have to face the hard decisions, danger, loss, and whatever other bullshit the future was going to throw at us. But time and tide waited for no man, and I could feel both slipping away from me.

"What are you going to do now?" Breck asked quietly.

"That's what Miranda asked me, too."

"Hmm. And what did you tell her?"

"What are *you* going to do?" I asked, answering his question with my own and taking the coward's way out.

He pulled away just so he could give me an inscrutable look. "Well, that partially depends on you."

My heart skipped a beat. That was one of the most terrifying things I'd ever heard, and one of the best. "I want to stay with you." Admitting that was the bravest thing I've ever done.

His smile blinded me. "I want to stay with you, too. It's not going to be easy, baby. I can be kind of a dick. Ridge and I have more in common than just incredibly good looks."

"Rumor has it, I can be pretty difficult to live with, too." I pulled him against me, kissing him. I missed the taste of the whisky in his mouth, so I urged him to take another sip.

"Are you trying to get me drunk and take advantage of me?"

"Sweetcheeks, I couldn't take advantage of you again tonight if you begged me."

His eyebrows rose, and with an evil grin he slid his hand up the leg of my shorts. "Really? Not even if I begged?" His fingers were cool on my skin as he tickled the hairs on my leg. "I thought you liked it when I begged."

I groaned. "You're going to kill me."

"And you're going to love it."

"Fuck yeah, I will," I breathed.

He pulled his hand out of my shorts and leaned his elbows on his knees. "But first, I want to apologize for fighting with you before the mission."

"It's over and done," I told him. "No use rehashing it. And you apologized already."

"Over the comms, when you were about to shoot me? Feels like a lame apology. And besides, I wasn't really sorry then."

I snorted. "Oh yeah?"

"I mean, I was sorry to be fighting with you. I hated having that hanging over us when we had a job to do, and I was sorry I got angry, but I didn't get it. Even then."

I frowned. "Explain."

"You said that you wanted to keep me safe. That was your priority. And I was trying to convince you that it was more important to take down Harlan and protect other people. I wasn't really thinking about what you'd been through with Asadi, or what you'd go through again if something happened to me." He took a deep breath, and his big blue eyes met mine in the moonlight. "I'm not saying that I would do anything different. I still who want. to be there. It felt so fucking good to look that bastard in the eye and tell him to fuck off . But I should have tried harder to under-stand your position, the way you tried to understand mine."

"Give and take," I told him. "It's not going to be easy, you and me."

"But it's worth it. And now we're free, both of us, to make a new start."

"That does sound nice. Does making a new start mean no more escorting for you?" I suppose I should have said I didn't give a shit if he chose to keep doing it. Hell, I'd never been the jealous type in the past, and I knew the difference between what Breck and I had and meaningless sex. But surprise, surprise, I found I *was* the jealous type, so I wasn't gonna say any of that.

Breck sighed. "I can't say I loved it, but it did make some really good money. I know you want me to quit."

"I want you to quit not because I judge any of it. It's just too dangerous. Unless I'm in the room, I can't really protect you. And even then, I can't prevent it. I can only avenge you. I can only hurt the people who hurt you."

"Like Harlan."

"Like Harlan."

Breck sighed. "I don't want to go back to college, and I want to stay with you. That's what I *know*. But I'm never going to be your button-sewer, Steele. So what are my options here?"

"Miranda said she wants you on the team, if you want."

His jaw dropped. "Really? She wants me to help? And we get to take down more assholes like Harlan?"

I shrugged. "Who knows? She could ask us to do anything from picking up trash off the beach to taking down a small nation. But, yeah, she implied very heavily that there would be more taking down of the bad guys."

"Vengeance will be ours?" he said with a smile.

I sighed heavily. "I guess."

"What's so bad about getting a little vengeance, baby? We stopped Harlan from hurting any more people. That's a good thing." He stood up, staring down at me with his hands on his hips. Even scowling at me, he was so beautiful, with his blond curls hanging down around his face and his strong, slender body. I reached for his hand. He took it suspiciously, but he let me pull him back down.

"I'm thrilled we took him down. And I can't deny it felt good. But vengeance." I shook my head. "It's never enough. It doesn't undo the hurt, it can't erase the memories. I'd rather try to keep you from getting hurt in the first place."

"I could die crossing the street."

Of course he was arguing with me. I had a feeling that was going to be a very common occurrence. "I know. But you do what you can to prevent it, right? You look both ways before you cross the street. You assess the traffic and make your decisions based on the most likely scenarios. You cross at the green, not in between."

Breck raised his eyebrows and smiled.

I mock glowered at him. "You do cross at the green, right? No jaywalking?"

He crossed his heart with a finger. "From now on, I promise. No jaywalking."

I pulled him onto my lap, and he ended up straddling me, his arms over my shoulders. He leaned in and kissed me long and slow. My hands went to his hips, thumbs stroking the soft skin of his abdomen. Maybe I *could* take advantage of him one more time. If I ate something.

He nipped at my lip and then pulled away. "You worry too much."

"No such thing," I said. "Do you know how easy it is for someone to kill another person? If you don't care about the consequences, you can walk up to pretty much anyone and shoot them. Stab them. You can shoot them from across the street if you're good enough. If you pick someone at random, someone you have no connection to, there's a good chance you could get away with it."

Breck pushed my hair back from my face, staring into my eyes. "But how do you watch out for that? You can't go through life assuming everyone is going to kill you."

I slide my hand up the back of his shirt. It was going to be a long time before I stopped needing to touch him to make sure he was still there with me. "Sure you can. *I* can. I'm a paranoid bastard, and I have all the best training Uncle Sam could provide."

He grinned. "But it sounds like you'd have to be around me all the time if you want to keep me safe."

"Probably, just to be sure. It's safest."

"Well, I guess I can live with that. So we're staying in Florida? Forced to live surrounded by all this luxury?" He bent down and trailed his fingers in the warm water, then flicked them at me.

"Looks like," I agreed. "For a little while anyway."

"Good. Besides, don't you want to see if Wes and Danny end up fighting or fucking?"

I laughed. "Nope. They're going to do both eventually."

"Yeah, but which one *first?* My money's on fighting, and the winner depends on how much of a shit Wes is beforehand."

"I'll take that bet. They're gonna fuck before they fight. Wes looks like he wants to throw the kid down on any flat or semi-flat surface and show him how well a gamer can handle his joystick."

Breck giggled.

"Want me to open it up to the other guys?" I asked. After all, now that Breck and I were firmly together, we'd need something else for everyone to gossip over.

"Yeah, just don't tell Josie," Breck said. "She'll rig it somehow so she wins."

Too fucking true.

My stomach growled loudly. Breck laughed again and slid off my lap. I whined, reaching for him, but he slapped my hands away. *"That's* what I forgot. I came here to tell you Josie said there's food. If you want."

"Oh, I want." I stood up and reached for him again, avoiding his slapping hands. "I want a lot of things, Mr. Pfeiffer. Starting with food, and maybe a new room. A bigger one. We're gonna need a lot of privacy."

Breck draped his arms over my shoulders and grinned. "Greedy, greedy, Mr. Alvarez."

"I'm a professional con," I reminded him. "Wanting more goes with the territory." I ran my hand down the smooth skin of his back and felt him shiver in response. Alive, whole, healthy, and grinning up at me with that devilish angel's smile. "But if there's one thing Charlie's ploy taught me, Brekkie, it's that there's only one thing I *need*. And as long as I have you, I'm satisfied."

Breck's eyes got watery. "I'm going to allow that disgusting sentiment just this one time because we're having a moment," he said. But the way he sniffled while he said it took away any sting. "Now shut up and kiss me again."

And so I did, all the while wishing that Charlie Bingham, wherever he was floating, was as happy as I was right then.

THE RECESSED lighting in the kitchen cabinets threw just enough light for me to read the labels on the bottles on Josie's precious bar cart. Bourbon, whisky, rye, whiskey with an *e*, Japan, Kentucky, Scotland, Charlie certainly had the fermented mash family covered. I was tempted to drink the Jack Daniels I'd found only because I knew it would have Charlie rolling over in his grave. I could almost hear him bitching at me.

Jesus, Shook, why do you treat yourself like this? Who hurt you as a child? Live a little.

I reached for the Johnny Walker Blue. High end and yet somehow common, it felt like the perfect thing to drink in memory of the slippery thief. Whoever had said crime didn't pay had never lived on a government salary. Sure, I had great benefits and job security, but I was starting to seriously question if it was worth all the bullshit and bureaucracy.

I dragged a chair over so I could put my feet up on the rail. Tilting the chair onto its back legs, I stared at the moonlight dancing on the Gulf. After twelve years bouncing around field offices in Texas and Arizona, Florida's humidity was hard to get used to. What was I even doing here in Florida? In this house?

The answer to both of those questions was the same: chasing Charlie.

Three years ago, I'd transferred to Miami office as the noose around Charlie had tightened. Ten years after this guy, and we were so close. Then the moron had gone and gotten himself killed.

I could leave. Unlike everyone else here, Charlie had nothing on me. There was no blackmail material, no Sword of Damocles hanging over my head. Well, at least none that wasn't of my own making. No. I was even more pathetic. I was here of my own volition. All because of a letter. That fucking letter. Handwritten in Charlie's Catholic school script on Bigolb stationery, it had come in the mail the same day I'd found out about his death. I'd read it through twice, then put in for a leave of absence.

My dearest Leo, he'd written. Even now, I had to laugh at that. *It looks like we're destined never to meet again. Now I'll never get that second date. I guess should have let you catch me after all, but I liked knowing you were out there, watching me. Watching over me. You were my safety net. I knew if things ever got too out of control, I could call you and you would come for me. At the time, the price was more than I was willing to pay. Now it looks like I've paid the ultimate price.*

My second biggest regret is the work I have left undone. Work I couldn't do while I was alive. I know playing by the rules frustrates you as much as it did me, albeit in a different way, maybe. Make a dead man happy. Come to the funeral. I think you'll be pleasantly surprised. And if I have seriously misread you, and you're hoping I'm roasting on a spit in hell somewhere, then think of it as a parting gift. Three of the FBI's most wanted, and a fourth I've had eye on for quite some time, gift wrapped for you. All I ask is that you wait a few days to arrest them. Wait until when? You'll know.

The rest of the letter got a little more personal. I kept it folded up in my wallet like a teenaged girl, but I couldn't think of a better hiding place.

The whiskey went down smoothly as I sipped it and watched a bat swooping crazy patterns in the air as it feasted on mosquitoes. With a sigh, I scratched at a bite on my leg with my bare foot.

I missed my cowboy boots. What would my life have been like if I had chosen to stay on the rodeo circuit instead of cutting my losses and heading for the Bureau? Been a long time now since I'd been on a horse. Longer still since I'd tried for eight seconds on a bull.

As if someone had read my mind, Toby Keith's "Should Have Been a Cowboy" blasted from my phone. Not my old phone, the new phone Miranda insisted we use with a phone number known only to a handful of people, all of whom were inside this house.

I glared at the phone, ready to send the caller to voicemail hell when I saw the caller name.

The display read: *Pick up the damn phone, Shook.* A pre-programmed number, then. Wesley?

"Wesley, I swear to God if you're calling me because you're out of Doritos and Mountain Dew, I will kick your ass to Mexico."

"Such a delightfully macho threat, Agent Shook. Is that FBI-approved?" The masculine voice on the other end of the connection sounded smoothly amused.

"Who the fuck is this?"

"I'm a friend of Charlie's. A friend with a vested interested in seeing that his final wishes are carried out."

Really? Who spoke like that? He sounded like Carson when he was trying to be British. "Listen, Masterpiece Theatre, Charlie didn't have any friends. So drop the shitty accent and tell me why I shouldn't hang up on you." Wesley had the phones set up to automatically trace and record all incoming calls, so I should be able to find out where this bozo was calling from.

"Jeez, Leo," he said in a normal voice. I'd put the accent at somewhere in the Middle Atlantic States. Nothing as distinctive as Boston or Brooklyn, but definitely somewhere north of the Mason-Dixon Line and east of the Mississippi River. "The guy's dead. Can't you show a little respect?"

I took a long sip. "Fine," I said finally. "Charlie, *may he rest in peace,* had no friends. Now who the fuck is this?"

"Call me Mr. X."

I almost snorted two hundred dollar a bottle whiskey out of my nose. "Not gonna do that. How about I call you Buddy?"

"You can call me Al, for all I care. All I want to know is your opinion of tonight's events."

Al sounded annoyed. I think he cared more than he let on. Poor guy. I was too tired for this shit. All I wanted was to drink, go to bed, block out the sounds of Steele and Breck doing what they couldn't seem to stop doing, and fall asleep wondering what the fuck I was still doing here. "It went fine."

"Don't bullshit me, Shook. I know you must have loved seeing that dirty politician screw himself over."

I snorted. That had been sweet. Harlan was exactly the kind of scum I itched to take down, but assholes like him always seemed to weasel out of everything. They had connections, money, and leverage.

Much like Charlie himself. I guess it really did take a thief to catch a thief.

I uncrossed my legs and let my feet fall heavily to the ground. "Look, Buddy. I'm not gonna lie. I loved it. And the team worked great. I wouldn't have believed it, but I had have to give Charlie that much. He assembled a perfect group to get the job done. What I don't get is why?"

"Why, what?"

"Why is he doing this? Why did he care? Why did he want to be some kind of posthumous Robin Hood?"

"Do you know how Charlie made his fortune?"

"I'm going to go out on a limb and say crime."

"Information. The real money and power in this world is in information, and Charlie was an information broker. He bought and sold knowledge, gossip, plans, a piece at a time. Sometimes in the course of finding out one thing, he'd find out about other things. Bad things being done by bad people. He took care of what he could, but most of the time he couldn't act on this information, not alone. And I think he was hoping that by ensuring that as many of these things as possible could be set right, in the next life he would be granted the peace he never did achieve in this one."

"Charlie never struck me as a particularly religious man. And I like to think I knew him better than most."

"That you did, I assure you. You knew him better than his own mother."

"That's not a high bar." Charlie's mother had abandoned him in a Wal-Mart when he was seven. I knew. I was an expert on all things Charlie-related.

"You don't have to be religious to be a good man, Leo. Charlie cared about things. He didn't seem like it, but he did."

I knew that, too, but I kept it to myself.

"But maybe Charlie just got lucky," Al said.

"I don't think Charlie ever just got lucky. The man was brilliant."

There was a long pause. "I think Charlie would be thrilled to hear you say that."

"And you know, he does have Miranda and Josie on his side. Miranda is terrifyingly competent. And Josie is a woman of many talents. Some of them even legal."

Al laughed. "Isn't she great? My advice is stay on her good side. You wouldn't like her when she's angry."

I snorted a laugh, almost sending some whiskey down the wrong pipe. "Now I have this image of Josie all green like the Hulk."

"Has she told you about how she and Charlie met?"

"Kind of. Said they were working on separate cons at the same place, same time."

"Technically, that's true. Why don't you grab a refill, and I'll tell you the whole story."

"How do you know I'm drinking?"

"Please, Agent Shook."

I could hear him rolling his eyes. I liked his voice, it was almost as smooth as the whiskey. "Fine. If I'm so predictable, tell me what I'm drinking."

"Hmm. Let me think." I heard the sound of ice cubes hitting the bottom of a glass, then something being poured. "I'm going to say some Johnny Walker Blue."

"Damn, you're good." I rolled the glass between my palms, and then went back into the kitchen, closing the sliding door behind me.

"Charlie told me that particular bottle always made him think of you."

"Why?" I gave myself a generous refill.

"He didn't say." Al launched into a long, detailed story of Charlie and Josie's meeting that had me laughing so hard, I was afraid I would wake up half the house.

I had no idea who this interested party was, but I liked hearing him talk about Charlie.

Part of the reason I'd taken the leave of absence was because I knew I'd gotten too wrapped up in Charlie. He fascinated me. He did everything with a signature flair, a brazen flaunting of his skills that rivaled any comic book super villain. He wasn't one to hide his illegal light under a bushel. And he never had been one to hurt innocent people.

I'd read over every scrap of information any law enforcement agency in the world had on Charlie, and most of his victims had been, as Al had so succinctly put it, bad people doing bad things. Granted, he had profited off those bad things rather than stopping them, but still. He wasn't a saint by any means, but I'd rather spend time with someone like him than some sociopath who'd murdered his family or wiped out a school.

My preferences hadn't gone unnoticed, and rumors had started to circulate that maybe I wasn't trying as hard as I could to capture Charlie. Maybe I had gone soft on him.

Maybe they were right.

I also hated hearing Al's stories. "Wow," I said, interrupting him mid-anecdote and pacing the dark kitchen. "Sounds like there was a whole part of Charlie I never knew about. I guess he did have friends after all."

"Charlie chose you to lead this team because you knew him better than anyone. And he appointed me to watch over you, because he cares about you."

Yes. Well. Moving on. "So where are you hiding, then?"

"Oh, here and there. Miranda keeps me updated. It was my idea to have Josie and one of her many special friends meet you in D.C."

"Thank you for that. But why aren't you here with us getting your hands dirty?"

Al laughed. "I don't need to get on your radar any more than I already am. I have too much respect for your skills, Agent Shook."

"So you're a criminal?"

"You might say that." He chuckled, soft and deep. "But then again, you are too now, Shook."

I couldn't argue with that.

"It's very late, Leo. Why don't you get some sleep? Soon, it'll be time for your next assignment. The men are going to need your professional help on this one."

"Great. Can you give me any hints?"

"You might want to ask Josie some hints on making cocktails. And buy yourself another bathing suit. Something sexy."

I laughed out loud. "I can't wait."

"Goodnight, Leo."

"Goodnight, Al."

I watched the waves rolling onto the shore for a long time after I hung up.

THE END

Get your **fake boyfriend** fix with PROS & CONS OF
DECEPTION (PROS & CONS #2)

FAKE IT TIL YOU MAKE IT, isn't that what they say?
Every time hacker Wesley Bond so much as looks at
Danny's smirking expression, the can't decide whether he
wants to kiss him or punch him. Pretending to be boyfriends
with gorgeous, vulnerable, much too young for him ex-
hustler will drive him insane. But if they want to take down
the bad guy, they're going to have to find a way to work
together.

"Hey, can anyone explain why my shirt drawer is empty?" Ridge Pfeiffer demanded, appearing on the patio where the rest of our little band had congregated. Our resident retrievals expert (read: *thief*) was naked from the waist up and scowling beneath his blue eyes and blond curls like the world's most overgrown, pissed-off Botticelli angel.

I pulled down my sunglasses to look at him, then slid them back up so I could focus on my phone screen. Right now, I was engaged in a long-term bout of spear phishing at Campbell Enterprises, and I was about to close the deal. This was way more interesting than anything Ridge was likely to share.

Janie, I typed, *I'm on a plane with Dal Anderson and he wants a four-paragraph summary of Thursday's press release so we can prepare talking points for the investors!! Can't access the secure server from here and I'm fah-reaking OUT!! Send me something? – Becks*

There. That ought to do it.

Becks, aka Rebecca Frankel, Junior Executive Assistant to the VP of Human Resources at Campbell, according to her LinkedIn profile, was adorably naïve and helpful. For example, when a friendly IT man had called the other day and asked for her credentials to verify a "suspicious login" from her site, she'd provided all the necessary info. Hell, if I'd asked for her astrological sign and social security number, she'd probably have given me that too.

Once I'd accessed her email, I'd had the keys to the castle. It had been easy to copy her writing style – hyper-friendly, with way too many exclamation points for a person over the age of thirteen – to learn that she was going on a business trip with her boss this week, and to find that she was smoke-break buddies with Jane DeVoor, Assistant to the CFO. As soon as Jane emailed back a summary of Thursday's press release to help her pal out, I'd make a few quick investment decisions like I'd somehow learned to predict the future.

Hint: Ditch your psychic friends and go phishing instead.

"Um, would we say the drawer is really empty, though?" Breck, Ridge's identical twin, asked from the lounge chair where he was stretched out in the sun practically on top of his boyfriend, Steele Alvarez.

"Close enough. The only things left are a pink tank top that says *I Would Bottom You So Hard* and this Pittsburgh Steelers t-shirt." Ridge held it up. "Neither of them is mine, and frankly I don't feel comfortable wearing either."

"Hey!" Carson exclaimed from the shade at the edge of the patio. "That Pittsburgh shirt is mine. I'd wondered what happened to it!"

"Well, you can fucking have it, dude," Ridge said, holding it out. "I don't know how it ended up in my drawer."

"Come bring it to me," Carson commanded, adding the little world-weary British inflection to his voice that seemed to drive all the boys wild. "I don't want to get out in the sun."

"Are you an actual vampire? Or is that just what you're impersonating this week?" Leo drawled. The FBI-agent-on-hiatus who liked to consider himself our leader barely looked up from his e-reader, which I happened to know contained nothing but dull biographies of politicians and a couple non-fiction books about religious extremism. *Ho-hum.*

"Yes, Leonard. That's it. I'm afraid you won't be able to resist my dazzling sparkles and century-old penis if I come any closer." Carson nodded thanks at Ridge as Ridge passed him the shirt. "You know, some of us are concerned about skin cancer."

Uh huh. I'd bet my original custom Alienware rig and all the classic games loaded thereon – current value: priceless – that Leo was on the right track. Carson was a con man with a dozen identities that we knew of and probably a dozen more we didn't. No doubt he was working a gig that required him to be pale as a ghost, though fuck if I could imagine what it was. Not for the first time, I was tempted to peek at the man's computer – child's play for any decent hacker, and I was way more than decent.

I wouldn't hack Carson, though, even to satisfy my curiosity, because of *trust* and *boundaries* and *being a team player*, and all the other happy horse shit my Aunt Ade had hammered into me. Blah, blah, blah.

"Can we back up the bus to the part where Angel-Face isn't comfortable wearing the Bottom t-shirt?" Steele began. The muscle of our operation paused as he realized what he'd said, then he started to chuckle. "Heh. Back up the bus."

Breck giggled like it was his job, and I rolled my eyes behind my glasses because Steele's joke didn't even make sense, let alone make me laugh. Must be nice to have someone appreciate your dumb jokes and agree with you all the time.

"Yep. There's nothing as hilarious as making assumptions about someone's sexual preferences based on their appearance," Danny bitched from his chair. As usual, he was lounging around in nothing but a Speedo as if clothes were against his religion. "You two are so cutesy. It's nauseating."

"Spoken like a guy who hasn't gotten laid in way too long." Ridge leered at Danny in a totally unconvincing way. "I could help you with that."

Danny didn't even open his eyes. "All set, thanks. Meet Lefty, my new boyfriend." He held up his left hand. "He knows exactly how I like it, he gets the job done, and he's always there when I need him." What he didn't say, because we all knew, was that Lefty was unlikely to assault him and abuse his trust like now-disgraced Senator John Harlan had, when Danny and Breck had been working as rent boys up in D.C.

"Aw. I think that's kinda sad," Breck said.

"And I think fuck you," Danny returned easily.

I ducked my head to hide my smile. What was it about Danny Munroe that got me? I mean, aside from the fact that subtle smartassery was my catnip and that the forty acres of smooth, tanned skin and lean muscles he displayed made me want to...

"Fuck both of you. Can we get back to the part where I have been stolen from?" Ridge demanded. "I mean, you think you're in a relatively protected environment, you think your shit is safe where you left it, and then suddenly, you find that things you care about are missing. I feel... violated."

There was absolute silence on the patio as each of us turned to look at Ridge. Leo put down his Kindle. Danny sat up and opened his eyes. Breck and Steele stopped eye-fucking. Carson leaned forward.

Ridge blinked, then tilted his head to the side, as though considering what he'd said. He shook his head. "No. Nope. This is not irony, you assholes. I have never stolen a man's shirts."

"Only because you couldn't get a fair price for them," Carson sighed, sitting back in his seat.

"Shook, you're an investigator. Find what happened to my shirts!"

"Sure," Leo said, swiping his finger across his screen like he couldn't possibly give less of a fuck. "Let's make a list of suspects. Who could wear your crappy shirts?"

"Well, me," Ridge said. "Danny, but God knows he doesn't wear shirts anyway." Danny snorted. "Wes, I guess." He looked at me. "But he doesn't have my taste. Or *any* taste.

And then there's, uh..." He looked at Breck and narrowed his eyes.

"Rather than stealing," Breck said, licking his lips, "which is such a harsh word, maybe it would help you to think of it as liberation?"

"You stole my shirts!" Ridge roared. "Jesus Christ. My own *brother*?"

"Well, I didn't have my own for a while, while all my stuff was back in D.C., and then... um... I guess I decided I liked yours better?" Breck grinned winningly.

"You couldn't borrow shirts from your boyfriend?"

"No. I mean... have you seen my boyfriend?" Breck ran a hand across the massive expanse of Steele's chest while Steele smirked like the smug bastard he was.

"*You* are a shithead, Breck Mason Pfeiffer," Ridge announced. "I expect my shirts back in my possession within the hour, or a reign of terror will commence the likes of which you have never seen."

Breck stuck out his tongue.

"See, all of this could be solved if you guys would only embrace nudity," Danny said sleepily. "Free the pecs."

I snorted under my breath, but of course, Danny heard me and lifted his head to give me a dirty look.

Jesus. Say one shitty little thing about a guy being a prostitute and suddenly he was giving me crap over every breath I exhaled, riding my ass day and night.

And not in the fun way.

There were times when I really didn't get what the fuck I was doing here. I mean, yeah, sure, Charlie had some dirt on me that I *really* didn't want to get out. But unlike the rest of these guys, I figured I had some dirt on Charlie, too. He'd been an information *broker*, but I specialized in information *acquisition*. I could find some shit on Charlie's companies— or make some up if I had to—that would invalidate anything he had on me. I could plant enough evidence to have Miranda arrested for being a high-profile madam – and no lie, the idea amused the hell out of me – before she could turn me in to the authorities. Hell, I could get each of these guys locked up without breaking a sweat.

And even though I liked them better now than I had in the beginning, sometimes it was hard to remember why I'd given up my cushy little set-up back in Elm Lawn to come down to the Island of Misfit Criminals.

I'd never exactly played well with others.

"Mail call!" Josie yelled, walking out onto the patio.

As usual, everyone turned at the sound of Josie's voice, primarily because the woman always seemed to be bringing us tasty food or alcoholic beverages. After a few weeks, the Pavlovian response had already been ingrained.

Today, Josie was wearing a short white skirt, white platform boots, and a flowery scarf. Was an Austin Powers sequel filming nearby? I wouldn't put it past her to be in it if there were.

"Mail call?" I asked. "As in, someone got actual physical mail delivered here?" People still mailed stuff?

"Only Ridge," she said, grinning. "But I've always wanted to say *mail call!*"

I smiled back. It was impossible not to like Josie.

She handed Ridge a magazine, and he quickly rolled it up and stuffed it in the back of his pants. Was he blushing?

"And for the second part of mail call, may I present the one and only Miraaaanda Bosley!" Josie threw her hands out like a gameshow host, giving us the jazz hands.

Miranda stepped out onto the patio in a blue sleeveless dress, carrying a briefcase in one hand and a bottle of water in the other. "Subtle, Josie. Thanks."

"You're welcome!" Josie chirped. "Listen, the fridge is full of snacks, there are steaks if you wanna grill 'em, but I've got an underwater demolition class in half an hour and I'm running late. You're on your own, boys...and Miranda."

Ridge frowned. "You're taking an underwater demolition class?"

"What? No!" Josie laughed. "God! Wouldn't *that* be a trip? Me, learning about underwater demolition at my age?" She shook her head like Ridge was hilarious.

"But you said..."

"Teaching it, Ridge, honey. I'm teaching the class."

Ridge stared at Josie like she was a unicorn, mostly because she was.

My phone buzzed in my hand.

A new email from Jane with a lovely little attachment and a smiley face.

God. If there was a bigger rush than this, I hadn't found it, and I was sure it couldn't be obtained legally. I fucking loved calling the shots, I loved being in control. I loved knowing I'd never be powerless again. And I loved that the buzz came with the added bonus of actually helping other people.

Of course, today's project wasn't anything particularly newsworthy. Obtaining info from a pesky little press release – information that would be made public in a few days' time anyway – wasn't the same as using a bot army to access vulnerabilities in a server, but I wasn't doing it to impress anyone. And besides, I much preferred the art of social engineering over smash-and-grab theft any day. Get some inside information, make some smart investments, profit, and make sure other folks profit too.

I preferred to think of it as redistribution of wealth rather than theft. Or, like Breck said, I was liberating the money from the ultra-rich so I could set it free with a charity that supported underprivileged kids in Chicago...or maybe hurricane victims down in Puerto Rico.

"Bond?"

I glanced up, startled to find Miranda standing in front of me. I'd been caught up in imagining all the good I could and hadn't heard her approaching. Why was everyone looking at me like....oh, damn. My eyes locked on the manila envelope in Miranda's hand. I knew that envelope. It was identical to the one Steele had opened a few weeks back that had led us to investigate John Harlan.

Looked like it was my turn.

"The other half of mail call, huh?" I said, grabbing the envelope.

"Hand-delivered. Nothing but the best for you," Miranda drawled. She hefted her briefcase. "Well. Good luck, guys."

"Wait, what? Aren't you going to stay while I open it?"

She shook her head. "Just like last time. Plausible deniability. You've got your limitless credit cards, all of Charlie's resources, and *Josie*, God help you. But if you get in a jam, you can call me."

"And the 'interested party'?" Leo demanded. "The other guy who knows about these missions?"

Miranda stared at Leo without speaking for a minute. "You don't call him. But he'll be around, too."

Leo watched her warily as she departed.

I stared at the envelope for a second, smirking at the low-tech-ness of it all. Just my name written in tidy block letters on a plain, manila envelope, but it felt heavy. Portentous. Charlie had sure as hell gone for the drama with these things.

I slit the top of the envelope, and my smirk died as I pulled out a stack of pictures and photocopied documents.

"What the fuck?" I muttered.

There were pictures of passports, maybe two dozen, in various shades of blue, green, and purple-red, all dumped in a box. *Republica de Honduras* was clearly spelled out on one and Guatemala and Colombia on a couple of the others.

I passed the photo to Leo, who'd stood and walked closer to my chair. Then I looked at the next one.

More passports, but this time a few were opened, with names and pictures visible. Some smiling, some serious; some presenting as women, some as men; all relatively young, and almost all from Central or South America.

"I don't get it," I muttered.

But as I passed that picture to Leo and looked at the next sheet, I thought maybe I did understand, and what I understood sickened me.

Missing person reports from various cities, all with pictures attached. My Spanish was rusty, but I got the gist. Dinorah had left her home in Esquintla for a short-term job and never came home. So had Fernando from Copan, Tomas from Guatemala, Isobel from Bucaramanga, Tala from Manilla, Mercedes from somewhere indistinguishable, and so on. The only differences were the dates and the cities. The circumstances were all frighteningly similar.

I passed those sheets off blindly and dove into the next set. Pictures again, but this time... a tropical resort, like maybe one of those bougie all-inclusive places? Women and men laying out on lounge chairs not dissimilar to the ones we were all lounging on. Crystal-blue pools and grass-roofed tiki bars, private bungalows and waitresses dressed in...

Oh. Oh, wait, *hold up*. I peered at one of the images.

"Leo!" I snapped my fingers without looking up. "Gimme the report about Tala Whatshername."

Leo or someone handed it to me, and I snatched it blindly, looking back and forth from the missing woman to the waitress. She was skinnier in the photo from the resort – like, count-her-ribs skinny – and her hair was longer, but the face was unmistakable. The tiny mole below the outer corner of her left eye was visible in both images.

"This is the same person," I said, glancing up. "The missing woman on the report is the waitress in this picture. And I bet if we look closely, every one of these other missing people is working at this resort, too."

Breck peered over Steele's shoulder while he frowned at the pictures of the passports. Ridge, Carson, and Leo studied the photos of the missing people. But Danny was staring at me, a tiny frown on his face.

"But how?"

"I dunno," I said. "Looks like some kind of human trafficking thing to me."

"So, what are we going to do?" he asked, serious and worried.

It was weird that in this sea of take-charge dudes – Twelve-Foot-Tall Steele, Head Bitch in Charge Leo, Man of a Thousand Faces Carson – Danny looked to me, the techie who pissed him off on the daily. Weird, but also kind of sweet.

My lips twitched the tiniest bit. "We're going to find them, and we're going to get them home."

Danny nodded once, a combination of agreement and conviction that we would get it done, all cute and earnest. Really, a guy who'd been through as much as Danny had shouldn't have been able to pull off innocent and sweet that way, but he did. Somehow, it made me feel better.

I flipped through the papers still in my hand. There were a few more resort pictures, including a close-up of the name and logo that I would use to obtain every microgram of available data about the place. But then there was a picture of a smiling, pregnant Tala with her arm around a man's waist. The man held a toddler who looked as happy as his parents.

Tala had a family. And her son had his mother's smile.

And that was when I remembered exactly why I was here – why I'd let myself be "blackmailed" by a dead man into taking down John Harlan, and why I'd stayed in this house ever since. One misanthropic hacker redistributing wealth could only do so much, but I was more than that now. I was part of a team.

Sometimes even the good guys needed to fight a little dirty. Sometimes, to bring the truth to light, you needed to employ a little deception.

Game. On.

MAN IN THE MIRROR (SHORT)

BRONZE STAR

SHOWTIME (SHORT)

THE COMPLETE VETERANS AFFAIRS BOXED SET

STAND ALONES

BELIEVE (FROM HEART2HEART #1)

FAIRYTALE OF LAGUARDIA (WITH BETH BOLDEN)

A dreamer and an idealist, Amy writes about people finding connection in a world that can seem lonely and magic in a world that can seem all too mundane. She invites readers into her characters' lives and worlds when they are their most vulnerable, their most human, living with the same hopes and fears we all have. An avid traveler who has lived in big cities and small towns in four different continents, Amy has found that time and distance are no barriers to love. She invites her readers to reach out and share how her characters have touched their lives or how the found families they have gathered around them have shaped their worlds.

Born on Long Island, NY, Amy has lived in Los Angeles, London, and Bangkok. She currently lives on the road in a Town & Country minivan. Honk if you see her!

Newsletter: http://aewasp.com/mailinglist

Made in the USA
Coppell, TX
26 August 2021

61223499R00215